Rhys

SAFE HARBOR

HJ WELCH

Hugs♡

HJ

Safe Harbor
Pine Cove Book One

Copyright © 2019 by HJ Welch

PROLOGUE

Three Months Ago
Robin

"WILL THE TORTURE NEVER END!" ROBIN COAL CRIED, slapping his hands over his face in despair. "The horror! The *nightmare!*"

Peyton, his best friend, patted his head as he flailed about on their couch. "There, there," she said in a deadpan voice.

Robin dropped his hands as his lip wobbled. "I can't take one more. Please, don't make me. If you love me at all, make it stop."

Peyton tutted and checked her phone. "I hate to be the bearer of bad news, but we still have a final applicant to see."

Robin collapsed against the arm of the sofa. "Tell my parents I loved them! It was a good life!"

Peyton laughed and tickled his sides. Robin shrieked and retaliated, not letting her get away with such a ruthless

1

assault. But in the end, when they were disheveled and on the floor, he had to face facts.

They were never going to find someone to fill their spare room.

It had been vacant for a couple of weeks now and they were getting dangerously close to when they needed to pay next month's rent. It would probably be okay this time, but if they didn't find anybody for when March rolled around, they would be in trouble.

Robin pulled himself back up to sit on the sofa. "Okay. Fine. Let's review. The guy with the weird fungus collection was a hard 'no,' right?"

Peyton nodded, sitting by his side. "As was the girl who was too high to function."

"And the girl with the notebook who measured our dust levels in millimeters."

"And the fitness fiend who said he'd ban junk food from the fridge."

Robin sighed and rubbed his nose under his glasses. "What about that couple? They didn't seem too bad."

"Are you kidding?" Peyton looked horrified. "The older guy wanted to divide every last egg and ounce of water down to the penny! I know we're not rich, but we don't need a tightwad like that!"

Robin looked miserably over the notes he'd made in a small hardback notebook. "What are we going to do, then?"

His best friend sighed and put her arm around him. As he was smaller even than her slim frame, he fit neatly. Not having had a boyfriend for quite some time, Peyton's hugs were the best Robin usually got these days.

"We'll figure something out. Hey, how about after this last guy we order some Thai food and open a bottle of wine?"

Robin bit his lip, already imagining what kind of train

wreck their final applicant of the evening would be like. "That sounds great, but I do have work tomorrow."

Peyton kissed his hair. "You worry too much, darling. A couple of glasses of wine won't harm. You know I'll look after you."

"I can look after myself," Robin grumbled, not really meaning it.

The truth was he'd love to have someone fuss over him from time to time. He just wished that could be a *boyfriend* for once. Instead, he allowed himself to be hugged by Peyton as they skimmed the last guy's application email.

"Alasdair Epping," Robin read out loud.

"Ex-Marine," Peyton added, raising her eyebrows. Her whole family was involved with the Corps in one way or another. She herself had gone into nursing. Robin could tell she saw that as a plus. But Robin wasn't too sure.

"What if he's all macho? What if he's not okay with…us?"

Peyton rolled her eyes. "If he was homophobic, why would he have responded to an ad looking for someone to join a queer house?" She looked up at the rainbow flag they had hanging above their sofa. "Besides, he's not serving anymore. This says he's a mechanic here in Seattle. How do you know that homophobia wasn't what drove him out of the military?"

Robin shuddered. "I hope not." That would suck.

"Look. He likes cooking and playing video games…" There was a knock at the door. Peyton checked her watch. "And he's punctual!" She skipped up to let this guy in.

Robin huffed. "Five dollars says he starts clipping his toenails right here in the living room."

Peyton rolled her eyes and opened their apartment door.

To a god.

Robin almost fell off the sofa again.

The guy standing on the threshold was beautiful. Shaggy

3

blond hair framed his sculpted jaw and warm brown eyes. He towered over Peyton at well over six foot, and his body, despite being covered up, was obviously impressive. Robin could practically see all the muscles rippling as he shifted his substantial weight from one foot to the other. He took a hand out of his bomber jacket and gave them a dorky wave.

Robin's heart melted into his slippers. Unfortunately, they were shaped like koalas and were probably the most embarrassing thing he owned, but until now, he hadn't cared. The potential housemates should know what kind of a geek he was.

Regretfully, now so did hunky Alasdair Epping. Robin tried not to blush.

Alasdair grinned, though, apparently unfazed by Robin's choice of footwear. "Hi! You must be Peyton? And Robin? I'm Dair."

"Dair?" Peyton repeated with a frown as they shook hands. "Oh! Short for Alasdair – cool. Well, come on in."

She let Dair walk ahead of her. As she closed the front door, she gave Robin an *'oh my god, he's gorgeous'* face behind him. Robin tried to ignore her and smile at Dair instead, but when he reached for his little notebook, he somehow managed to flip it up and smack himself in the face.

"Ow," he said sheepishly, rubbing his cheek.

"Are you all right?" Dair asked with genuine concern, sitting on the sofa opposite him.

Robin laughed. "It's cool." He picked the notebook off the floor where his dignity was probably also lying around. "So, um, you're looking for a room to rent?" he asked, then cringed. Of course he was, that was why he was there. What other reason would Robin have to be in the same room with a guy who looked like that?

Peyton came and sat beside him again. Dair linked his large hands together between his knees. His large frame dwarfed the couch he'd lowered himself into. Dear lord, the things Robin could do under a body like that-

Inappropriate! He shoved that thought into a box in his chest and slammed the lid down.

Dair didn't seem to notice Robin struggling not to have a minor seizure. He smiled ruefully at them. "I've been living alone since me and my girlfriend split up, and rent is damned expensive in Seattle. I was hoping to share, meet some new people. Not just find four walls to sleep between."

Ex-girlfriend. Damn. Robin managed a smile, realizing that was actually a very *good* thing. If they were going to live with this guy, it would be better if he was straight.

Not that they were sure if they were going to accept him yet. Other than the fact that as soon as Peyton had opened the door, Robin's heart had leaped and screamed *'yes!'*

He and Peyton shared a glance. "That's exactly what we're looking for," Robin agreed. "A friend."

"It turned out the last guy wasn't shy, he was an asshole," Peyton informed him, nodding sagely. "We're hoping to find someone we vibe with this time around."

Robin swallowed. It was always scary to have to come out, no matter how many countless times he'd done it in his life. But sadly, it was a necessity of any queer person's life.

"So, um, the ad mentioned we're both gay." Robin pointed at the rainbow flag above their heads. "Is that, uh, all right?"

Dair blinked and frowned. "Of course. Unless – did you specifically want someone else gay too?"

Robin's eyebrows rose and Peyton mirrored him. "No," he said truthfully. "So long as the person was comfortable with it, it wouldn't matter if they were straight."

Dair's face split into a beautiful smile. Robin's heart ached. "Great! That's awesome. One of my best buds in the Corps was gay. He and his husband have this Instagram account where companies actually pay them in products and, like, to go on trips and stuff. Just for posting pictures of themselves being all happy and with their tops off showing their abs. Isn't that cool?"

He laughed and shook his head. Wow…Dair was kind of adorkable. Robin tried very hard not to sigh audibly.

Dair made a little 'oh' noise and pointed toward the kitchen. "So I'll be honest. I kind of like cooking. For other people, not just me. It's like my yoga. Would it be a problem if I was in the kitchen a lot?"

Those inappropriate crush-like feelings rattled against the lid of the box in Robin's chest.

"A problem?" he squeaked.

"Mine and Robin's specialty dish is having the Thai place around the corner on speed dial," Peyton explained.

Dair gave them that kilowatt smile again. "I have a recipe for green curry I've been meaning to try out."

Peyton's face was completely serious. "Forget taking the room. Will you just marry me?"

Dair's laugh was infectious.

Uh-oh. This was a problem. Dair was obviously a perfect housemate. He was fun and generous and had a steady job, which made him reliable.

But something very dangerous was unfurling in Robin's chest. It was like the whole world was brighter just from having Dair in the room. Robin's chest ached and his heart pounded and his palms were damp.

Robin was falling head over heels for a guy he'd met all of five minutes ago.

A straight guy. Who Robin was going to have to see every day.

But Peyton was already walking back over to the sofas with three beers, discussing the lease. It was as good as a done deal. So Robin smiled and did his best to join in the conversation without getting tongue-tied.

Time, that was all he needed. This silly little crush would fade soon enough, he was sure. Until then, all he'd have to do would be to wrap a chain around the box in his chest and make absolutely sure no one ever found out about these feelings. They'd be gone soon enough.

At least…he hoped so.

DAIR

"THERE YOU GO, MA'AM. ALL FIXED."

Dair wheeled himself out from underneath the Chevrolet Spark he'd been laboring over, wiping his oily hands on a rag. The car's owner bit her lip and rubbed her chest anxiously. She was an exhausted-looking middle-aged mom with a toddler testing the length of the leash attached to their dinosaur backpack. They were desperately trying to reach Dair's toolbox to play with the grimy wrenches. He subtly moved the kit a few more inches away before getting back to his feet.

"What was wrong with it?" the mom asked over the racket of the other guys in the auto shop. They were joshing with each other and clanging against the vehicles they were working on. Dair scowled but quickly smoothed it out to address his client again.

"You had a coolant leak. The hose came loose – maybe when you went over a bump or a ramp? Over time, the coolant began to leak, making the engine overheat, and then the fluid that had been leaking also heated up, causing all that smoke."

"Oh…my." The mom looked stricken. "I had no idea."

"There was a warning light," Dair said gently. He led her to the driver's seat and opened the door to point where the indicator had been flashing. "Just in case it happens again. Now you'll know what that little fella was telling you."

"That's what that light meant." The mom shook her head and looked devastated. "I just thought it meant…well, I didn't realize it was anything urgent. I feel so stupid."

"Hey, it's fine," Dair said sympathetically. "It could happen to anyone."

"But I had to call that tow truck. And now the repair. How much will all that cost? My husband is going to be so mad. Oh god, what am I going to do? I'm so *stupid.*"

Then your husband's an asshole, Dair thought privately. Why would any guy make his wife feel guilty for something she didn't know about? Not everyone was into cars.

Dair's military-trained observation skills kicked in before he'd even thought about it. The model of the mom's phone was at least four years old. Her sneakers were all scuffed up, her jeans fraying, and her sweater had a couple of small holes in it. The car itself was several years old and not in great condition. The toddler ran one way, then another, wrenching the mom's arm left and right as she clung on to the leash. She was so worried, she didn't even seem to notice.

Making a decision, Dair quickly scanned the garage bay to make sure his boss wasn't around. "Oh, don't worry. We don't need to charge you for this. It was just a simple little fix on the hose, and the tow is a complimentary service. I'll just write up the paperwork on your behalf."

The joy on the mom's face was overwhelming. "Are you sure? Oh, I, thank you – thank you so much. I swear I'll never ignore another little light again. I'll come get it serviced on time."

Dair smiled. He wasn't sure how he'd square this, but the

tears of relief in her eyes were worth it. "I also gave your oil a quick top-up and checked the washer fluid. You should be good to go."

The mom didn't need telling twice. "I really need to get home and get dinner on. Thank you so much. You've been an absolute star. I bet your wife doesn't have these silly little problems!"

Despite the wave of melancholy that rolled through him, Dair smiled. "You drive safe now, ma'am," he said as she began wrestling her child into the car seat in the back. "Are you okay reversing out of the shop, or would you like some help?"

Having clipped the squirming, wailing child in, the mom turned to Dair, her keys clutched between both hands. "No," she said determinedly. "I've got it. Thank you *again*. You really saved my day."

Dair smiled and waved her off. Then he turned to head to the office to try and figure out how he was going to balance out a couple of things. If he didn't charge for his time (which honestly hadn't been that long anyway) he could just put the tow truck down as a company expense that he himself could pay back, then...

"Hey, Double Dair!"

The catcall was accompanied by several snickers that made Dair roll his eyes. When the guys in his unit had called him that nickname, it had been with affection and respect. But the jerks he had to work with in the auto shop had discovered it and used it with a decidedly more mocking tone.

Dair knew he had to take the ribbing, even if he found it childish and irritating. Otherwise, the guys would call him a sissy and a bunch of other pathetic shit.

The guy that had called out to him was messing about on

his phone despite it not being his break. "You gonna pay for the freebie you just doled out from your own check?"

Dair grit his teeth. He was hoping he'd be able to get away with just docking his own time and paying back what he owed for the truck. But now he'd have to pay the shop's cut on top as well. "Of course I am," he said out loud. After all, no good deed went unpunished.

"You're such a pussy, man. At least tell me you got her number? She was hot, in a desperate kind of way. I bet she'd let you do all kinds of freaky shit." That got a round of cackles from the guys.

Dair grimaced. "It really was a simple job. I was just trying to help her out."

"Oh – *I'd* help her out all right!" Several of the guys hooted and began miming thrusting hips and cocks in mouths. Dair rolled his eyes and left them to it.

He was fully aware that a lot of the guys had talked shit back over in Afghanistan, but that was different. When you faced death every day, everyone knew it was okay to let off steam and try and out shock each other in the crudest ways possible.

These guys were just morons.

Dair sighed as he got to work and billed himself for the whole damn service call. Shit. That was going to make him a bit tight this month. Never mind. He'd find a way around it, he was sure. He would never have taken money from the business, just himself, so paying the whole cost probably wasn't that much different. It just summed up the whole ethos of the garage.

Profit before people.

He really wished his coworkers weren't such immature jackasses. Especially when Dair often worked late on Friday and Saturday nights so they could go out or go home to their families. He had hoped he could be a bit of a good influence on them. But after a couple of years, they were still no better.

He didn't regret leaving the Marines when he had. It had just been the right time for him to move on. Or so he'd thought. Since returning to Seattle, he and his longtime girlfriend had finally had The Talk. When he'd been deployed for such long stretches at a time, they had been happy to coast along. But when it came down to it, he wanted kids and she didn't. There wasn't really much they could do about that. At least the breakup had been amicable.

But Dair had been naive to think his new coworkers could ever fill the void left by the loss of his Marine family. Having no real biological family and being single for the first time since high school, Dair had hoped to find his place in the world here at the auto shop.

As more crude laughter rang across the garage, he was reminded how much that hadn't happened.

Then he thought of home.

He smiled and leaned back against his chair. He *did* have his housemates now, didn't he? It wasn't the same as having a girlfriend or a wife, but it was sort of like having a family. Peyton was really cool, but Dair especially liked Robin. Maybe because he was quieter and a harder challenge to get to know than Peyton.

In fact, Dair had spent the entire first month thinking Robin didn't even like him. He still wasn't sure. They had appeared to get along when they'd met at his interview, but for the first few weeks, it was like Robin turned into a mouse and scurried off with a squeak every time Dair was home.

Slowly, though, Dair had won him over via his stomach with his mom's trusted macaroni and cheese as well as his special chicken Kievs. Then he'd asked Robin if he wanted to play Black Ops 4 on the PlayStation. Seeing as he was a software developer, Dair figured he must be into gaming too. He'd been right.

Nowadays Robin was still extremely shy, but it was like when he forgot himself, he opened up the floodgates with rambling streams of consciousness that Dair thought were funny but also really cute. Was it too much to hope that the two of them would become better friends with time? Dair was sure Robin's buddies at work were much smarter than him. But despite the fact they had nothing in common, Dair couldn't help but feel they'd get along just great given time.

In fact, wasn't Robin's vacation starting tonight? Yes, because Dair had made a mental note to swing by the store on his way home to get supplies to cook something special. Probably Thai. That was what they all loved most in the apartment. But just his luck, right at that moment another emergency customer crawled into the auto shop with a banged-up trunk and bumper from a small accident.

Naturally, seeing as it was almost the end of the day, the rest of Dair's coworkers melted away into the back rooms.

Dair didn't mind, though. The old boy driving the car was pretty rattled, having been shunted by a young kid he suspected had been drinking. Dair worried the other guys might have belittled the older man, but Dair took his time to assure him everything would be fine and they'd have his car back to him by tomorrow. Dair waited with the gentleman for his son to come pick him up, then got to work.

By the time he'd finished the repairs to the dinged car, Dair was the only one left in the garage. He didn't really have time to go shopping for ingredients as well as cooking. But this was Robin's special vacation. Peyton said he was going home to his ten-year high school reunion. That didn't happen every day.

After closing up the garage doors on the shop, Dair checked his bank balance on his phone. It wasn't pretty, especially once the payment from today came out. But screw it. He could put a takeout order on his credit card. That wouldn't be too much to pay back next month.

This was his chance to show Robin that he wasn't so intimidating. That they could be real friends. Dair knew him being straight was a bit of a barrier for one reason or another to Robin, but Dair honestly didn't care about that kind of stuff. His coworkers were all painfully straight, and look at what assholes they were.

Besides, Robin worked too hard. Dair knew he himself never took vacation either, but he hardly ever had a reason to. Robin would no doubt have to be dragged away from his laptop for an event he'd been planning for months. In Dair's short time in the apartment, he had found food to be the best method for this. And beer.

He already felt a little better as he walked to where he'd parked his truck, swinging his keys around his finger. If he was going to do this, he decided to go all out. He didn't have work the next day, after all.

He may not have his own family or girlfriend, and his coworkers were jerks, but he was lucky to have a couple of unlikely friends. Time to prove to Robin that Dair was there for him, that he could count on him.

Like the old saying went, the best way to a man's heart was through his stomach.

2

ROBIN

"Peyton! Hey, no! Give that back!"

Robin Coal leaped helplessly from the sofa as his best friend snatched his phone away from him and danced away. "Nuh-uh! This is supposed to be the start of your vacation."

Robin knew she was only teasing and meant well, but his eyes darted anxiously to his cell. "Um. About that…"

"Nope." She shook her head as well as the phone. "You did your handover. You've got the whole week off. They'll survive without you."

Robin bit his lip. "Well, see there's this thing about the build server being down, so they want to compile locally and push to production. But that would be a *seriously* bad idea, and they don't seem to be getting that! So I just thought I'd-"

"La la la!" Peyton skipped away from him toward the kitchen area of their open plan apartment. "I told you I'd bully you if I had to, so this is me being your bestest friend ever." She opened the fridge and chucked the phone in by the milk and Dair's protein shakes.

Robin squeaked.

"Um…what if Dair calls? He's already late. I'm worried

about him." It was a feeble attempt to get his phone back, but Robin tried it anyway.

Sure enough, Peyton blew a raspberry. "He's a big, tough Marine. I'm sure he's fine. Stop trying to change the subject. You're *going* to this reunion."

She was right about Dair, of course. And about Robin. He'd booked this time off work months in advance. But now he'd left the office and signed off from his current projects, the panic was starting to creep into his chest. He was never not on call. Being a software developer for Ticking Clock Entertainment might not seem that vital to most people. They operated a small chain of high-end leisure facilities in the Seattle area, including arcades, bowling allies, and escape rooms. But without Robin and his team, the whole business would crumble.

"I just promised I'd keep an eye on things," Robin tried to protest. Peyton crossed her arms and cocked a sculpted eyebrow at him. He squirmed. "Actually, I'm not even sure I'm going to go home-"

"I knew it!" Peyton cried. She pressed her hands to her head and looked horrified. "Robin, no! This is your ten-year high school reunion. Your brother has been working on this for half a year! You'll break his heart. But more than that, when was the last time you even went home?"

Guilt pulsed through Robin and he chewed his lip. He talked to his twin brother, Jay, almost every single day, and he was fully aware how much heart and soul he'd poured into the reunion. Not to mention that it had been months since Jay's last visit to Seattle due to work and Robin was going stir crazy not seeing him.

"I know," he agreed, raising his hands. "But the office is crazy right now and I think it's just too much to leave them in the lurch. I'm sure Jay will understand. I'll just-"

A squeaky bark interrupted him. Robin looked down to

see a small ball of fluff sinking his surprisingly sharp teeth into the hem of his jeans, then begin to tug with little grunts.

Peyton laughed. "See, Smudge agrees with me. Don't you, Smudgy?"

The little ball of fur growled and tugged some more, his tail wagging furiously. Robin sighed and picked up the latest addition to Dair's menagerie in his arms to pet. They weren't technically allowed pets in the building, but their superintendent almost never came over.

Robin and Peyton had been at their wit's end trying to find someone to fill the third room in the apartment after the last guy moved out. Everyone they'd interviewed had been a total weirdo. Then Dair had walked into their lives and was an instant yes. As an ex-Marine, Peyton's own military family loyalty had demanded they take him in. They'd both liked that he had a steady job and just generally didn't seem like an asshole. Plus, his favorite food was also Thai, so that had sealed it.

It didn't hurt that Robin thought he was hot as all hell in a scruffy, unpolished sort of way. But he was also straight, so there was no danger of anything happening or getting awkward. Even Peyton didn't know about his silly little crush.

Dair was more than a hunk, though. He was funny and kind. Perhaps a little too kind, as the small zoo in their apartment attested. But they'd only realized he was a package deal *after* they'd offered him the room. Neither Robin nor Peyton had wanted to take back the offer, so they just risked the three cats and two dogs that Dair had taken in over the years.

Apart from the new puppy, Smudge, the others had come all the way from Afghanistan, where Dair had served a number of tours in the Marines. It seemed like strays just flocked to him like he was a Disney Princess, if Disney

Princesses benched two hundred pounds and ate more in a day than Robin usually managed in a week. It was worth it for those insane washboard abs…

…and Robin was locking that thought safely back in his secret crush box which no one ever needed to know about.

Cuddling with Smudge had bought him a few seconds, but Peyton wasn't letting up.

"Rob, I know you're like a computer wizard and they'll struggle without you. You have the vacation days – use them before you lose them! I promise I'll give you back your phone if you go so you can check in. But right now, it's Saturday night, and we're going to have some fun."

Robin sighed. Smudge (so called because his nose was black but the rest of him was tan) wriggled around so he could lick the end of Robin's chin. He couldn't blame Dair for rescuing him from behind that dumpster. He was an adorable mutt, even if they had no idea what breed he was other than 'floofy.'

He and Peyton had music playing, so they didn't hear Dair approach until he rattled his keys and opened the door to the apartment. "Hey!" he called out, grinning at them both as he kicked the door closed, his hands full of bags of Thai food. "Hello, hello! Yes, I know!"

Robin's heart flipped at the sight of Dair's stunning smile. Damn. He actually *had* been worried that Dair was late. Robin needed to watch that this crush didn't get out of hand.

At his entrance, old Jimmy the bulldog had bumbled over to greet his dad, slobbering over his sneakers. The cats, Spot, Trixie, and Jolly Roger, all unfurled and came to investigate too. The poor things were all missing bits of ears, toes, and tails, even an eye in Roger's case. But Robin thought they were all gorgeous. He couldn't help but smile at the way huge Dair cooed over them. He probably knew ten different ways to kill a man, yet here he was making kissy noises at his fur babies.

That silly crush tried very hard to push at the lid of the box in Robin's chest, but he kept it firmly closed.

"Sorry I'm late, but I bring food," Dair announced, depositing the bags on the kitchen counter. He also clinked two six-packs of beers down. "Happy start of vacation, Robin!"

A mix of embarrassment and pride flushed through Robin at Dair paying special attention to him. He gratefully helped himself to one of the beer bottles to distract himself.

Dair popped the lid off his own drink. "I tried to call to say I was getting takeout rather than cooking, but there was no answer."

"Takeout is always good," Peyton informed him through a mouthful of cracker.

Robin smiled sheepishly. "Peyton put my phone in the fridge, sorry."

Dair blinked. "In the fridge?"

"Yeah," said Payton. "He was being a doofus. Oh, is that crispy squid?"

The delicious smell of hot noodles, rice, and curry made Robin's stomach growl, so he was glad to use food as an excuse not to talk about what was bothering him. He delved into the food boxes, finding his favorites to dish up, purposely avoiding eye contact with both Peyton and Dair.

It wasn't that he didn't want to go home. It had been a crazy amount of time since he'd last visited, after all. But the thought of abandoning his work was making him feel kind of sick. As he weighed the decision up again, the few mouthfuls of tangy noodles and beers swirled in his belly, making him feel suddenly a bit queasy. Damn, he couldn't go. He just *couldn't*.

"Robin?" Dair asked as they dropped into their sofas around the coffee table. "Are you all right?"

It made Robin's insides flip at the best of times when Dair used that concerned tone on him. The man had no clue how hot he was when he turned that efficient, proactive Marine thing of his on.

Robin found it crazy that a guy like that even wanted to be friends with someone like him. Initially, he and Peyton had tried looking for someone else gay, but that hadn't worked out, and it didn't seem to bother Dair that they were both queer. Dair was always happy to cook for them or test Peyton when she had exams or play video games with Robin. He was a good guy.

Robin sighed, poking at his food with his chopsticks, suddenly not hungry. He couldn't keep distracting himself with Dair. He had to face facts about the reunion.

His twin, Jay, would be devastated if Robin bailed at the last minute. Jay was on the reunion committee and had been working twenty-four seven organizing a whole week's worth of activities. The thought of that much socializing made Robin nervous. Both at work and play, Robin preferred to be hidden behind a computer monitor. But it really was his job that was causing him to consider not going back to Pine Cove.

When he didn't respond to Dair's question, Peyton did. She was a nurse, so Robin was stuck with two caring, protective friends. Damn them. "Robin's seriously considering not going to his high school reunion."

She reached over and squeezed his knee with a sympathetic look. The back and sides of her head were shaved close, leaving an inch or so of hair swept toward her eyes. On someone else the look might have been harsh, but Peyton's slim frame and androgynous aesthetic made it look stunning. Or so Robin thought.

"Wait, what?"

Dair raised his eyebrows at Robin. He was sitting on the other sofa with his pack loitering around him. In fairness, all of them apart from Smudge had settled down to nap. But that little fluffball was hopping around Dair's feet in the hope of catching any scraps of shredded beef that dropped to the floor.

"But..." Dair continued, still looking at Robin, "you've been planning this for months."

"Work's just crazy right now." Robin sighed, his heart heavy. Peyton made a noise at the back of her throat and narrowed her eyes at him. "What?"

She edged slightly further away along the couch. "Don't be mad..."

Robin frowned. He couldn't think of a time he'd ever been angry with her. "Why would I be mad?"

"Do you think you not wanting to go has anything to do with Mac also attending?"

Robin hadn't heard that name in a long time. His insides dropped as he shook his head in confusion. "No. No. I mean, I don't...no. That's got nothing to do with it." He'd been trying his very best to not even *think* about seeing him again. He felt like he'd jumped into a freezing lake, and shivered.

"Who's Mac?" Dair asked. His attention was so focused on Robin he'd even put his food down (on the table, away from Smudge's reach). Robin couldn't remember seeing Dair abandon food in the whole time he'd been living with them.

Peyton sighed. "Mac is Robin's psycho ex-boyfriend."

Robin spluttered. "'Psycho's is a bit strong, don't you think? I mean, he *was* kind of an asshole. But-"

"If he didn't get his way, he had a meltdown!" Peyton cried. She'd never met him, as she and Robin had become friends later at college. But she'd heard a few stories from

Robin. He suspected she'd heard even more from Robin's other siblings too, since she knew them all.

He bit his lip. "Okay, yeah. There's a reason we broke up. But it was as much my fault as his."

"Bullshit," Peyton said angrily. "He used to go through your phone without asking and text nonstop if you went out. He had strict rules for eating tacos. He called you 'Binny.' He *punched* you after losing at a goddamned video game!"

Dair's head snapped around to Robin. "What?"

"It wasn't like that!" Robin fanned his hands, trying to get them both to calm down. "Okay, look. We were, like, seventeen. I came last at Smash Bros, so I started tickling him so we'd both be last together. I stupidly thought it would be sweet and funny. When he lost, he pinned me down and thumped me in the ribs. There wasn't even any bruising. And I shouldn't have dragged him down just because I was bad at the game myself." He looked between them both.

Dair blinked slowly. "He *hit* you."

"More than once," Peyton muttered under her breath. Dair's expression was horrified.

Robin laughed and tried to break the tension from the room. "Guys. I swear it wasn't that bad. I'd honestly forgotten he was going to be at the reunion. He wasn't what was making me think about not going."

He was mostly sure that was true. Almost.

"Look, whose relationship is perfect as a teenager? We broke up when I went to college and he didn't. That was it."

That wasn't it, but that was what he told people. The real truth was too painful. But it was also irrelevant, so Robin didn't see the need to elaborate.

Peyton scoffed. "You mean you dumped his ass." She leaned over and clinked her bottle against the one he was still holding. "Well done you. But still – do you think it's *possible* that's part of your reluctance to go home? That you don't want to run into him again?"

Robin opened and closed his mouth. Now he was being forced to really think about it, it had been *years* since he'd gone across the state to visit his family. They generally came to see him in small groups, and they spent their holidays away in California or Hawaii.

He frowned. "I mean…no. I don't really want to see Mac again. But work-"

"Already thinks you're off for the week." Peyton waved her hand dismissively. "Your phone is staying in the fridge until I say otherwise. They'll cope without you. If Mac wasn't going to be at the reunion, would you be thinking of ditching?"

Something dropped in Robin's chest as he envisioned his ex not going to all the events this week, let alone the big Saturday night party. Damn. Suddenly all he could picture was seeing his twin and all their old friends. He thought of his parents' house and his older brother and younger sisters. Even the thought of eating at the old diner and strolling Pine Cove's famous boardwalk made his heart squeeze with longing.

"Oh," he said sheepishly. "Yeah, actually. I guess maybe I do want to go."

Perhaps there was some part of his subconscious that had been trying to avoid Mac, after all?

"Right," said Peyton in her no-nonsense voice. "I'm not letting you bail because of that grade A twatwaffle."

"Hell no," Dair agreed sternly. "If anything, he's the one that shouldn't be going. You have every right to be there, not him."

Robin rubbed behind his neck and tried to pick his chopsticks back up. But they jumped from his hand onto the floor, where Smudge raced to sniff them. Embarrassed,

Robin put his beer down, picked both the dog and his chopsticks up, then looked dejectedly at the others.

"Well, he *is* going. Jay told me. So like I said, maybe it's best if I just stay here, seeing as work is so crazy."

Dair was shaking his head and scowling. "No. He doesn't get to win this. Abusive asshole."

Peyton raised her hand for a high five without taking her eyes off Robin. The pair of them slapped hands, then dropped them back into their laps.

"Won't your friends look after you?" Dair asked with real concern.

"Of course they will," Robin said. "But…"

"Robin's twin and friends are completely awesome, but they all kind of look like Robin." Peyton waved her hand up and down, indicating Robin's small, slight frame. "And the last we saw of Mac on Facebook before Robin blocked his ugly face was him looking like, well…" She waved her hand over at Dair. "Mac was never intimidated by sharp wit. Only other dumb jocks."

Dair's eyebrows disappeared under his shaggy blond hair. "What you need is a wingman to scare that douchebag off."

Peyton gasped and shook Robin's knee. "Oh my god! If you showed up with a big hot boyfriend, I bet Mac would think twice about giving you grief."

Robin rolled his eyes, hard. "I don't need a *bodyguard,* for crying out loud. Besides, I don't have any kind of boyfriend, let alone a big hot one."

The awful truth was Robin hadn't had a boyfriend at all since Mac. It was something he was deeply insecure about. Sure, he'd had several hookups, even some that could have been called dates. But he'd told himself he was focusing on his career, not his relationships.

But after the realization about not wanting to go home because Mac might be there, he wondered if he'd been holding back from getting a boyfriend for similar reasons. His relationship with Mac had been hard work and complicated, and Robin had never felt able to try that again with someone else.

Urgh. That was something to hash over another time. He couldn't magic up an impressive buff boyfriend, so Peyton's observation was irrelevant.

Dair's brow was creased in thought, though, as he petted one-eyed Roger the cat. "Think about it a minute. If you went home with a guy who happened to be bigger than your ex, do you think Mac would stay away and let you enjoy the reunion?"

Robin raised his eyebrows, not sure where Dair was going with this. "Uh, maybe?" He closed his eyes and took a slow breath as he tried to picture it. Him, with a gorgeous man on his arm, protecting him from any shit Mac might try and pull. "Yeah, I guess. But-"

"Great!" Dair's cheerful tone surprised Robin, making him open his eyes to see his housemate beaming. "What if I pretended to be your boyfriend for the week and tagged along to your events? Obviously we'd just be there as friends, but it might make that dickwad back the fuck off. You'd be safe."

He'd started off excited, but by the time he'd stopped talking his words became almost a growl. Something fluttered in Robin's chest as several thoughts flew through his mind. Did Dair really care that much about him that he wanted to protect him from Mac? But was he seriously suggesting...?

"You want to pretend to be my boyfriend?" Robin repeated. "For a whole *week?*"

Peyton's hands had already covered her mouth at Dair's idea. "Oh my god, I love it," she whispered between her fingers. "It's diabolical. Dair, this is genius! Robin – yes!"

But Robin was still reeling. "Uh, but – well, you're straight?" Smudge whimpered and pawed at his chest. Robin hugged him close, the contact making him feel better.

Dair frowned. "Yeah, I suppose. But it would just be for show. That's cool, right? I wouldn't be, like, taking advantage of LGBT culture or anything?"

Peyton blew a raspberry. "Hell, no. You're one of the best allies I've ever met."

Robin looked down at Smudge, who gave him a toothy smile and panted, his tongue lolling out of his mouth. "This is crazy. I couldn't lie to everyone like that. Could I?"

He would have been a total fibber if he tried to deny that the idea of even just pretending to date Dair didn't sound amazing. Nothing would happen between them, obviously. But to spend a whole week together, for everyone to think they were a couple...Robin had to admit that would be a dream.

But even if he could convince everyone else, surely he could never convince Jay? They spent half the time they spoke on FaceTime. He'd know Robin could *never* hide a secret like that on his face. They'd be rumbled before they even began.

It seemed he was in the minority with his worries, though.

"Look," said Dair in that firm Marine voice that made Robin's toes curl and his cock tingle. "You have every right to go to this thing. I don't care if it was ten years ago – that fucker hit you. So if you want, I can come with you and make sure he doesn't lay another finger on you. He won't even look your way if he knows what's good for him."

Robin was taken aback by the ferociousness of his words. "Wow. Um, thanks, dude. That's really nice of you. But – okay, let's say I agree. What about your work? It's a bit last minute to take off."

Dair shrugged, all smiles again as he picked up Jimmy the bulldog to lay on his lap. "I haven't taken a single vacation day in a year and a half. They owe me."

Peyton bounced on the couch, looking between Robin and Dair. "This is awesome. Robin – don't overthink it! You guys go and have a fun vacation, Mac stays the fuck away from you, and you get to enjoy the reunion. It's a win-win!"

Robin bit his lip. He did his best to look at Dair, but shyness overcame him. "And, um, you'd be okay with the whole, um, boyfriend part?"

He glanced up as Dair smiled warmly at him. Dair leaned over and squeezed Robin's thigh, sending shivers all over his body that he barely contained. "Of course. We'll keep it simple and say we literally just started dating. If we're taking things slow, then no one will be surprised if we aren't making out all the time."

Even just the thought of making out with Dair made Robin's vision swim. "Uh, yeah. That sounds smart."

"It's brilliant," Peyton announced. She grabbed both her beer and dinner again, then held the bottle aloft. "I declare this our first apartment caper as the Three Musketeers!"

Dair also raised his bottle. "Would you come along, too?"

Peyton took a swig of beer. "I could, yeah. After my Friday shift. So I'd be around for reunion day. Do you think your family would mind, Rob?"

"Not at all. They love you," Robin said truthfully. He shook his head and laughed. "Okay. I guess we're really doing this?" The other two nodded. So he raised his bottle as well, all of them clunking together as they made their toast.

"The Three Musketeers!"

Smudge barked and jumped to the floor, chasing his fluffy tail in happiness.

Robin watched in a kind of daze as his friends resumed their dinners and cracked open more beers to celebrate. This was really happening. A laugh bubbled up from his throat. It was insane, but…it might also be a total blast. His laugh made the other two cackle as well.

Soon, there were more beers, then vodka and rum. They turned the music up and danced around the mostly eaten takeout with Smudge scampering between their feet.

Robin's phone stayed in the fridge the rest of the night, totally forgotten. If anyone called from his work, someone else would just have to deal with the problem for the rest of the week.

Robin had a reunion to go to.

3

DAIR

WELL, THIS CERTAINLY WAS A TURN OF EVENTS.

Despite his pounding head, Dair had been forced out of bed too early on Sunday morning by various pets jumping on his face, demanding to be fed and walked. After a street run with Smudge and a lazy walk around the block with Jimmy, Dair had called his boss to request the vacation time. Sober, it had seemed like more of a big ask.

Sure enough, his boss was an ass about the last-minute request. But he couldn't deny that Dair hadn't taken a single personal day all year, and there wasn't actually anybody booked off the next week. So, begrudgingly, he allowed Dair the vacation time.

Unpaid.

Dair could think about the implications of that later. Right now, he could live off his credit card and hopefully pick up a bunch of extra shifts when he got back.

That settled, Dair showered, then raided the fridge for breakfast, removing Robin's very cold but luckily still functioning phone. Sadly, he hadn't had the wits about him to save the rest of the Thai food, but there hadn't been loads left anyway. Instead, he set about whipping up some hot, greasy carbs to ease his unsettled stomach and pounding head.

It was easier to make a selection of food for more people. So he got out eggs, pancake mix, bacon, potatoes to make hash browns, as well anything else he could find to douse in maple syrup for the three of them. Hopefully, the smells of frying food would lure his housemates out soon enough. Until then, he'd let them sleep.

A deep contentment was in his bones when he thought of the events of the night before. They'd had Saturday night dinner all together several times now, but this was entirely different. He felt included in a way he hadn't in a very long time.

He was going to go to Robin's hometown and meet his family. And pretend to be his boyfriend. That was a bit unexpected, but not in a bad way. It was the family part that Dair had been excited about.

Dair had lost his own parents a long time ago. As an only child without any cousins his own age, he'd adopted the Marines as his family as well as his ex-girlfriend. Since drifting away from them, he'd always hoped he'd date someone with a big loving family. Obviously this wasn't *actually* dating, but it was the closest Dair had gotten in a while.

Now though, a sliver of doubt was trying to squirm its way into Dair's mind. This was a big deal. Robin's family was important to him. Could Dair really lie to them for a week?

He was mulling this over when he ripped open one of the packs of bacon. Immediately, he found himself surrounded by excited pets, winding through his legs or, in Jolly Roger's case, unashamedly jumping up onto the counter.

"Okay, this isn't for you guys," Dair said with a chuckle. They still had plenty of food from their breakfasts that Dair had sorted first thing, so he shooed them off. Then he got the stove on and began heating up a couple of pans.

Like they'd said last night, they weren't really going to be lying to Robin's family. They were just going to say he and Robin had gotten together recently and keep the details vague. So long as Dair was there to act as a barrier between Robin and Mac, everything else would be fine.

Dair realized he was gripping the spatula so hard he was in risk of snapping it. He shook his hand out, then got to cracking some eggs into the oil. They sizzled and popped while he poked at the edges.

Robin had been pretty insistent that his ex hadn't smacked him around. But the fact remained that Mac had hurt Robin back in their high school days. It didn't matter that Robin had normalized it in his mind. It made Dair's blood boil.

Robin was gentle and delicate. The idea of anyone threatening him was totally unacceptable. Dair simply wouldn't allow anything to happen to him, and he wasn't going to let him be bullied into ditching the reunion. If he had to tell a couple of white lies to achieve that, so be it.

He knew his natural inclination was to look after most people and animals smaller than himself (which, to be honest, included almost everyone). But there was just *something* about Robin that made all Dair's protective instincts flare.

He sighed and looked down at Smudge who was dancing around his feet. The others had wandered off again, full from their own breakfasts. But Smudge knew damn well there was still bacon up on the counter, and he wasn't going anywhere.

"Bad boy," Dair murmured, reaching down to scratch behind the pup's ears. "You know Daddy's a softie, don't you?"

Smudge yipped.

The sound of Robin's door opening made Dair look over his shoulder away from the frying pan. Robin stumbled into the living room, rubbing his eyes and wincing, his reddish hair sticking out at all angles. He looked so adorable.

Dair wasn't sure how cool he'd be if – or *when* – they ran into Robin's abusive ex. The idea anyone would hit teenage Robin – when he would have been even smaller than he was now – was abhorrent. Dair didn't care if had been part of a game or just in fun: you didn't hit your partner.

Ever.

"Is this real life?" Robin croaked, holding his hand up to blot out the sunshine from his eyes. He staggered toward the kitchen island like a zombie, plucking his wayward glasses from where they were hanging off a lampshade.

Dair chuckled. "If you were still dreaming, breakfast would already be on the table."

Robin blinked, focusing on Dair. "You're making that for us too? Maybe I am still dreaming."

They shared a laugh, then Robin fumbled to get the coffee going, groaning as he bumbled from one side of the kitchen to the other. Dair realized he was watching him, amused. But he couldn't help it. Robin was cute.

"Oh, my phone." Robin inspected it where Dair had left it on the island, but the battery was dead. Instead of plugging it in though to check his messages, Robin shrugged and found himself a mug. Dair was proud. He was starting to let go of work already.

"So how are you feeling?" Dair asked him.

Robin sipped some sugary coffee and sat at the kitchen island. "Are you referring to the hangover or the Scooby-Doo, Hardy Boys-esque caper we've got planned?"

Dair barked a laugh, which made Smudge yap too. Dair caved and dropped him a small morsel of cooked bacon. "Is it really that crazy? If we're going to be getting separate motel rooms, all we'll have to do is hold hands occasionally."

Was it his imagination, or did Robin blush? Maybe it was the heat from the coffee going to his cheeks. Dair waited while Robin coughed and cleared his throat. "Yeah. Just a little hand-holding. No biggie."

"The rest will be a bro's trip. I bet you're excited about going back home. Peyton said it's been a while."

Robin sighed. "I guess I didn't realize just how hard I've been avoiding my ex."

He rolled his eyes. They were blue with a ring of jade green around his pupils. The two colors blended together to make them kind of shimmery topaz blue. Dair wasn't sure he'd even seen eyes quite like them before.

"Screw him," Dair said firmly, that hot anger bubbling again. "You're a hundred times the man he is."

Robin smiled bashfully and ran his hand through his unruly hair. Then he began petting Jolly Roger, who had appeared by his side. It made Dair happy how easily Robin always fussed over his fur babies.

"It's difficult, I guess," Robin said suddenly, "not to be embarrassed. None of this would be necessary if I just had a boyfriend already."

Dair shrugged and flipped the bacon. The smell was making his mouth water. "It's just timing. Peyton and I don't have girlfriends right now either."

The small smile that tugged at one side of Robin's mouth suggested that thought hadn't occurred to him. "True." He sighed and rubbed his topaz eyes under his glasses. "I guess if I'd dated anyone properly since Mac, it would be less awkward. I just feel…'less than' facing him now." He used air quotations, then dropped his hands dejectedly.

"I get that," Dair said sincerely. "I'm sorry. But you're not anything 'less.' Trust me."

Something rash washed over him. If Robin was going to confess a personal secret like that, so would Dair. Then they'd be on an even playing field.

"You know what? I've never dated *anyone* aside from my ex. The idea of even sleeping with anyone else still seems weird to me."

Robin's eyebrows rose and a little 'oh' noise escaped his mouth. "You mean…she's the only one?"

Dair knew plenty of guys who'd be ashamed by that fact, but Dair figured life was too short to get hung up on shit like that. "Yep." He nodded and sipped his own coffee. "So don't worry about what other people think. What's the point of having sex if you're not into the person? It's not a competition."

"I've had a few hookups…"

Robin frowned, then looked up at Dair. The smile that he gave him made Dair's heart skip unexpectedly. It was nice to have someone look at him like that again. Like he'd made a real difference. Seeing Robin cheered up made himself feel more complete somehow.

"You're right. Not that it's anyone's business, but I don't need to measure myself like that." His forehead creased again. "Damn, maybe I didn't need to pretend to have a boyfriend after all?"

Dair raised an eyebrow. He wasn't letting Robin get out of this. "Nuh-uh. Not giving a damn about this asshole doesn't mean I'm going to allow you to face him alone. I'm your muscle, remember?"

To prove his point, Dair flexed his biceps through his T-shirt. He wasn't sure, but Robin might have made a sort of squeaky noise. But at that same moment, Dair's timer went off, and he hurriedly flipped over his hash browns, forgetting about Robin's reaction.

"Ass-rimming son of a juggler and a priest!"

Dair and Robin both jumped as Peyton came stumbling out of her bedroom, half falling against the sofa as she clutched at her head and moaned. Her shorts and T-shirt pajama set had murderous-looking bunny rabbits on it.

"Oww," she hissed, blinking at the morning sunshine streaming through the apartment's windows.

"Hello, sleeping beauty," Robin said with a grin. "How's your head?"

"I've had many, *many* complaints." Peyton stumbled over and snagged Robin's coffee from the island to swallow a big glug. "Whose idea was it to get the whiskey out?"

"Yours," Dair and Robin said in unison.

Peyton grimaced. "Yesterday me is a whore."

Robin rolled his eyes as Dair chuckled at Peyton's potty mouth. She relented and gave Robin back his coffee before going to get her own and sitting down at the island.

"I hope you're hungry." Dair finished dishing up, then turned around with two overflowing plates for his friends.

Peyton made a sound embarrassingly close to what Dair guessed was her orgasm moan. "Can you be *my* fake boyfriend?" she joked, attacking her breakfast with vigor.

As Dair sat with his own plate, he spied Robin dropping a chunk of bacon for a very naughty Smudge before he picked up his own knife and fork. Dair smiled, glad he wasn't the only softie here.

For a few moments they ate quickly but quietly until they'd all absorbed enough carbs to take the edge off their hangovers and enough caffeine to kick-start their brains again.

"Okay," Peyton said, slowing down her ravenous pace to something more civilized. "I had a thought – no – two thoughts. One, Dair, do you want to say you're bisexual?"

"Err…" He hadn't really thought about it.

Robin waved his fork and nodded. "Oh, good idea. People

are going to be all 'ohh, are you *gay* now?' But seeing as you were with a woman for over a decade, it might make more sense to say you're bi instead?"

Dair nodded, touched he had remembered that little detail. "Sure." That made sense to him. In fact, it was kind of nice to pretend he had this new side of his personality. It felt oddly right.

Robin chuckled to himself and looked down at Smudge, who was still loitering hopefully for more tidbits. "I have a bi boyfriend, Smudgy. How modern am I?"

Smudge barked and wagged his fluffy tail.

"Thought numero dos." Payton held up two fingers. "Speaking of the wild pack. If I'm going to be here by myself working twelve-hour shifts most days, we're going to have some problems. One small but destructive problem in particular."

All three of them looked down at Smudge. The pup stopped wagging his tail and looked back up at them expectantly.

"Ah," said Dair in agreement.

The cats would sort themselves out, and Jimmy slept most of the time these days. But Smudge? There was a reason none of the lowest cabinets had knobs on them anymore and Dair only had one completely intact pairs of sneakers. And that was with three of them in and out of the apartment most of the time.

"It's okay. I've already thought of a brilliant solution." Peyton grinned. "You take Smudge with you."

"To Pine Cove?" Robin spluttered, almost choking on his coffee.

"Yeah," Peyton confirmed. "I'm pretty sure I Googled last night before going to sleep, and it looks like a crazy dog-friendly town."

Robin wiped the coffee off his chin and appeared to

consider her words. "True. Most businesses had a dog if I remember correctly."

"Is your family allergic?" Dair asked. He didn't want to leave Smudge alone to destroy the apartment. Also, the little fella would be upset and lonely if he did. But he didn't want to be an imposition to Robin's folks either.

"No," Robin said, still frowning. "We had a dog growing up. I'm sure they'd love to have a puppy visit."

"And I *definitely* checked the motel you'd be staying at accepts pets. Isn't that cool? You need to remember to book those rooms before you go, by the way."

Robin nodded. "Okay. Yeah, sure. I think that would work? Dair, you okay bringing Smudgy?"

"Absolutely. The more, the merrier."

Thankfully they were planning on leaving the next morning, on Monday. So Dair would have the rest of the day to make arrangements for bringing a dog with them across Washington. He could pop to the store and make sure he had plenty of food, bowls, and toys, and he'd bring Smudge's usual bed, which would smell of home for him.

This was going to be fun, he was sure. Not since he'd served had he felt this tingle of excitement and anticipation. Of course this was in no way as dangerous. Nobody's life would be on the line. But they were still venturing into the unknown.

And Dair was surprised to realize just how excited he was to be doing it with Robin. Hopefully, this was going to be the start of the next phase in the friendship. Who knew how close they'd be after an escapade like this?

4

ROBIN

As they left the bay area of Seattle behind them, Robin tried not to be too conscious of the fact he was alone in a Ford Ranger extremely close to his crush.

Crush. It was like he was already back in high school again. Did grown men even have crushes? It seemed the right word for how he was feeling, though. So seeing as he didn't have to say it out loud, he was going to keep using it.

Dair was the poster boy for chivalry. Here he was, rescuing Robin from his ridiculous situation with a smile on his face as he hummed along to the radio. He even opened and closed the car doors for Robin when he was getting in and out of the car.

Robin didn't really deserve such kindness, but it felt so nice he allowed himself to enjoy it just a little bit. A handsome ex-Marine was coming on a road trip with him, playing along with this silly game just to make him feel better.

If nothing else, Robin hoped the two of them might at least become proper friends out of this. After all, coworkers went on bonding weekends as team-building exercises. Jay had made buddies at other friends' bachelor parties. Why couldn't he and Dair get a deeper friendship from this escapade? Sure, they didn't have much in common. But neither did Robin and Peyton, and they still got on like a riot.

Unfortunately, he spent the first half hour of the drive on his cell to his colleagues, who were indeed going into a meltdown without him on the first day. Honestly, he knew he was good at his job, but it was like they didn't even want to try. They just wanted to sit back and let him do it all. Eventually, Dair had poked Robin's thigh with one of his large fingers and mouthed *"you're on vacation"* to him.

As much as Robin didn't want to let his company down, he was also not keen to blow what could be his only ever chance to go away with Dair. So he managed to close the call after a few more minutes, telling them they could Google anything they really didn't understand, then switched his phone off. He was avoiding messages from his family anyway, so the damn thing could stay silent in his bag for a while.

The countryside became more picturesque as they drove east. It would take them three to four hours to reach Pine Cove, and they weren't in any hurry. They'd left after the city's morning rush hour, but that still meant they should arrive in the early afternoon.

Robin had been too chicken to tell his family in person that he was bringing a 'boyfriend' with him for the week. Especially Jay, who he was still worried would smell a rat immediately. So he'd sent a message to the family group chat, then put his phone on silent before shoving it to the bottom of his bag. He wasn't sure how they were going to react. Robin hadn't brought a boy home since Mac, and it was no secret now how relieved they'd all been when Robin had mustered up the courage to dump his ass.

It hadn't been easy. In fact, Robin had been forced to do it several times the summer before college as Mac simply wouldn't take no for an answer. At the time, Robin kept getting flattered that a guy as gorgeous and athletic as Mac wanted him that much, so he kept being convinced to try *one more time.* Eventually, it had taken Robin moving out of town to go to school that had finally made Mac see their relationship was over.

Had it ever really been real? It wasn't like they were the only gay kids at school. The LGBT society had been a thriving community, in fact. Robin was looking forward to seeing some of his friends again after so long, especially the outrageous Emery Klein, this week. But Robin had never expected to get himself a steady boyfriend. Not with his fabulous, charming twin next to him.

He'd often wondered if it was simply the flattery of having someone like Mac be interested in him that had kept them together for a year and a half.

He was pulled from his reverie by a certain ball of fluff scampering back into his lap from the back seat. Dair had placed Smudge's bed in the truck, but Smudge seemed far more interested in tormenting Daddy and his friend in the passenger seat.

"Whoa! Hello there!" Robin cried, scooping the little mutt up in his arms. "You're going to cause an accident, you maniac!"

Dair laughed from behind the wheel. It was one of the things that tugged pitifully at Robin's heartstrings. Dair was so easy to laugh, so free with his smiles and time and patience. How else would he have ended up on this trip with Robin?

Robin wasn't an idiot. He knew it was going to be a hard sell to convince people that someone as stunning and manly as Dair would be dating him. But fuck it, that was kind of part of the fun. For a week, Robin could live in this little fantasy land where Dair *did* like him that way. Then they'd have an amicable little 'breakup' in a few weeks' time, no one would be any the wiser, and they could continue being friends. Hopefully better friends than before.

As Dair drove, they talked about their backgrounds. Things they might know if they'd started dating recently. They decided to say they'd gotten together about a month ago, which would mean a couple of months after Dair had moved in. That seemed reasonable to both of them.

Robin was sad to discover that Dair's parents had died suddenly in a car crash during his junior year of high school, so a little over a decade ago. His ex-girlfriend, Malory, had been his rock during that time and the years following, always there for him when Dair came home from deployment. But after Dair was discharged and began his new life in the States as a mechanic, they'd drifted apart and split more or less amicably.

Dair seemed pretty upbeat despite this slightly sorry tale, so Robin tried not to make too much of it either. He helped Dair memorize his siblings' names and who was the oldest to youngest. He talked a little about his town and then meeting Peyton at college, then his job that he'd had since moving to Seattle.

Dair talked a bit about working as a mechanic, using words that meant nothing to Robin as he knew zilch about cars. But Dair didn't have a clue about Javascript or refactoring code either. They'd had a nice moment of appreciation for each other's professions.

Then Dair asked a question that woke Robin right up.

"So. Who made the first move on who?"

They'd stopped for burgers and fries at this quaint log cabin sort of diner, and Robin almost dropped his bun into his lap. It bounced like a live grenade in his hands, somehow not completely falling apart before he could grab it securely again.

"Um, what?" he asked awkwardly through a mouthful of meat.

Smudge snuffled in his sleep by their feet. Dogs weren't allowed inside, so they'd grabbed one of the outdoor picnic tables and tied his leash to a bench leg.

Dair had a sparkle in his eye. "How did we get together? How did it go down?"

Robin could feel the heat rising in his cheeks and he desperately tried to will it away as he swallowed his mouthful of burger. "Um, I don't – I'm not sure?"

He had limited experience with this. Mac had kissed him on his parents' sofa after he'd invited Robin over to watch Saturday Night Live and sneak some beers. Mac had been in charge of the whole affair, and within minutes, they'd been up in his room, naked and jerking each other off. Typical desperate and horny teenagers.

His Grindr hookups and dates had always had an air of expectation about them that lacked a certain magic that Robin always yearned for. What did he really want? This was his pretend relationship. What was the most romantic thing he could think of?

Did he really want to look too closely at that, though? It wasn't like he hadn't already imagined several different scenarios where Dair had revealed the secret feelings he'd been nursing for Robin. Where he'd lean in and ask if he could kiss Robin...

Robin squirmed in his seat, hoping Dair didn't notice. "Um, well. I thought you were straight. So, maybe you, uh, asked me out?"

"To dinner and a movie?" Dair grinned before popping a fry into his mouth. "Maybe I just obliviously thought we were hanging out. Then you pointed out we were on a date. That's kind of cute, right?"

Fuck. Was Dair *trying* to destroy him?

"Yeah, that's definitely cute," Robin agreed helplessly. His heart was fluttering.

"Then, when I realized we were actually on a date, I discovered I was into it, and the rest has just been us taking it slow while I explore this bi thing. Watching Netflix and going on walks and stuff?"

Robin nodded, his throat thick. "Sure."

"Oh. First kiss." Dair nodded, giving it real thought, by the looks of it. "How about I gave you a peck on the check that first night? Then a proper kiss the next night? When I got brave enough."

He waggled his eyebrows, clearly comfortable discussing this. Robin felt a little dizzy. "I can't imagine you ever not being brave," he managed to mumble.

Dair licked his lips and put his food down. After a moment's pause, he wiped his hand on his napkin, then reached it over the table to the halfway point. "Thanks," he said. "But I've been plenty scared in my life. It's all about how you deal with it."

Robin looked at his hand. Was he suggesting...?

Robin glanced around the outside area of the diner, but there weren't many people near them, and nobody appeared to be paying them any attention. Cars hurtled by on the freeway, and the trees rustled behind the building. It was just them, no one else.

Time to be brave. He cleared his throat and laughed as casually as he could. "Do you want to practice holding hands?"

Dair bit his lip. "When you said that just now – if you'd have been my ex, Malory – I'd have reached for her hand. So

I figured it might be nice to reach for yours. If you're comfortable with that?"

Dear lord. He really had no clue what affect he had on Robin, did he? That was so sweet. Robin really needed to play it cool and act like this was totally fine. Not like his heart was trying to thump its way out of his chest.

"Yeah," he said, trying to sound confident. "Totally. It's probably a good idea to be relatively comfortable around each other, right? Practice a bit so we don't jump if the other touches them, or, you know, whatever." He was babbling. He needed to stop babbling. So he brought his hand up and dropped it into Dair's as fast as he could, not overthinking.

Except the skin-to-skin contact lit his insides up like he'd been struck by lightning. He suppressed a shiver as his body reacted to feeling Dair's warm, callused palm against his own.

Dair grinned. "Easy," he declared.

"Sure," Robin squeaked.

Dair appeared to be analyzing the feeling of holding another man's hand. Or…was that even it? It sounded like he'd had literally no intimacy with someone else aside from his ex. So maybe it was just having another human being's hand pressed against his own that was a new sensation.

He rubbed the back of Robin's knuckles with his thumb. "Is this okay?"

Robin took a second before he answered, trying to compose himself. "Y-yeah, fine. So long as you're comfortable?"

Dair nodded and raised his eyebrows. "Of course. It's no different, is it? Just two people sharing a moment. I don't know why folks would get upset because you're a guy and not a girl. If you close your eyes, it doesn't matter. A hand is a hand. It matters who it belongs to. Like the relationship you have with that person."

Robin marveled at him. Being a progressive thinker shouldn't be that fucking hot. "Yeah," Robin croaked. "If only everyone saw it that way."

Dair grinned, selecting another fry to dip in his ketchup, licking the salt from his fingers. Robin was amazed at himself for not whimpering.

Dair was still casually holding his hand, lightly stroking the back of it. "My folks were just so chill about this stuff, you know? They talked a lot about how other people are marginalized, like the LGBT community, people of color, the differently abled. Then, in the Marines – well, no one gave a shit who you were. Everyone ragged on everyone else, and every fucker watched their teammate's back. Equal on every level. I just think I have a very low tolerance for bullshit."

Robin was incredibly brave and caressed Dair's hand just a tiny bit with his own thumb. "Agreed." He cleared his throat. "I mean, in that I wish people were treated a bit more equally. Or that some folks acknowledged the prejudice and struggles that other people went through. I think I let too much bullshit go on sometimes."

Dair squeezed his hand twice. "Hey. We can't fight every battle. We do what we can."

Robin's heart ached. Dair was too damn perfect. Except he was straight – as hard as that was to believe with his strong hand wrapped around Robin's.

As if to make the situation even more unbelievable, Dair's eyes lit up as he made another suggestion. "Hey! If we're going for realism, do you want to take a selfie and post it on your Facebook or whatever? That would make it look a little more believable than me just showing up out of nowhere, yeah?"

His words made total sense. Yet panic flared through Robin. That felt like crossing a line in some way. Physical evidence of this sham relationship. But what did he expect would happen? If Dair was going as his date to all these things, there would be photos. People were going to talk to him. He'd promised himself he was all in for this escapade, so that meant building up the illusion of his and Dair's relationship before they arrived back in Pine Cove.

"Great idea," he said with the best smile he could manage. "If not somewhat nefarious. You're good at this."

"I prefer to think of it as resourceful," Dair said with a wink. "Right, come on. Let's get an adorable selfie to make everyone jealous."

Trying not to let his hand tremble, Robin got his phone out and switched the camera setting around so they could take a picture of themselves. When he flubbed the first few, he winced, expecting Dair to get annoyed.

"Why not try angling it this way?" he suggested instead, surprising Robin. He posed patiently, making sure Robin was totally happy with the final result.

Unfortunately, Robin's glasses made things difficult with the light reflecting off the lenses, but his contacts were somewhere in his bag. He just felt so dorky next to Dair, but if anything, Dair hugged him closer.

"Try one last time," he murmured against Robin's ear. "Don't overthink it."

So Robin just snapped a few pictures wildly. To his surprise, he got the best photo by far doing that. "Oh," he said faintly. He genuinely loved the way he looked in that one. But even more mesmerizing was the way Dair was drawn back in the image, looking at Robin with what appeared to be such affection. He was probably just hoping Robin would hurry up and take the shot. But for a moment, Robin could pretend Dair really was his boyfriend.

Within minutes, the moment was over. They paid the check and hustled Smudge back into the truck, the mountains of the Pacific Northwest looming over them as they pulled once more onto the freeway. But Robin was captivated, editing their selfie to make sure it looked just right. Even more than that was the caption he was working on.

In the end, he put: 'Excited to be heading home with someone so awesome by my side.' Because it was true.

Dair just didn't need to know *how* true it was.

5

DAIR

ALTHOUGH DAIR HAD LIVED IN AND AROUND THE SEATTLE area his whole life – Lakewood, Olympia, and the like – he'd never really traveled out very far east of Snoqualmie or Monroe. As they drove through the Okanogan-Wenatchee National Forest, he wondered why the hell not. It was breathtaking.

Purply-blue mountains capped with blinding-white snow rose above the swathes of deep green pine trees that had presumably given Robin's hometown its name. Telephone poles often followed the roads as they wound through the ups and downs of the terrain, leading them closer to the place Robin had avoided for so long.

Yet again, anger simmered under Dair's skin, and he gripped the steering wheel slightly tighter. He didn't want Robin to see he was having a moment of fury. Luckily, Smudge was distracting him with sloppy kisses to the face while Robin laughed and tried to keep singing along with Britney on the radio.

It was difficult to stay mad with Robin looking so light and carefree after the prospect of this reunion had made him so stressed a couple of days ago. But the reason he had denied himself this beautiful countryside and time with his family was a subconscious drive to stay the fuck away from that bastard Mac.

Dair was friends with a few guys from his unit who had escaped poverty and abusive home environments. He knew a guy whose family had been rich as sin but complete assholes. There were plenty of reasons to turn your back on the place you'd grown up in. But to be driven out, to feel like you weren't able to return because you were unsafe...

He tightened his fingers around the wheel again, making the leather creak.

"Are you okay?" There was concern in Robin's topaz-blue eyes as Dair glanced over at him.

"Yeah, fine," he lied. He gave Robin a smile that was genuine, though.

Ultimately, he was there to ensure nothing happened to Robin and try and make this week go by as smoothly as possible. He was just there to run interference so Mac didn't start anything.

He was *not* there to punch Mac in the face should they run into each other.

However, as they drove closer to Pine Cove, it was clear Robin was getting more anxious.

For Dair, Seattle and the surrounding towns were his only link to his parents. But it was also a stark reminder of all he'd lost. Not just his folks, but the life he'd hoped to build with Malory.

She still lived in the city as well. The chances of running into each other were extremely small, so neither of them had minded the other sticking around. But there were so many restaurants and parks and theatres they'd created memories in together. Dair didn't so much miss her as the *idea* of them that that had seeped into the very brickwork of the city.

Sometimes, though, what you wanted as teenagers doesn't last. He and Mal had been great together. But ultimately, he'd wanted kids and she didn't, and that was just the way it was. He was glad they were still friends.

So it wasn't like he wanted to leave Seattle or would even know where to go if he did. However, he could see why people chose to uproot themselves from their hometowns.

But Robin? From everything he and Peyton had said about his family, they sounded loving and supportive. They certainly seemed to treat Peyton as an adoptive extended member of their brood, despite having enough kids to begin with. She had gushed to Dair about how great the Coals were even before Dair had suggested this escapade.

If it wasn't for Mac guarding his hometown like a junkyard dog, would Robin have been back long before now?

"Hey." Dair reached over to the passenger seat and squeezed Robin's thigh. "Are *you* okay?"

It was funny, but it didn't feel strange at all to be physical with Robin. He'd appeared slightly startled when Dair had suggested taking a selfie together earlier, but then they'd had fun getting a really great shot. Maybe this whole fake boyfriend thing would be easier than Dair had imagined.

Dair removed his hand from Robin's leg and placed it back on the wheel but glanced over to see Robin look at him and gulp. "I'm being silly. It's just jitters. Once I get home, I'll be fine."

A sudden thought occurred to Dair. Was Robin embarrassed by him? Robin was super smart, so it wasn't a leap to assume his family was well educated too. Dair had barely made it out of high school with his diploma. It had always made so much more sense to him to be elbow deep in grease and car parts or pushing his body to its limits. Books caused his head to swim.

Was Robin anxious over what his family was going to think about this guy he was supposedly dating?

Dair shifted in his seat. "I'll do my best not to embarrass you," he said, aware the comment was sort of out of the blue. But he felt he needed to make that promise.

He saw Robin's head snap back to look at him from the corner of his eye. "What? Why would you – Dair. That's nuts. You're an *ex-Marine* and you're *gorgeous.*"

The compliments took Dair by surprise. Or more, the fierceness with which Robin gave them. Dair's heart warmed. It was kind of nice to know Robin felt like that. "Oh, um, thanks. But I'm not smart like you. I don't want your family to think you're dating a doofus."

Robin's cheeks had gone red and he rubbed the back of his neck, looking adorably flustered. Dair squeezed his leg again in assurance before making a turn.

"From the crazed messages and many – *many* – gifs I half looked at in our group chat, my family is just thrilled I'm dating anyone," he mumbled. "Not that – you know." He waved his hand between them. "This is real. But they don't ever need to know that. They worry about me. Besides, they're going to love you. Don't even give it a second thought. They'll be stunned I managed to bag someone so hot. If anything, *that's* what will give the game away that we're lying."

A slightly manic laugh bubbled up his throat. He'd gone the color of beets and was now staring determinedly out the window at the passing trees. Dair frowned, glancing between him and the road.

Several thoughts flew through his head, the first of which was that Robin had called him both hot *and* gorgeous in the space of a couple of minutes. Dair hadn't thought about how it would feel to have a gay man tell him he was attractive. Especially when he hadn't even bothered with so much as a haircut in months. He'd felt liberated not to after always having to have it short in the Marines. He kind of expected himself to freak out, but all he could feel was flattered.

He didn't like the idea that Robin assumed they were mismatched. "Dude, not to get weird or anything, but you're hot too. Objectively speaking, as your friend. Like, seriously cute. Don't put yourself down."

Robin spluttered and shook his head, determinedly petting Smudge, who was trying to nip his fingers. "You sound like Peyton."

"Then you're two for two and we must be right," Dair said proudly. He was relieved to hear Robin laugh again and visibly relax. "Look – I know we're going to stretch the truth a little and tell people we're a couple. But I am still here as your actual friend – right?" He raised his eyebrows over at Robin. "I'm like a cheerleader and a bodyguard all rolled into one. I believe in you."

Robin puffed out a breath. Dair could feel him looking at him for a moment before punching him lightly on the arm. "Thank you."

Dair winked over at him. "You're gonna nail this reunion, okay? If there's anything I can do to ease the nerves, just shout. I'm your guy. Your cheerleader-guard...cheerguard!"

They shared a smile for as long as Dair could keep his eyes off the road. Then he concentrated on following the directions his phone was telling him. They didn't talk much for the remainder of the drive, but Robin remained relaxed enough.

Until they pulled into his parents' drive.

"Oh, god." He unclipped his seat belt, but remained sitting in the car. "I guess this is it. Boyfriend time." He gave Dair two thumbs-up and a grimace.

"Yeah."

Dair licked his lips. For all he'd given Robin the pep talk

about being awesome, he had failed to analyze his own feelings after Robin had called him gorgeous. Suddenly this felt like a much bigger deal than it had back at their apartment when they'd been getting drunk.

The only parents he'd ever been introduced to had been Malory's. He supposed there had been buddies at school whose folks he'd met. But they'd faded into obscurity, so the experiences couldn't have been that memorable. Malory's family, though, had been a big deal.

Her dad was the financial director of a big law firm in Seattle, her mother an interior designer, and her older sister a paralegal. They had warmed to Dair well enough, but at family gatherings, he'd always felt like he'd been on the outside looking in.

How was Robin's family going to receive him? The two of them might not *actually* have been dating, but the Coal family didn't know that. What if they deemed a gruff mechanic unworthy of their refined, educated son?

What did it matter? He wasn't really going to be going out with Robin once this week was through. He was just here to make sure Mac stayed away. Yet he couldn't shake the feeling that he wanted their approval. It was important to do Robin proud and maybe give him some of that confidence he was lacking in himself right now.

So Dair plastered the best smile he could on his face as the front door swung open. "No going back now," he said discretely to Robin through his teeth. A small middle-aged woman with bushy brown hair skipped onto the front porch and began waving frantically, as if Dair and Robin might miss her. "Your mom?" Dair guessed.

Robin made a sort of squeaking noise.

Right, game on. This was a mission, and Dair needed to focus. Before Robin could move, Dair was out of the truck, striding around the back and opening Robin's door for him and Smudge, like his pops had taught him before his passing. Just because Mr. Epping had envisioned his son dating women didn't mean Dair had forgotten what chivalry was.

"Oh, thanks," Robin said faintly, hopping out of the Ranger. Smudge was on his leash and immediately began straining against it in Robin's hand, determined to sniff every inch of this new terrain.

The Coal family home was three stories high and made entirely of a light-colored wood. Logs held up the roof over the porch and the triangular-shaped garage, and large square windows let plenty of natural light in. Dair had observed as they'd driven through the outskirts of town that many houses were situated on their own smallish plots rather than next to each other on streets. The Coal house was the same, surrounded by pine trees at the end of its own driveway about a hundred feet long. Dair inhaled deeply, filling his lungs with the rich pine scent.

He already loved it here.

"This is beautiful."

Robin didn't say anything as the truck door swung shut. He offered his mom a nervous smile but appeared reluctant to walk toward her.

This wasn't the Robin Dair knew at all. Where was the guy who debated for hours about the physics of warp drive on Star Trek or thrashed Dair at Call of Duty? Where was the guy who had apparently stood up to his manager a couple of months back when he'd had tried to wrongly overrule him? Where was the sweet, fun-loving guy who skipped around the apartment to Carrie Underwood when he thought no one else was looking?

Okay. This was what Dair was here for. To be The Perfect Boyfriend and protect Robin any way he could. If that also included some surprising, last-minute nerves at seeing his family again, that was fine. Dair reached down to take

Robin's hand, squeezed it twice, then nodded toward the house.

"Right, yeah," Robin stammered.

Smudge was desperate to meet Mrs. Coal and tugged them both toward the porch with his leash.

"Oh, Robin!" his mom cried. Her eyes looked shiny behind her glasses as she rushed down the stairs to throw her arms around her son. Dair expected him to let go of his hand, but if anything, Robin held on tighter. "You look wonderful. I swear you've grown. How was the drive? Have you eaten? Dinner's on, so I hope you're hungry. Everyone's coming over. Oh, it's so *nice* to have you back!"

Dair felt a pang in his chest. Malory's mom had been nice enough but never as warm and open as that. It was painfully obvious how much Mrs. Coal loved her kid. Dair clung to the memories of his own mom tightly, but it scared him how much they'd faded over the last decade. He had never been away from his parents long enough for them to miss him that much. Would his mom have been this emotional to see him after several months away?

"My goodness. This must be Alasdair." Mrs. Coal didn't fully release Robin but kept one arm around him as she turned to look at Dair. "It's such a pleasure to meet you, darling."

Dair's chest contracted. He wished he was *really* meeting his partner's parents. Mrs. Coal already struck him as someone kind and welcoming. The feeling only lasted a second, but it was powerful and almost overwhelming. Then he remembered he had a job to do, so he smiled and offered his hand for her to shake.

"It's a pleasure to meet you, ma'am."

She batted his hand away and launched her arms around his neck, standing on her tiptoes. Dair was so shocked he didn't have time to even think about hugging her back before she let him go.

"Sorry, sorry," she said from under her cloud of bushy brown hair.

It seemed to have doubled in size with her excitement. She yanked a hairband from around her wrist and pulled the mass into an attempt at a ponytail. Her cardigan had a bumblebee brooch on the lapel along with several small holes in the wool from where she'd maybe stuck other pins in. The knees of her faded blue jeans were engrained with mud that refused to wash out.

"It's just a bit overwhelming." Mrs. Coal waved her hands in front of her moist eyes. "Robin has never bought a boy home, and you seem like a real gentleman. And who's *this* darling?"

Poor Smudge had been dancing around, desperate for some love. So when Mrs. Coal dropped to her knees on the dry ground, he hurled himself at her, tail thwacking Dair's leg and her shoulder as he licked all over her face.

"Steady, steady!" Dair placed his hand over Robin's to tug at the leash. "Sorry, ma'am."

"Why would you be sorry?" she cried as she laughed, smooshing her face into the puppy's. "He's a treasure. Is he yours?"

"He is," Dair replied fondly.

"Dair rescued him," Robin said. Dair heard the pride in his voice and it made his heart warm. "All his cats and dogs are rescued. The others came all the way from Afghanistan."

Mrs. Coal pulled a clean tissue from inside the sleeve of her cardigan and wiped her face before standing up again. "Aren't you an angel? We had a collie while Robin was growing up. But when she passed…" She shook herself and smiled, but her eyes behind her glasses were definitely shining. "Anyway. It's lovely to meet you, darling. Bobbin didn't say how handsome you were." She winked. "Won't you come in?"

"*Mom*," Robin protested. Dair wasn't sure whether it was in response to the pet name that had slipped out or her calling Dair handsome, but Dair enjoyed it all the same.

"Bobbin?" he asked as they trailed up the porch steps after her.

"Kill me now," Robin moaned. But the big smile on his face suggested he perhaps didn't mind as much as he was making out.

They left their bags in the trunk to take to the motel later. For now, Dair allowed Robin and Smudge to lead him into the house.

His first thought was that there were photos *everywhere*. Hanging on the wooden walls, standing up on the furniture. There was even some sort of wind chime they passed on the porch that looked like it contained several baby photos. Dair knew there were five children, but as the photos were of them all at every age possible, he was still none the wiser as to what they all looked like.

Except Robin. He was the only redhead, his auburn hair shining in every picture. As there were so many of him with another black-haired boy of the same height, Dair guessed that might be his twin, Jay. But the rest were a mystery.

There were lots of well-worn rugs on the wooden floorboards and almost as much terracotta pottery around as photo frames. The smell of roast chicken floated through the air, making Dair's mouth water, even though they'd stopped for burgers and fries.

"I'm afraid your sibs are mostly still at work, but your dad's tinkering in his workroom. And Kes – KES!"

She absently hollered upward through the house as she bustled into the large open kitchen, not looking to see if Dair and Robin were still behind as she realized a pan was boiling over on the stove.

"Jiminy Cricket!" She yanked the pot from the flame and held it aloft while the water inside calmed down.

Dair found himself in a spacious kitchen that instinct told him was the heart of the house. The counter wrapped around the walls in an L-shape, and a freestanding island divided the space between the kitchen itself and the dining area. A large wooden table with thick, twisted and gnarly legs stood proudly with a large bowl of colorful pebbles in the center. At a glance, Dair surmised from the mismatched shapes and hues they weren't store-bought rather rescued from beaches unknown. Each probably held a family memory.

Once he'd turned eighteen and left for the Marines, it had felt too painful to try and deal with the sale and emptying of his parents' home. He'd packed a couple of boxes to put into storage, then left his aunt and uncle to unravel his folks' lives while he went off to basic training.

In years to come, he'd realized how selfish that had been. Not only that, but he'd lost the right to any keepsakes that he wished hadn't been distributed amongst extended family members or simply taken to Goodwill. If he had more tangible items from his childhood, would he feel less disconnected from it now he was an adult? He guessed he'd never know.

"Are you burning the house down again, Mom?"

"I never – that was *one* time," Mrs. Coal protested with a huff, dropping the pot back on the stove.

A teenage girl with a pixie haircut grinned as she flounced into the kitchen, phone in hand. Then she jumped and clutched her heart in an exaggerated fashion at seeing Robin sitting at the kitchen table next to Dair.

"Jesus! We're being robbed!"

"Ha-ha." Robin rolled his eyes as he stood to greet his sister with a hug. "Nice to see you too, Kes."

"It's *Kestrel*," she corrected pointedly, pocketing her phone. But she was soon distracted. "PUPPY!"

Just like her mom, she threw herself on the floor to be voluntarily mobbed by Smudge, who'd been released from his leash. She even went so far as to roll onto her back and let him climb onto her chest.

"Oh, you're such a good puppy, aren't you? Yes, yes, so adorable." She paused in their wrestling to look up at Robin and Dair. "And who's this mountain man you've let wander in after you?"

"Kes!" her mom snapped.

Robin lightly nudged her twig-like arm with his foot. "Be nice," he growled. Dair hadn't been aware that Robin could growl. "This is Dair."

Dair waited a beat before waving down at her. If Robin was too shy to be the first to tell the white lie, Dair would do it for him. "Robin's boyfriend. Lovely to meet you."

Kestrel harrumphed and rubbed her nose against Smudge's. "I'm sure I don't have to tell you to treat him well or I'll push you into the lake, but...treat him well, or I'll push you into the lake. Understood?"

Kestrel probably weighed a third of Dair's body mass and had spindly legs poking from her shorts like a giraffe. A stiff breeze would most likely knock her down. But she shot him a look that could have frozen hell over. If Dair had ever been lucky enough to have his own kid sister, he imagined her being exactly like Kestrel.

"Understood," Dair repeated back to her with a grin.

"Oh, for goodness sake, Kes. Stop showing off." Mrs. Coal checked the oven, the delicious smell of roasting chicken wafting into the room.

"Kestrel," Robin's sister corrected without looking up from her new best friend, who was licking her ear.

"Sorry," said her mom patiently. *"Kestrel.* Please go tell your father to wash up. Dinner won't be long and the others will be back soon."

Kestrel gave a dramatic sigh and reluctantly put Smudge back on the floor. But before she went to get her and Robin's father from wherever he was, she turned back to where Robin had sat back down, draping her arms around his neck.

"I'm glad you haven't forgotten where we live." She kissed his cheek, then skipped off out of the room.

Dair looked at Robin just as he turned to glance at him. As they held each other's gaze for a moment, Dair reached out to squeeze his friend's hand. It was crazy how quickly that had become an easy habit.

He gave Robin a look that he hoped conveyed how he was feeling. Their worries had been unfounded, at least so far. His family was delighted to have both him and Dair here. They had even made Dair feel at home right away. There were still other family members Dair was yet to meet, but he was getting a very good vibe already.

Robin responded with a small smile and a relieved sigh. Dair couldn't help but feel he was still holding something back, but for now at least, the homecoming was going as well as Dair had hoped it could.

They just had to get through a whole week of this, and they'd be fine.

6

ROBIN

"I THOUGHT WE HAD AN EVENT TONIGHT?" ROBIN SAID BY WAY of greeting when his twin walked through the front door.

Jay grinned, used to Robin being as blunt as a spoon. Robin tried to mask it with other people, but why bother around Jay? They could read each other like books.

"I missed you too, bro." Jay threw his arms around Robin and squeezed so tight he lifted Robin off the floor an inch. They were the same slim, small build, but Jay had always been the more confident of the two. Robin was sure it wasn't true for all twins in the world, but in their case, the older twin was certainly the more dominant.

"Yeah, yeah, of course I missed you," said Robin, patting him on the back. "Now get off me."

Jay laughed loudly and tickled him. Robin wasn't kidding. He'd missed his twin like he'd miss a limb.

To anyone looking closer it was obvious they were brothers, despite their different hair colors. They had almost exactly the same facial features, subconscious mannerisms, and were even both left handed. But that was where a lot of the similarities ended.

Robin loved being around Jay because it gave him a sense of completion. Like he could never truly be calm unless his twin was there to balance him out.

It had been a shock to them both when Robin had upped roots and relocated to Seattle.

At the time, Robin had been so blindsided by getting into his first choice of school he'd sort of simply assumed Jay would come with him. After all, you could do teacher training almost anywhere. But Jay had insisted it would do Robin the world of good to go out on his own. For a while, Robin had been left feeling hurt and abandoned, even though it had been him who had split them up. But ultimately, Jay had been right. Of course. Robin needed space to breathe on his own without relying on Jay or without Mac strangling him.

Robin may have flourished out in the big wide world, but Jay was still the extrovert to his introvert. During school, Jay had shone in the drama club, actually making it cool for a few years as everyone wanted to get on stage with bright, talented, hilarious Jay Coal. Robin had been to every play, sitting in the front row brimming with pride. But heaven forbid the spotlight should ever turn on him.

Robin liked being the quiet one, watching from the shadows. People were such hard work to him. He never had the easy patter Jay did in groups, where he was effortlessly entertaining. Too long in social situations drained Robin completely within a few hours, leaving him unable to do anything else but run off to hide somewhere to recharge. Preferably with a loud video game so he could shoot lots of aliens.

Which was why Robin was eager to know what they'd be doing that night. Jay hadn't said, and when he'd knocked at the door, Robin had raced to let him in so they could have a moment to themselves. He realized belatedly that had left his mom alone with Dair, but they seemed to be getting along well enough. Smudge was still there to act as a buffer, if necessary.

Even though it didn't mean anything as Dair wasn't really his boyfriend, Robin was still pleased that his mom liked him already.

"You're safe," Jay assured him, closing the door and ruffling Robin's hair. "Tonight is just a family dinner. I thought you might nope out if you realized we'd all be here to meet your new man, so I *might* have let you believe there was something official planned for the reunion."

"Asshole," Robin grumbled. He supposed it wasn't too bad, but it was a lot for Dair to deal with at once when he wasn't even getting the advantage of a girlfriend in return.

"Speaking of which…" Jay raised an eyebrow and fixed Robin with a stern look. "Boyfriend?"

Robin did his very best not to squirm. "Yeah, boyfriend," he agreed, hoping he didn't sound as defensive as he felt.

"You never mentioned any *hint* of a boyfriend before."

"Well, because I knew you'd get like this, didn't I?" Robin waved his hand up and down Jay's frame as he crossed his arms. "I do date, you know. It's just all the other guys were terrible and I ditched them pretty fast. Or well, you know, they ditched me. But that's not the point."

"And what is the point?" Jay asked in amusement at Robin's rambling. Jay never rambled.

"The point," Robin said firmly, scrambling around for a point to make, "is…that Dair is the first guy to stick around long enough to warrant mentioning. And I happened to be coming to the reunion. So…ta-da!" He waved his hands in a weak attempt at jazz hands. "Now you know I have a boyfriend. No big deal."

"No big deal?" Jay repeated. They both knew that was bullshit, but Robin wasn't going to let Jay dwell on it.

"Yeah. He's already met Mom and Kestrel."

Maybe his dad had come in by now. Robin didn't know. But their older brother Swift and younger sister Ava were still at work, hopefully coming home soon. Robin didn't want to be hanging around waiting for them to have dinner. It gave everyone else more time to interrogate Dair, and that was dangerous for their charade as well as Robin's nerves.

Jay narrowed his eyes. "What's he like?"

Robin rolled his eyes and threw open his arms. "Boyfriend shaped," he cried in exasperation.

"Well, come on then." Jay practically danced down the hall, leaving Robin to scurry after him. He trusted Jay wouldn't do anything mean or upsetting to either him or Dair, but Robin was still anxious.

The last time they'd met a significant other of his had been Peyton, his best friend. But she'd been more than spunky enough to handle several Coals at once. The only boyfriend he'd ever had was Mac, and that was a long time ago. They'd always been respectful of him at the time, but they hadn't held back in their disdain of him after. It made Robin embarrassed to think he'd put up with Mac's nonsense for that long.

Robin shrugged that off. He would prefer it if his family liked Dair, as Robin fully intended on staying friends after this week. But at the end of the day, they weren't really boyfriends. So whatever happened, it would be okay.

Right?

Jay was already giving Dair a hug by the time Robin got back to the kitchen. Maybe he should have warned Dair that his family was so tactile before they'd arrived, but Dair appeared to be coping just fine standing from his chair every five minutes. Another flare of pride rushed through Robin until he reminded himself that this wasn't real. He needed to be careful he didn't let his family get too invested in Dair if they were just going to 'break up' in a couple of weeks' time.

"Wow." Jay stepped back and lightly slapped Dair's thick, muscular arm. "Swift is going to love having you around. Finally someone who can talk bench-pressing and protein shakes."

Dair looked a bit uncomfortable and Robin could have smacked Jay. He was only kidding, but Dair was desperate not to come across as some dumb jock.

"Dair can talk about lots of things," Robin blurted out firmly. "He likes old Hong Kong action movies, and he's always cooking Thai for us, and he fixed tanks while he was in the Marines. As well as Smudge, he's got another rescue bulldog and three cats. Oh, and he *almost* beat me at the latest Far Cry the other week, which you all know is *very* impressive."

He laughed and put his hands on his hips. There was a beat of silence.

Damn. He'd been babbling again. But if they were really dating, it would be okay for Robin to be proud of Dair's accomplishments, right?

Jay gave him a look that Robin read as 'I was just kidding – chill.' But Dair looked at him with appreciation. Robin tried not to blush. Hopefully Dair didn't mind him cataloging so many details about him. It was all for the sake of their charade, after all.

"Aww, you two." His mom put her arm around Robin and shook him. "You're adorable together."

Robin glanced at Dair, but he smiled warmly, reminding Robin that he was okay with this whole thing.

Smudge decided he hadn't had enough attention in the last two minutes, so began chasing his tail and yapping. Everyone laughed and crowded around to fuss him.

"You guys already got a dog?" Jay asked. Robin didn't miss the slight note of concern in his voice.

"Oh, no." He laughed and waved his hands. "He's Dair's."

"But Robin's great with all my little guys," Dair piped up immediately. "He never forgets to top up their water and walks the dogs when I'm at work and lets Smudge sleep on his bed, even though he shouldn't."

Robin looked at him. He supposed he did do all that stuff. But hearing the way Dair describe it made it sound remarkable. He was touched.

"Well, will you look who it is?"

Robin's heart swooped as their father walked into the kitchen. He was wiping his hands on a dish towel, then kissed their mom on the cheek as he hung it off the oven door.

"Dad." Robin rushed over to hug him. Like most of the family, Joe Coal was on the short side and bespectacled. His thinning hair was combed back and kept short. Even though he'd been out tinkering in his carpentry workroom, he still wore a shirt that he'd tucked into his pants over his rounded belly.

"That's not your car outside," he said as he patted Robin's back.

"No, sir. It's mine. Alasdair Epping, nice to meet you." He shook hands with Robin's dad as his mom tutted.

"I won't have this 'sir' and 'ma'am' business. We're Deb and Joe, and we're just thrilled to have you here, aren't we, Joe?"

"You check the oil and tire pressure before you set out?" Robin's dad asked with a raised eyebrow to Dair.

"Oh, Joe!" His mom whacked him with the towel he'd just been using. "Quit it."

"Naturally, sir – Joe." Dair winced, clearly not comfortable addressing Robin's parents by their first names.

Robin huffed. "Dair's a *mechanic*, Dad."

Jay laughed as he set about fixing people's drinks. Robin's mom insisted Robin and Dair sit while she and his father finished up dinner, making idle chitchat asking how Robin's job was going. They didn't really understand any of his technobabble, but it touched Robin how much they cared.

Kestrel reappeared not long after with the oldest of the Coal kids in tow. "I found another one," she cheerfully announced before sitting straight back on the floor again with Smudge.

Swift waved to the room at large as he trailed behind his little sister.

Being a family all named after birds, Swift perhaps would have been better off if he'd been called Cuckoo. As birds who laid their eggs in other birds' nests, it meant they often looked vastly different from their adopted siblings. Although Swift wasn't mistakenly part of the family, to anyone looking on, he was clearly the odd one out.

While the rest of them were small and either delicate or compact, Swift was your all-American hunk. Tall and blond with an overabundance of muscles. He could easily fill the stereotype of the alpha male jock, bullying the other geeky kids. But Swift had made himself his twin brothers' protector the moment they had stepped into school, then his sisters' as well. A gentle giant, he was probably the quietest member of the brood.

Just like seeing Jay, Robin immediately felt comforted as he hugged his big brother. "Swift, I'd like you to meet Dair – my...boyfriend." He only tripped slightly saying the word for the first time. Hopefully it would get easier from now on. "My boyfriend," he tried again with more conviction. "I have one of those now."

"Hey, man," said Swift as Dair rose to greet him. They slapped hands before shaking them and nodding.

"Nice to meet you," Dair replied. "So, you're the big bro?"

"That doesn't make him the boss," Kestrel piped up from the floor.

"She's *definitely* the boss," Swift said with a chuckle. "Who can say no to the baby?"

"Nobody, it's my superpower."

"Kestrel, please get off the floor and set the table." Robin's mom sounded slightly exasperated.

Kestrel hugged Smudge tighter on her chest and turned her big eyes on Swift. "But *I* couldn't possibly move the adorable puppy!" she cried with a pout.

"See?" Swift sighed and went to go grab the cutlery.

"So, Dair," Jay said, always the conversation starter. "You're a mechanic?" Dair came and sat by Robin again, opposite Jay.

"Yep," Dair replied, pride clear in his voice. "I went into the Marines right out of high school, then trained as an engineer equipment mechanic. I moved into operations later, then switched to regular cars when I came back home."

"A practical man, I like it." Robin's dad waved a pair of tongs from where he was dishing up by the stove.

Robin listened while his family asked Dair about his life in Seattle, carefully skirting around the issue of his breakup with Malory when it came up. They seemed to accept his explanation of discovering his bisexuality without question.

Robin loved his family, but it sounded hilarious to his ears that Dair would have some sort of sexual awakening because of him. They were apparently buying it, though, so he continued to play along.

Robin's mom told them Ava, the sister between the twins and Kestrel, was going to be late but had texted to say they should go ahead and eat. The only sibling living at home right now was Kestrel. Everyone else had their own place in town and was just visiting for the evening. But as the wine and beers flowed with dinner, Robin got the impression everyone would be staying over. Except them. Their bags were still in Dair's trunk and Dair declined Robin's dad's offer of a second beer as he'd be driving.

"We're going to stay at one of the motels," Robin explained. "The pet-friendly one. I didn't get a chance to book a room yet, but I'm sure it'll be fine."

In truth, he was going to book two rooms to give them both some space. If anyone asked, he'd say the second one was for Peyton. She'd share with him once she arrived, after all. But even if he and Dair got a room with two beds, that felt like a step too far. They were getting to be better friends, it was true. But sharing like that so soon would be too much.

That was the plan, anyway.

"A motel?" his mom asked in horror as she passed around a bowl of green beans. "Robin, you can't be serious."

"Mom, it's fine." He wanted to be firm without making a big deal of it. However, it became quickly apparent that he was totally outnumbered.

"You're taking Smudgy Budgie away from me?" Kestrel scooped the puppy into her arms in horror.

"Dude, Swift and I are both staying," said Jay as he swirled his glass of red wine. "How else do you think I'm going to make it to class tomorrow?"

"Jay teaches drama at our old high school," Robin explained to Dair, giving himself a moment to scramble around for some composure. Dear lord, they weren't actually going to try and convince him and Dair to stay here, were they? *Share* Robin's old room? His heart began to race in panic.

"And I made sure I didn't have a client first thing," Swift added, nodding at Dair. "I'm a personal trainer."

"Does this mean I don't have to go to school tomorrow?" Kestrel asked, waggling her eyebrows.

"No," said several voices in chorus from around the table.

Robin's mom looked stricken. "Come on, Bobbin. You can't bail on us. You guys are the guests of honor!"

"Mom," Robin started, looking to Jay for help. To be fair, his twin's expression was sympathetic, but he wasn't exactly jumping in to help Robin out either. So Robin glanced at Dair, who raised his eyebrows, clearly unsure what to do.

How did Robin fight this without sounding completely suspicious? As far as his family knew, he and Dair shared a bed all the time. So he went for a different approach.

"We – we wouldn't want to put you out by making up any beds."

Kestrel snorted. "Like she didn't do all that laundry yesterday. Who do you think got pillowcase duty?" She pointed at her chest.

"It's no trouble at all." Robin's mom had a hint of pleading to her voice. "We haven't seen you in months, honey. We'd really like to make the most of the visit. But I understand if it's too much for Alasdair?" She turned her wide eyes on him.

Robin squeezed his hand twice under the table, like Dair had done to him outside the house. Ultimately, this came down to what Dair – the straight guy between them – felt comfortable with.

"Wow. Whose cat died?" Ava strode into the kitchen in her biker leathers, helmet cradled under her arm. Her chestnut curls tumbled around her shoulders as she entered the room smelling strongly of firewood. "Oh, look. There's a puppy. That's new. How are you all sad when there's a puppy?"

"Mom's not *angry* with Robin for ditching us for a motel," Kestrel said devilishly. "Just *disappointed.* That's Dair, by the way. He was a Marine. This is his puppy, Smudge, that I'm stealing."

Ava paused where she stood, midway through dishing up

some dinner into a Tupperware box. She held her fist out for Dair to bump. "Cool, man. Robin, do what Mom says." She stuffed a roll into her mouth, nodded at the rest of the table, then walked out the door again.

"Ava's not staying," Robin protested as the front door slammed behind her. He could feel the back of his neck heating up and his breaths getting shallow. Not that he didn't appreciate what his family was saying. But he and Dair couldn't sleep in the same bed. They just *couldn't.*

"Ava lives ten minutes away," Robin's dad pointed out evenly, carefully dissecting a potato. "I'm sorry this is a surprise to you, son. But we all assumed you'd just stay here."

"You can stay at the motel if you really want, though," said Swift, ever the peacemaker.

"But why waste the money?" Damn Jay for having the foolproof argument. None of them were struggling financially, but who would willingly throw hundreds of bucks down the drain when they had a perfectly good place to stay?

As much as Robin didn't want to hurt his family, this was ultimately not about them. Dating or faking, he wanted Dair to be comfortable and happy. So Robin turned to him, ignoring everyone else and the rushing in his ears, and looked him in the eyes.

"It's up to you. This is a lot to take on in one day."

There might as well have been no one else in the room as Dair broke into a beautiful smile. He raised Robin's hand and kissed the back of it, then rubbed the knuckles with his thumb.

"Of course I'm happy to stay here with your family, babe. Thank you so much for offering, Mrs. Coal."

"Deb." She waved her hand and blinked her eyes. Oh crap, was she *tearful?* Robin bit his lip. She was already charmed by Dair, he could tell. He couldn't blame her, but damn it was going to upset her when it all 'ended.' "Wonderful, that's wonderful. Who wants dessert?"

"We haven't finished-" Robin's dad began, gesturing to the table still mostly filled with food. But his mom was already up, pouring more drinks and getting a banana cream pie out of the fridge.

Robin looked at Dair, then squeezed his hand twice, trying to say 'I'm sorry.' But Dair shook his head ever so slightly and leaned in. His lips brushed against Robin's ear, and he had to work damned hard not to shiver.

"It's fine. Don't worry." Dair's words were barely a murmur. No one else could have heard. "Just relax."

Robin did his best.

But all throughout the rest of dinner, then the drinks and chat afterward, he felt like he had a hand wrapped around his heart. His breaths weren't quite deep enough and his vision swam every now and again.

Alasdair Epping was going to spend the night in his childhood bedroom. He was going to have to fake it for a whole week here in front of Robin's family, twenty-four seven. This was all a terrible mistake. And for what? To try and prove something to Mac? To the town?

Robin didn't need a boyfriend to define him. He knew Dair had some idea that Mac was dangerous, but that was crazy. They'd played rough as teenagers, but Mac would never actually hurt Robin, not physically. The worst he'd realistically have to face was an awkward conversation, which he would probably still have to face with this whole 'boyfriend' situation.

He could have faced Mac alone, but here he was now having to *bedshare* with the man he had a huge, embarrassing crush on. There was no way this wasn't going to end in disaster. He could feel the edges of that box in his chest heaving under the strain.

All too soon, the yawning began. Jay and Swift had work in the morning, Kestrel had school, and Robin's parents had always been early birds rather than night owls. As the general procession began upstairs to bed, Robin and Dair fetched their cases from the car as well as Smudge's bed. They set him up in the kitchen, hoping it wouldn't be destroyed come morning.

Robin felt like he was in a daze as he led Dair upstairs, toward his room. This was it. No going back now.

"I'm so sorry!" Robin blurted in a whisper as soon as the door to his room was closed. "My family are maniacs. We don't have to share a bed. I'll sleep on the floor. It's fine."

But Dair didn't even seem to hear him for a moment. He was too busy looking around Robin's old room.

It hadn't changed much since he'd left after high school, except the photos of him and Mac had been burned under Jay's supervision. It looked like his folks had possibly repainted at some point during the few years since Robin had last been back. The walls looked fresh and things weren't exactly where he remembered them being. But he still had his cork board hanging up, filled with photos and flyers and ticket stubs from his teenage years. The door to his built-in wardrobe was open and appeared to have his mom or his sisters' winter clothes hanging in it. But his old mirror was still on the inside with the rainbow stickers he'd added around the edges when he and Jay had first come out at thirteen.

That would all be tolerable, but the posters of koalas tacked to the walls and behind the door made Robin bite his lip and wince. There had been some of popstars and actors before, Robin was sure. But his parents had just kept all the fuzzy, cuddly koalas. There was a big stuffed koala on the bed too.

He cringed and glanced at Dair. "Not exactly a bachelor pad," he said, weakly attempting to make a joke.

But Dair grinned at him. "It's cute. It's very you."

Was it?

Dair picked up his duffle bag and dropped it on the bed. "I hope I wasn't too much back there, kissing your hand and stuff. I just thought it would be good to play along. And your family aren't maniacs, they're lovely. It's normal to think you'd want to share a room with your boyfriend. But don't worry. I don't mind sleeping on the floor at all."

Really? He was going to brush off Robin's childish, geeky bedroom just like that? What a relief. But that left them with their original position of the sleeping arrangement.

"No, no." Robin couldn't have Dair sacrificing himself to the floor. "This whole situation is my fault. I'll take the floor."

Dair considered the bed. "It looks big enough for two. Besides, if anyone walked in, they'd think we had a fight. Unless you kick in your sleep, I'm happy to share."

How was this situation getting worse? Robin wasn't going to banish Dair to the floor after everything he was doing to help him. But he got the impression Dair wouldn't let Robin martyr himself either. Besides, he was right. If anyone saw them, their ruse might be up.

But Dair would be *so close.* And *sleeping.* It didn't get much more intimate than that.

A thought suddenly occurred to Robin. If he made a big deal of this, Dair might guess that Robin wasn't comfortable. If he asked why, Robin would struggle to keep the lid down tight on his dumb crush box, he was sure. So he plastered a bright smile on his face and did his best to make his heartbeat calm down.

"Sure, no problem. Yeah, that makes sense. Totally fine." Robin took a deep breath and forced himself to stop babbling. "Do you want to use the bathroom first?"

Dair smiled and unclipped the top of his bag. "No, you go. I need to dig for my toothbrush."

Robin didn't know if he should go as fast as he could or dawdle. Mac had never stayed the night while they'd been dating as teenagers. Robin's parents had been keen to maintain some boundaries. So he'd never had to do this particular dance across the hall with anyone, knowing his immediate family was around, risking bumping into a boyfriend in his underwear or something equally embarrassing. But the universe was kind to them for once as it sounded like everyone else was already in bed.

After brushing his teeth, flossing *and* rinsing with mouthwash (because he'd die if Dair smelled any bad breath from him), Robin dashed back across the hall. He almost knocked before going back into his own room. Was that weird? Probably. Instead, he cleared his throat and hit his knuckles against the wood before turning the door handle at half speed. In theory, that would give Dair enough time to cover his junk if he was naked.

Dear lord. Robin couldn't decide if a naked Dair would be amazing or just give him a genuine heart attack.

He was greeted with a halfway scenario. Dair was not in fact naked. But he was only wearing a pair of tight briefs and a tank top with a logo so faded it was unreadable. Even after three months of living together, Robin had never seen Dair so intimately. But Dair seemed totally oblivious.

"Found my toothbrush," he said cheerfully, waving it at Robin. "Is the bathroom easy enough to find?"

Robin nodded and pointed weakly. "Second door on the right," he managed to croak.

In record time, Robin hurriedly changed into long pajama pants and a T-shirt while Dair was doing his thing. He turned off the main light and just left his bedside lamp on, thinking it would be easier to plunge them into darkness once Dair returned. But as soon as the door opened, Robin realized from his position lying in the bed that he'd accidentally set the scene for a seduction.

Naturally, he jerked his hand out and sent his glass of water flying. "Shit!"

At least there was no danger of seduction now as he scrambled to fling the sheets off himself, dive to the floor, and scoop up the glass before it completely emptied. He reached up to grab the box of tissues conveniently left on the nightstand. But when he turned around, Dair was already there, using a towel he'd presumably brought back from the bathroom with him to mop up the wetness.

He'd squatted down, so there was no ignoring the bulge in his underwear. Robin could see almost every inch of his perfect body through his skin-tight clothes as he swooped in to Robin's rescue yet again. The outline of his cock was clear through the material, and it wasn't small.

So much for there being no risk of seduction. Robin's own cock twitched to life in his thin cotton pajamas, and there was a very real possibility he could get half a hard-on right there and then. In a flash, his mind was suggesting to Robin how he could launch himself at Dair. Or even better, how easily Dair could lean over and pin him down, their cocks rubbing together through their pajamas...

Robin leaped back up and shoved his glasses up his nose as Dair got the last of the spillage. "Oh! Um, thank you!" While Dair draped the damp towel over the back of Robin's desk chair, Robin scurried back under the covers, hiding both his disobedient cock and his skinny body he was so ashamed of.

Once again, Dair seemed calm and relaxed as he placed his toothbrush back in his bag. He hummed as he picked his clothes off the floor. They must have dropped there when

Robin had knocked over his glass and Dair had jumped across the room to help him.

Dair folded his clothes with military precision, unsurprisingly. He smoothed down the edges and placed each item on the dresser, one on top of each other, quickly but carefully. Then he turned around and pointed to Robin's now mostly empty glass. "I can refill that for you."

"Oh, no," Robin tried to protest. But Dair had already strode across the room and plucked the glass from the dresser. "Thank you," Robin said sheepishly. Dair winked at him.

Maybe it wasn't completely terrible of him to enjoy being doted on, just a little. Robin still smacked his forehead and groaned when he had a few seconds alone.

"Klutz," he hissed.

Dair returned from the bathroom with a full glass of water, which he handed to Robin. Then he turned off the hallway light and closed the door, leaving them in the almost-darkness as he slipped into Robin's bed.

Robin had never shared this room with *anyone*. When his family had moved here, he and Jay had been twelve and treated it as a small act of God that they'd been granted their own private rooms, having doubled up their entire lives. Of course, not long after, the Big Gay Panic had begun and there had been many nights where Robin had snuck into his twin's room, desperate for company but not entirely sure why. Jay had never slept in here, though. Nor Mac nor Peyton nor anyone.

Until Dair.

They were far enough apart that they weren't rolling into each other, but Robin wasn't sure he'd ever been more aware of his scrawny little body, and he'd been plenty aware his whole life. He had an Adonis of a man beside him and he was *straight*. Robin was seriously tempted to suggest he sleep on the floor again just to put some space between them, but wasn't sure how he could bring it up without sounding hysterical.

He pulled his glasses off and dropped them on the dresser. "Um, so, goodnight?" He glanced briefly at Dair before looking back at the ceiling. His skin was prickly and his breathing shallow.

"Are you okay?"

Robin had to turn and look at Dair for that. They were now lying side by side, a couple of feet apart, their heads resting on the pillows. They were close enough Robin could still see all the details of his face. "Am *I* okay?"

Dair raised his eyebrows and nodded. "Big homecoming, small white lie. Not your average Monday."

Robin bit his lip. "I guess not." He never did anything remotely this interesting, he knew. It was kind of exciting, in its own way, once Robin ignored all the panic he was feeling around Dair. "But it's fine. Thank you, again. For being here and well, everything."

"No problem."

Dair's stunning smile was imprinted on Robin's eyes as he killed the light and turned on his side to face the wall. Robin had never been more conscious of each breath he took in and out or every tiny time he fidgeted. It was like after all his life trying to avoid it, he was finally in that spotlight.

But eventually, Dair's breathing evened out to adorable little snuffles and Robin felt like he could finally let go.

It would still be a long time before sleep finally claimed him.

7

DAIR

DAIR WAS WOKEN UP BY THE BONEY KNUCKLES OF A HAND slapping into his mouth.

"Ow!" His whole body twitched into consciousness.

Several thoughts assaulted him at once. This was not his bedroom. It wasn't the room in the apartment he shared with Robin and Peyton either nor his other apartment or the old house with Malory. He wasn't on tour or at the barracks.

So where the hell was he?

His training told him to be as still and silent as he could be until he had worked out his position. Then it all came flooding back.

He was with Robin. In his bed, of all places.

The whole situation had gotten a little out of hand at the dinner table, but nothing Dair couldn't handle. He tried to shift his bulk without bouncing the mattress too much, which was kind of difficult considering his sheer body mass. But when he had moved enough to see Robin, he could tell he was still fast asleep.

This was so much more than he'd signed on for, but he

was continuously surprised at how unbothered he was by each new turn of events.

He'd ended up sleeping next to Robin for the night. So what? Dair could – and had – sleep through a damned artillery attack, so even if Robin snored, it wouldn't have been an issue. He'd felt the tension radiating off Robin's body as they'd initially got between the sheets together. Dair would be an idiot to ignore the sexual implications of such an act. But now Robin was relaxed in sleep, and everything felt so much more normal.

They were just buddies in a pinch. Sure, Dair had never shared a *bed* with any of his unit, but he'd bunkered down in camp beds with dozens of guys side by side. This wasn't all that different, really.

Robin stirred, making Dair realize he was staring at the poor man. So he quickly rolled onto his back to look at the ceiling, waiting to see if Robin woke up fully. He was squirming sleepily, but suddenly Dair felt him freeze. So Dair glanced over, not surprised to see Robin's topaz eyes were wide.

"Morning!" Dair gave a little wave, then wasn't sure why he'd done that. So he laced his fingers over his stomach to try and make them behave. "Sleep well?"

Robin blinked. "Uh, yeah." He sounded uncertain as he reached for his glasses and slipped them on his face. "You?"

"Fine," Dair agreed, shifting his weight to face Robin more.

It was in that moment he realized his problem.

Shit. He tried not to let it show on his face, but his cock was doing what it almost always did in the mornings.

Waking up.

He reckoned he wasn't even at half mast, but his dick was certainly hard enough he felt it against his briefs. Damn it. He definitely didn't want Robin to realize and get uncomfortable. It was just a natural human occurrence, but Dair would absolutely hate it if Robin was to feel embarrassed, confused, or even, heaven forbid, threatened by it.

The sensible thing would be to lie there and let it go down, but it didn't feel like it was going to calm itself anytime soon. Besides, Dair wasn't okay knowing he had the beginnings of an erection next to someone who had trusted him to be a gentleman during this fake boyfriend endeavor.

"I'm feeling kind of gross after the drive yesterday," he said, not exactly lying. "Do you think I'd be all right to take a shower?"

"Oh, sure. I'll check it's free, but I think everyone else should have left by now." Robin swung his legs out of the bed and padded across the carpet. He looked out the door and down the hall. "I think you're good. Use whatever shampoo and stuff you like."

He rubbed his eyes under his glasses and gave a sleepy sigh. It made something…strange…happen in Dair's chest. It wasn't like he'd never seen Robin in his PJs before. But there was something new Dair was feeling. He couldn't identify it, though, so he did his best to shrug it off.

He had bigger problems right now.

"Great. Thanks." Dair needed to move, but Robin was looking at him expectantly. There was no way he'd miss the morning wood if Dair got out from under the covers now. "I might be in there a few minutes. Did you want to pop in first?" He knew there were other bathrooms, but it was the only thing he could think of.

Luckily, Robin gave him a shy smile. "Um, yeah, actually. I'll just be a minute."

Dair dove from the bed the second the door closed behind Robin. He found his toothbrush and deodorant, then picked out fresh jeans and a T-shirt, which he carefully held in front of his junk while he waited for Robin to return.

"All yours." Robin gave Dair a double thumbs-up as he walked back in. Dair nodded and made a run for it.

By the time he got under the hot water, his cock was still not behaving. In fact, as soon as he touched it with a slippery hand, it got even more excited.

"Fine," Dair grumbled, rinsing the suds from his fingers and using the water as lubricant. He'd definitely locked the door, but it still felt wrong to start jerking off in his friend's parents' bathroom, even if they were alone in the house now. He wasn't sure how else to make his dick deflate, though. Thinking of all his usual boner-killing stuff was doing nada.

He closed his eyes, letting the hot water run over him and the steam fill his lungs. He wanted to be quick, so he flicked through his go-to Rolodex of hot porny images and tried to satisfy himself as soon as possible.

Sexually speaking, he was a pretty simple man. He'd loved having sex with his ex, but a blow job was his particular favorite treat. They were always such fun, which was Dair's priority during sex. He wanted to smile and laugh and tease his partner.

Obviously, he didn't think of his ex anymore when he tugged one off. But usually a vision of a generically pretty woman did the trick. Except today it felt like he was chasing that sweet spot but not quite getting it. "Come on," he muttered to himself. An imaginary blow job was easy enough to get his head around. Yeah, there were better and worse ways to do it, but pretty much any combination of mouth on cock felt good to Dair.

Would Robin know how to do it any differently?

The thought shocked him so much Dair's eyes flew open, and he inhaled a lungful of shower water, making him splutter and wheeze. What the hell?

Well, it was only logical to assume that when both you and your sexual partner had a cock, you'd have a better understanding of what felt good. That must have been what had triggered the thought. But in almost twenty years of jerking off, Dair had never considered two guys before. He knew he didn't have much of an imagination, but simple ideas with a woman had always been enough.

He wrapped his hand back around his shaft. There was no denying his dick had perked up and his insides flipped at the concept, however.

So while Dair banished any thought of Robin from his mind – that just wouldn't be right – he couldn't help but stick with the idea of two dudes, one sucking the other off. Not himself, of course. That would be weird. But two generic attractive guys going at it seemed to be doing the trick for Dair's cock, finally.

It was unusual, but fantasies were just fun, weren't they? More importantly, they were private. So when the guy doing the sucking off started stroking his own cock in Dair's mind, Dair went with it. That *was* hot, imagining them both coming together. He'd always worried blow jobs were a bit one-sided.

As he sped up his hand, he screwed his eyes closed and stifled a grunt, gripping the tiles for support. He could feel his climax building, and his breathing was ragged.

Without warning, the guy getting head morphed into Dair. He was too into the fantasy and too close to release to stop now. So he ran with it.

In his mind's eye, he used the heat of the shower to imagine the heat of a mouth over his shaft instead of his fingers. Yeah, the idea of his mystery lover jerking himself off on his knees below was fucking *scorching*.

It was just as Dair's mind decided that the other guy's hair could be red that Dair came, biting his lip to stop himself crying out too loud as he spilled all over his hand.

He panted, allowing the still running water to wash away the physical evidence of his debauchery as his cock softened in his hand. Wow. That had been…wild. He expected feelings of guilt or shame to start creeping in at jerking off to the idea of a guy sucking his cock. But they didn't arrive. Instead, his post orgasmic euphoria tingled through his body, making him feel like he was floating.

Well, he hadn't done anything wrong. So if that was what had made him feel good this particular morning, then so be it.

Aware he'd been in the bathroom a fair while, he finished washing his hair and body as fast as possible. Then he shut the water off, feeling bad for letting it run so long. As he dried off and brushed his fingers through his hair, he hummed. By opening the window, some of the steam escaped, and soon he was able to dress without getting his clothes too damp.

The mirror had half defogged and he looked at himself. He had forgotten to bring a razor with him and he was looking kind of scruffy. In the Marines, he'd just kept his chin and head as closely shaved as possible at all times. But since coming home, he'd kind of let everything grow a bit unruly, only getting a five-dollar trim every couple of months. For the first time since probably his teenage years, he carefully studied his reflection and wished maybe he'd made a bit more of an effort for Robin.

He was supposed to be showing Dair off as his handsome boyfriend, after all. But right then, Dair felt a bit more disheveled than delicious. His hair was a mop and his stubble almost long enough to be considered shapeless scruff.

He bit his lip, turning his face left and right. Would it be possible to find a barber before the big Saturday night reunion? It was still just Tuesday, after all.

Even if he did, the smartest thing he'd brought was a blazer to go with his jeans. The solitary shoes he had that Smudge hadn't chewed were his sneakers. Would that be good enough? It had seemed so back home. Dair had been taught to present himself immaculately for inspection while in the Corps. But since re-entering civilian life, he was pretty sure he hadn't even worn a suit.

He didn't just want to be a wall of muscle between Robin and Mac if he showed up. Dair wanted people to look at him as Robin's boyfriend and be impressed. He was only a mechanic, so he wasn't going to wow anyone with that. But he was feeling very strongly now he should do something to smarten up.

Decision made, he finally left the bathroom. Robin wasn't in his room when Dair dropped his things off, but there was music coming from down toward the kitchen area. So Dair gave his hair one more rub with his towel, then jogged downstairs. The sound of Duran Duran got louder as Dair approached.

He stopped at the threshold to the kitchen, marveling at what he saw. Robin had Smudge on his hip, dancing as he stirred something in a pot. The warm smell of rich oatmeal reached Dair, as well as bread toasting, coffee percolating, and the tang of freshly cut strawberries on a chopping board.

It was a perfect domestic scene, and something twisted badly in Dair's chest.

This was what he craved. Sharing a home with someone wonderful where they cooked meals together and walked the dogs in the nearby park and curled up in one bed at night. A home that could grow with children and accommodate extended family whenever they wanted.

In that moment, Dair wished this was real with all his heart.

But Robin was a guy, and they were only pretending. Dair would have to keep searching for a family like the Coals to call his in-laws.

For now, he could enjoy this weeks' vacation. Just because Robin wasn't really his boyfriend didn't mean Dair couldn't still enjoy his company as friends. So he mustered a smile and pushed himself off the doorframe.

"That smells great."

Robin didn't stop dancing as he turned and beamed at Dair. "I wanted to make you breakfast this time!" He handed Smudge over to Dair, wiggling his butt to Hungry Like the Wolf. "Is this okay? I can get us some sausages too?"

Dair shook his head as he sat down, cuddling his puppy in his arms. "This is perfect."

It really was.

8

ROBIN

"Yep. No, I understand that, but I'm on vacation. Have you tried redownloading the branch from source control, reinstalling the packages, then compiling? Well, then, I suggest you start there. If that doesn't work, try *Google*. And, dude, StackOverflow is a thing. Use it. Okay. Yep, no problem. Bye." Robin grimaced and closed the call. "Sorry about that."

Ever patient, Dair just smiled and shook his head. "I've been admiring the scenery."

Robin had never really appreciated how pretty his home town was growing up. But showing Dair around on their first full day there gave him the opportunity to see it through fresh eyes. Dair was delighted at all the rustic buildings that Robin used to think were old fashioned but now agreed were quaint and charming. The sun was shining, and the fresh, pine-scented air filled his lungs, putting a spring in his step.

They walked down Main Street holding hands. Robin had almost protested when Dair had slipped their fingers together, but then he remembered that was the whole reason Dair was there. So Robin had chatted with Dair about the local history of the place until his heart rate calmed down again. He was getting quicker at chilling out in response to Dair's touch. In fact, it was almost becoming normalized.

They passed the barbers called Turkish Delight where Smudge made friends with another fluff ball. She'd been asleep upside down with her little legs sticking up in the air until Smudge raced over. They sniffed each other's butts and chased each other in circles on the sidewalk.

"Pom?"

A stunning guy in his early thirties with black hair, square jaw, and tawny skin approached the open door. He wore an apron and was cleaning a straight razor. When he saw Robin and Dair holding hands, he paused. Robin had just enough time to panic before the guy's face broke into a shy but sweet smile.

"I think your dog likes mine," he joked. His voice was soft and his honey-brown eyes sparkled.

"Smudge is a hooligan," Dair said, shaking his head. "Sorry. Hey, gently, *gently!*"

Smudge bowled Pom – who Robin thought was a Pomeranian and had to laugh at the name choice – over and they scampered back toward the barbershop. Dair tugged on Smudge's leash to break them apart before something got broken.

"It's fine," said the barber with a gentle chuckle. "She's tougher than she looks. Have a lovely day."

There. Robin and Dair had survived their first encounter in town as a 'couple' and the world had not ended. Robin let out a breath and laughed, glancing at Dair.

"Piece of cake," Dair said, apparently understanding Robin's thoughts. He gave Robin's hand a double squeeze like he had done at the dinner table the night before. Double Dair, like his old Marine nickname.

They continued heading toward the boardwalk with the

old-fashioned arcade and all the restaurants and quaint shops. They walked in amicable silence for a while, but Robin became slowly aware he was doing something.

He was darting his gaze everywhere, keeping a fervent eye out for Mac.

Jesus. How could he have been so oblivious that Mac was still screwing with his head so badly? He'd been aware of his reluctance to date, but had honestly put that down to being so focused on his career. Same with this whole reunion. Until Peyton had pointed it out, he'd genuinely thought his last-minute panic had come from his job.

But all this anxiety was apparently stretching all the way back to his high school ex.

That was pathetic.

Robin was furious with himself. If Peyton or any of his other friends devalued themselves to the point they only saw their worth through their love life, he'd shake them. Peyton wasn't the sum of her girlfriends. She was an outstanding nurse, a caring friend, brilliant dancer and terrible influence. He loved her for everything she was. If she allowed a past relationship to dictate her life now, Robin would be horrified.

But that was exactly what Robin was doing.

He was exhausted, imagining countless scenarios of what he would say to Mac when they eventually ran into each other. Ideally, Robin would love to think he'd be cool and say something cutting about how great his life was and how he had forgotten all about their relationship. But the truth was he knew he was far more likely to either burst into tears, shout at Mac for being such a shit, or both.

It was kind of nuts in the cold light of day how he'd justified Mac's actions. Robin really had thought the way he'd shoved and pushed him around was just normal guy behavior. Perversely, Robin had *liked* it, because it meant he was dating a 'real' man. Like that validated his gayness and signaled his arrival into his new life.

But there was nothing manly about slapping or thumping the person you were supposed to love, even if it was 'just horsing around.' It made Robin feel kind of wobbly to revisit now. At the time, he hadn't picked up that Mac only did those kinds of things when they were alone.

Robin shook his head and tried to focus on the beautiful summer's day, the clean air, and the gorgeous mountain rising in the distance. He was in the here and now, and he knew that ten years ago he hadn't been *totally* clueless. After all, he'd been the one to break up the relationship. Even if Mac had wheedled them back together a couple of times, Robin had eventually done the right thing, stayed strong, and called it quits for good when he'd moved to start college. With Peyton as his new BFF, he'd ultimately blocked Mac from his life, not just online.

"Robin?"

He startled as Dair squeezed his hand twice as he called out his name. "Sorry, what?"

Dair chuckled. Robin realized they'd reached the pier along the boardwalk. It offered a spectacular view over the town's lake, which was a few football fields large. Grassy shores met the waters on the other side, with hundred-foot-tall pine trees reaching for the blue sky. Looming over them were the purply snow-topped mountains Robin had dismissed in his childhood as an ordinary, everyday sight. Now they stole his breath with their magnificence.

"You were miles away," Dair said. "Is everything okay?"

Robin considered before he nodded. "Yeah," he said truthfully. "Just got a bit lost down memory lane."

"I'm not surprised."

Robin smiled up at him. Something powerful was

unfurling in his chest. "Thank you," he said through the slight lump in his throat.

Dair cocked his head. "For what?"

"For helping me come home." Robin swallowed the lump and blinked back tears, allowing himself to smile. "This is my town, and...well, I didn't quite realize what I was doing by avoiding it."

He swung their hands, trying not to let embarrassment overwhelm him while they were connected. He felt raw and vulnerable. But Dair did that double squeeze thing again, giving Robin confidence.

"You make a seriously awesome cheerguard. So, thank you."

Dair had the leash looped around his wrist, so his hand was free to reach up and touch Robin's chin, tilting it slightly upward to look at him. Robin blinked in surprise at the intimate gesture.

"You're welcome," Dair said sincerely, then released his face.

Robin laughed, attempting to ease the unexpectedly intense moment. Thankfully, Dair joined in with him and the tension eased a little from Robin's chest. They leaned against the pier's fence and let Smudge sniff around.

Robin cleared his throat, hoping to dispel the last of the mildly heightened atmosphere. "So, you like it here? In Pine Cove?"

"It's gorgeous." Dair shook his head, mildly disbelieving. "I can't believe how relaxed I feel here. It's like I've been here before, but at the same time it's like nothing else."

Robin was surprised with how proud that made him feel. "It's pretty awesome, isn't it? I kind of forgot."

Dair's unruly dark blond hair glinted in the beautiful sunshine as he smiled down at Robin. The sight almost took his breath away. Luckily, Dair didn't seem to notice as Robin covered it up with a cough.

"So, you must have spent all your summers on this lake?" Dair asked.

Robin couldn't suppress his shiver. "Oh, no. I can't..." He took a breath and smiled. This wasn't anything to be ashamed of. "Actually, I can't swim."

"Really?"

Robin tried to keep his voice light. "It's this weird thing I've always had. I, um, have nightmares that I'm underwater and I can't breathe-"

He barely finished before Dair tugged his hand and turned them around. His arm was around Robin in an instant as they walked back toward the boardwalk. "Dude, I'm so sorry. I didn't realize."

Robin laughed. He couldn't think of a time he'd *ever* laughed in response to his little phobia. It was crazy how safe he felt with Dair next to him. "Don't worry," he assured him. "I'm okay looking at it. In fact, I think it's beautiful. I'm just not eager to get in or on it."

Dair shook his head, but at least he was grinning. "Okay, good to know."

"Right, are we going to lunch?" Robin asked. "My treat."

He'd noticed earlier that Dair had been frowning over his wallet, which added to Robin's suspicion that Dair had taken unpaid leave from his job for this trip. So Robin was doing his best to cover everything and not think too hard about how warm and fuzzy it made him feel that Dair would lose several days' work for him.

Dair raised an eyebrow. "Well, I could eat for sure, but I'm happy to split it."

Robin shook his head. "You wouldn't be here if it wasn't for my dumb situation. And you're always cooking at home. Let me pay you back."

After a beat, Dair gave him a grin and squeezed his hand twice. "All right, sugar daddy."

"Eww," Robin cried with a laugh. "Shut up and follow me."

They didn't have to meet Jay until later that afternoon. There was a reunion of the LGBT society happening, focused on their class, but people from the years before and since were coming too. Robin was actually sort of looking forward to it, as crazy as that felt for someone who wasn't keen on crowds and parties. As it wasn't until the evening, he and Dair had the day to themselves while everyone else was at work and school.

There was only one place Robin wanted to go after all these years away. He just hoped it hadn't changed too much in his absence.

Sunny Side Up was the only greasy spoon to go to in Pine Cove. There had been a couple of other dives that had tried to set up on the roads into town, but everyone around knew that Sunny's was the place for comfort food. Their hash browns were the stuff of legends.

Sunny Perkins had opened the place up in his twenties some thirty or forty years ago. Although he came across as a grumpy bear, the whole town knew he had a heart of gold. He spent most of his time back in the kitchen, banging pots, flipping eggs, and singing along badly to the radio.

Luckily, his husband, Tyee, was always out front ready to give customers a warm welcome along with their Great Pyrenees dog, Peri. It had always been that way, although Peri had been a pup when Robin had left town ten years ago. Now he was an enormous white cloud that lumbered up when Robin stepped into the diner with Dair.

He didn't expect Tyee to recognize him after all this time. Robin was just a customer who used to come in with his twin brother on sporadic Saturdays. But to Robin and Jay, seeing a married gay couple running a beloved restaurant in their town was the most remarkable thing. It had made them feel less alone before they'd come out to their family at thirteen, then the world at large at fifteen.

Peri might have grown five times over since he was a puppy, but Tyee looked exactly the same. His long black hair was poker straight and flowed below his shoulders. He was still wearing that familiar old sleeveless denim jacket over a checkered shirt, just with a couple of new buttons stitched on. His skin was the same copper brown with hardly any new laughter lines, and he still wore the Shoalwater Bay yellow-and-black beaded bracelet on his wrist, always remembering his tribe. Robin sighed, feeling comforted at just the sight of him.

Robin didn't have any LGBT relatives. But he and Jay had always thought of Sunny and Tyee as their distant gay uncles, even if they didn't know it.

To his surprise, though, Tyee immediately rose from the servers' station and threw his arms out, making Peri bark. The dozen or so customers already sitting down all turned to look, and Robin's cheeks burned.

"Robin Coal! As I live and breathe! You must be in town for the reunion?"

Robin was too stunned to speak as Tyee hugged him. "Uh, y-yes," he stammered after he'd let him go. Warmth blossomed in his chest. He couldn't believe Tyee remembered him. It felt fantastic and somehow validating.

"It's been too long, too long. You look very well. We see Jay all the time, of course. But I trust he's well?" Robin nodded. "And who's this handsome fellow?"

Robin quickly reached back and took Dair's hand. "This is Alasdair, my boyfriend." It got easier to say each time. "He came back with me for the reunion. And this is Smudge." He was naturally already trying to make friends with Peri. But the enormous old dog just sort of looked at Smudge in bewilderment as he danced between his legs, yipping and growling playfully.

"Excellent." Tyee laughed at the dogs and clasped Dair's free hand with both of his. "Please, come and sit. A window table so you can see the town. She's missed you!"

Robin smiled and shook his head as he followed Tyee. When he and Dair took their seats, Peri forced his way in between their feet, using his body as a big hairy footstool and resting his head on Robin's messenger bag. Smudge tried to climb onto his back like a child attempting to mount a pony, but it didn't go very well. After he slid off the third time, poor little Smudgy huffed and settled by Dair's feet.

Tyee chuckled as he came back with menus for them both. "See, Peri says you're not going anywhere!"

When the diner resumed its business again, it felt like just Robin and Dair alone in their booth. It wasn't exactly private as the sides didn't go above their shoulders, but there was no one around in their immediate area, at least.

"Wow," said Dair, glancing around the place rather than looking at their menu. "Folks are real friendly here, huh? It's like everyone knows everyone."

Robin shrugged. "Small town," he said by way of an explanation. He told himself when he'd relocated to Seattle that he didn't miss everybody getting into each other's business. In fact, he'd convinced himself it was people being nosy. But today just felt like they cared. They wanted to know he was happy and well.

He was, he realized with a jolt. Happy and well. He loved his job and he had great friends, and for the first time in forever, he'd felt able to come back to the place that would always be his home. Best of all, he was getting to share the experience with his newest friend, who was starting to also become one of his closest friends. That was pretty awesome.

They ordered food and chatted easily and fussed the fluff

monsters at their feet. It wasn't until they were heading back to Robin's parents' place did Robin realize that he'd stopped obsessively looking everywhere in case Mac showed up.

"What?" Dair asked from behind the driver's wheel.

Robin was grinning at him. But he couldn't very well say thank you again. He also didn't want to admit he'd been nervously looking for Mac in the first place. So he just shrugged.

"I've had a nice afternoon, is all."

Dair grinned back.

"Me too."

9

DAIR

Dair had never been inside a gay bar before. He wasn't one much for nightclubs, anyway. Peyton and Robin had invited him out a few times, but it had felt like he would be intruding on a space meant for them, so he'd never gone.

As he looked around Pine Cove's premier gay bar, The Aquarium, he felt unsurprisingly lost. He was used to sports bars. Here, the walls were covered in blue glitter paper, there were disco balls reflecting in a dazzling display, and a high proportion of the dudes were half-naked and being very tactile on the dance floor. It wasn't that it was gay that was the issue, per se. It was that it was just *so much*. The music was pounding, and people were spinning, and the colored lights swirled frantically.

Then he felt Robin's hand slip into his own, and everything calmed just a little.

He looked down at his friend and smiled. But Robin's expression was concerned. "Do you hate it?" he shouted over the music.

Dair blinked in shock. "Hate it? Of course not! It's just…a lot."

Robin rubbed his other hand against Dair's arm. "Shall we go out back for a bit?"

Dair nodded gratefully. "Would you like a drink before we go?"

Robin's face changed from worry to something happier, which made Dair happy in turn. His whole purpose here was to be Robin's support. Dair was struggling with the riotous atmosphere, but he could still buy his buddy a beer and continue the evening somewhere quieter. At least for a little while.

When they each had a beer in hand, Robin led Dair across the dance floor toward the back of the club. Dair was surprised when he felt a couple of hands trail across his back or down his arm. But when he looked, no one was really trying it on with him. It was like these guys were just saying hello.

Huh. Like holding hands or sharing a bed with Robin, he figured he would have been more freaked by that. But it felt fine. Nice, even. Like he was being welcomed to visit a world he didn't really belong in.

The courtyard outside was beautiful. Fairy lights were wound around all the trees and the trellis fences. Seashells, mermaids, seahorses, and starfishes were nestled subtly in the lush green foliage, and wind chimes made from shells tinkled gently overhead.

The throbbing music from the dance floor was reduced to a low pulse and the humid air from so many panting bodies was swept away by the clean night breeze. There was a slight nip to the evening, but after the clawing atmosphere inside, Dair found it welcoming.

Pine Cove High School's LGBT society had booked a seated area of the bar for people to congregate at the start of the night, and Dair had met a dozen or so people already. But out in the courtyard, he and Robin found some familiar faces.

"Hey!" Jay cried, standing up from the picnic bench he'd been straddling.

It was funny how he was like Robin but also not. There were some shockingly similar mannerisms they shared. In particular, they both flicked their hands in exactly the same way and had a little quirk of the mouth that Dair had spied. But Jay's hair was so dark it was almost black, and he seemed to be animated all the time, whereas Robin only allowed himself little outbursts of that kind of exuberance.

It was clear how much Jay loved his brother, however. He looked slightly tipsy as he skipped over and threw his arms around Robin, then kissed his cheek noisily.

Jay wasn't the only Coal sibling there. Their sister Ava nodded and raised her beer bottle at them. Apparently, she was bi and quite the queer activist. From what little Dair had seen of her so far, she came across stoic and kind of scary. She'd almost made the Team USA archery team the last Olympics and was now an instructor at one of the town's outdoor centers. Dair had a feeling the two of them would probably get along, given the chance.

Despite not being outwardly animated, she seemed perfectly at home in the sparkly, hectic Aquarium bar. Dair thought he could probably take a leaf out of her book.

They made their way to join her at the picnic table, when a squeal pierced through the air. Dair didn't exactly jump, but he was instantly on alert as his head whipped around just in time to see a glittery blur launch itself at Robin.

"Oh em *gee!* You bitch! How long's it been? It's okay. She still loves you, even though you're a big city ho now. Fuck me till Sunday, I love that you're here, baby!"

Dair stepped back as a small, shimmering, Asian American guy wearing very short shorts, cowboy boots, and a cropped lace T-shirt enveloped Robin. He jumped up and down as he hugged him, lifting Robin off the ground and kissing him all over his cheeks, leaving glossy pink lip shapes.

Robin was laughing, so Dair relaxed. He was pretty sure this wasn't Mac.

"Emery Klein," Robin said once the human glitter hurricane released him. "I'd like you to meet my boyfriend, Dair Epping."

Emery pulled a fan from the back of his shorts and thwacked it open with a loud crack. He peered at Dair over the top of it. "Are you open to sharing?"

"No," Robin said with a laugh.

"Mother, may I at least have him on Tuesdays and every other Saturday?"

Robin slapped his arm, transferring some of whatever was making Emery's whole body glimmer to Robin's palm. "Get your own."

"Oh, she will." Emery snapped the fan shut again, then offered his free hand out to Dair like he was a woman in a historical film waiting for her knuckles to be kissed. Dair wasn't sure what to do, but his manners dictated he comply. So he gently took Emery's hand and pressed his lips to the fingers.

Emery gasped, reclaimed his hand, then dropped onto the bench beside Ava. "Oh, *honey!* Wherever did you find this one? Keep him. Don't *ever* let him go."

Robin glanced at Dair, smiling shyly. "I don't intend to."

Those words did something funny to Dair. He knew they were just pretending to date, but he supposed it spoke to his need to feel like he belonged somewhere. Robin probably meant the apartment. They'd struggled to find someone for the room before Dair came along. Yeah, that was most likely it.

"Soooo," Emery drawled. He draped himself over Ava, who automatically stroked his dark, neatly trimmed hair. They must be friends as well. "I'm Emery. I'm a Leo – but not like a regular Leo, I'm a cool Leo. I went to school with these two delicious crumpets. I was gay before it was the in thing to do. However, I love these two very much, so I didn't mind sharing the limelight." He cracked his fan and lightly wafted it against his face.

"You came out of the womb with a confetti cannon singing Barbra Streisand," Jay said, rolling his eyes. "I'm not sure anyone in history was gay before you were."

Emery preened. "True. Now, your turn, G.I. Joe. You have twenty seconds to convince us you're good enough for our little Robin here."

Dair felt his eyes widen. Robin patted his arm. "He's kidding. You're *kidding*," he informed Emery sternly.

Emery flicked his eyebrows and threw Robin a positively sinful look. "Am I?"

Ava banged her beer bottle on the table and cocked her head toward Dair and Robin. "How's Peyton?"

"Peyton?" Dair repeated.

Ava blinked once. "You know. Your housemate."

"We know who Peyton is," Robin said with a laugh. "I mean, yeah, she's great. She's hoping to visit for the weekend. Why do you ask?"

Ava picked her beer up again and downed half of it. "No reason."

"Robin?"

The whole table turned to face the speaker who standing a few feet from the table, including Dair. His head jerked back a fraction in surprise.

He may not have been gay, but even he could see this guy was fucking gorgeous.

He looked like a movie star with golden wavy hair, bronzed skin, and perfect white teeth behind a tentative smile. He wasn't quite as big as Dair, but his physique was clear through the simple white T-shirt and blue jeans he wore. He was ripped. As he moved closer, Dair saw his sparkling blue eyes twinkle in the fairy lights, and as his smile grew, a little dimple popped in his left cheek. He was like an Abercrombie & Fitch model.

Dair's hand, which wasn't holding Robin's rose to the scruff on his jaw. This guy was so polished it made Dair feel like a hobo in comparison.

"Wow, Robin," the guy said, taking another step toward the picnic table. "You look amazing. It's so great to see you."

Robin stood, but he was still holding Dair's hand. It was only then that Dair noticed the grim expressions on the three other faces around him.

"Mac?" Robin queried.

Mac?

Dair shot up to stand beside Robin, holding his hand a little tighter. "Mac?"

Mac tore his gaze from Robin and gave Dair a friendly smile. "Oh, hey man. Are you here with Robin? I'm Mackenzie. We all used to go to school together."

Emery thwacked his fan open so hard it was amazing it didn't break. "Did we? I don't remember." He glared at Mac.

But Mac just chuckled and rubbed the back of his neck. "Yeah," he said slowly. "I guess it's been a while. Robin, could we maybe talk for a minute?"

"You're talking now," Jay snapped.

Dair looked down at Robin and raised his eyebrows, asking him silently if he wanted to go talk with this guy. Dair hoped if he did, they'd just move across the courtyard so he could still see them. But Robin was his own man. Dair wasn't going to tell him what to do or speak for him. Even though he was sorely tempted to inform Mac that Robin wasn't going to be going anywhere with him.

Robin looked back at Dair, then something appeared to relax in him. He pushed his glasses up his nose where they'd slipped, and turned back to face Mac. "Actually, Dair's only just met everyone. I'd rather not abandon him." He cleared his throat and looked like he was struggling with something. "Dair's my b-boyfriend."

"Oh, really?" Mac nodded. "That's great. Nice to meet you, man. If Robin's looking this well, you must make him really happy. That's awesome." He shook his head. "Look, I just wanted to say I'm sorry. I know I was a jerk when we were kids, and that wasn't fair on you at all. I know I did wrong and I didn't believe in you enough. You're in computers now, right?"

Robin licked his lips. "I'm a software developer," he said.

"He's a genius," Dair chimed in, rubbing Robin's back. He wasn't buying Mac's nice guy act. People could change, sure. But Dair wasn't going to abandon Robin just because of a cute smile and a pretty apology. "He basically keeps the company going."

"Babe," Robin said bashfully.

Babe. It was a generic pet name that Robin was probably only using for effect in front of Mac, but it warmed Dair's heart in a surprising way.

While everyone's eyes were on Robin, a couple of chubby guys holding hands maneuvered their way around Mac, who was in the thoroughfare. The expression flashed across Mac's face for less than a second, but Dair was certain he caught a sneer. Then Mac was all smiles as Robin looked back at him.

Hmm.

"That's incredible," Mac said in response to Robin's job title. "You always were so damn smart. I'm proud of you, Binny. Well done." He held up his hands suddenly. "Sorry. You never liked that name, did you? Robin." He nodded to the group and took a step back. "Well, I'll let you get on with your evening. Hopefully I'll see you guys around. Dair – pleasure. See ya, Robin."

The five of them watched Mac re-enter the club. Then a loud bang snatched their attention back to the table. Emery had slapped his hands down on the wood, his pretty, black-lined eyes narrow with fury. "We need shots. Now."

He stormed away from the table to the outside bar. Ava nodded as she stood to follow him. "Yeah. Sounds like a sensible plan."

Dair looked down at Robin.

He was shaking ever so slightly.

Without thinking, Dair wrapped his arm around his small frame and steered him toward the table to sit again opposite Jay. The twins immediately reached a hand out to each other to hold.

"Are you okay?" Dar murmured.

His blood was pulsing in his ears. That wasn't how he'd expected Mac to be at all. He'd envisioned some drunken redneck with a pot belly, not a charming guy with movie star looks. It had caught him off guard, but hopefully he'd taken care of Robin well enough.

Robin cleared his throat and shook his head. "Yeah," he rasped, then tried again with a more normal voice. "Yeah, I'm fine. That was fine, right? He was okay? I told you he wasn't a psycho. He was nice. He was nice to me." Robin was nodding, his brow slightly creased. It looked like he was replaying the encounter in his head.

"Just because he was nice doesn't mean shit," Jay snarled.

Robin frowned. "People change."

Dair smiled and gave Robin's shoulder a little squeeze. "The important thing was that you've seen him and there wasn't any drama. As long as you're okay, we can forget about him and enjoy the rest of the night."

"Speaking of forgetting," Emery announced as he and Ava came back to the table. They had a tray each, and when they placed them down, Dair was horrified to see they were covered in shot glasses filled with alcohol of every color.

Some of them were on fire.

His manners activated on instinct, and he reached for his wallet with his free hand. That many shots must have cost a fortune.

Emery stuck a polished nail in Dair's face. "No, she doesn't," he said firmly.

Ava shook her head as she began placing glasses in front of people. "Em's loaded. Don't try arguing with him. Just drink your forgetting juice. It'll make you grow up big and strong." Her eyes flicked up and down Dair. "Big-*ger* and strong-*er*."

Dair toyed with the purple drink he'd been handed. They'd gotten an Uber across town, so he didn't mind indulging. But he wanted to make sure Robin was truly okay before they started getting tanked.

"How are you feeling, really?" he asked as the other three started taking selfies with the carnage spread across the table.

Robin blinked and looked up from the small glass dangling between his slim fingers. "Honestly, fine," he said. There was a hint of incredulity in his tone, like he couldn't believe what he was saying. He let out a laugh. "All this time I've been letting this idea of what we were mess with my head without even realizing. But he was totally normal, wasn't he? Polite and friendly and he acknowledged he was a jerk." He shook his head. "I'm so relieved."

Something strange reared in Dair's chest. Was that *jealously?* No, that didn't make sense. But there was definitely something in his gut warning him that Mac still wasn't to be entirely trusted.

"As long as you're okay?" Dair said diplomatically.

Robin nodded, clinking their glasses together. "It's like – maybe I wasn't such a terrible judge of character? Maybe I didn't waste all that time with him getting messed around? *Not* that I, like, want to get back together or anything. But yeah. I feel better. Less embarrassed about the whole thing."

Perhaps it was the shot they downed together or the three more they did with the group, but as the night went on Dair couldn't agree that he felt better after meeting Mac in person.

In fact, he was pretty sure he felt worse.

10

ROBIN

APPARENTLY, SOMEONE HAD LET A STAMPEDE OF RHINOS RUN through Robin's bedroom last night, and they were currently dancing on his head. He groaned in pain as daylight pierced through his eyelids, and he licked his dry teeth and lips.

He was the wrong way around in his bed, hugging a pillow for dear life with Dair's large feet poking into his hair. From his soft snores, Dair was evidently still asleep. But Robin felt too nauseous. He needed a glass of water, some aspirin, and to brush his teeth.

Mercifully, he still had his jeans on, but only one sock. He sat up and pulled the other one off too, padding toward the door barefoot. Their jackets, shoes, and shirts from last night were strewn across the desk, office chair, and dressers. There was a pizza box half hanging out of the wardrobe and empty beer bottles littering the furniture surface tops.

Jesus. What had they gotten up to last night? Robin remembered the shots outside The Aquarium, then dancing in the club. There had been a drag queen...and maybe some karaoke? He rubbed his head and grimaced. Okay, they had definitely ordered an Uber to take them home after they'd picked up the pizza from the only place in town that stayed open late enough to serve food to drunken revelers. That was a relief.

Had he and Dair continued dancing in his room? He honestly couldn't recall. There was some vague recollection of him claiming that pillow and curling up on the bed...

Had Dair pulled the comforter over him?

He rubbed his stubbly jaw. Maybe?

Shaking his head, he turned and reached for the door. He could continue his detective work after he'd taken measures to diminish this hellish hangover. But as soon as he opened his bedroom door, a fluffy ball shot inside. "Smudge! No!" Robin hissed. But he couldn't grab the puppy before he launched himself onto the bed, scrambling on Dair's chest.

His naked chest.

For a moment, Robin forgot his panic that the puppy would wake Dair up with a hangover just as bad as his. He stared as the bed sheets slipped down a little, revealing taut pecs and rippling abs...

...and Robin was being a creep. He screwed his eyes shut, managed to snag Smudge off the bed, and fumbled back out into the hall. Somehow, Dair was still asleep, so Robin closed the door, then deposited Smudge back down on the wooden floor.

"You're a terror," he chastised.

Smudge licked his black nose and wagged his fluffy tail.

First, Robin hauled himself into the shower, the scalding hot water soothing his aching body. Once scrubbed up, he popped a couple of painkillers, had a quick shave, then snuck back into his room to grab some clothes. Dair was still sleeping soundly, all snuggled up under the blankets.

Robin sighed to himself. 'Cute' wasn't a word he would have thought he'd use for the large, handsome ex-Marine. But right then, he did look kind of adorable.

Before heading down to the kitchen, he found his phone in yesterday's jeans. The battery was dead, but he unplugged his charger to bring with him.

It transpired he wasn't the first of his siblings to make it downstairs. He hadn't realized how early it was, as Jay was still there. Granted, he was already dressed for work and eating cereal, but Robin would have thought he'd be out of the house by now.

Ava was sprawled across the kitchen table, her head lying on her arms. From the looks of her clothes, he wasn't convinced she'd even been to sleep at all. She moaned at Robin's entrance without looking up but otherwise didn't react to his presence. Robin wasn't sure she was even fully awake.

Someone, probably Jay, had put Smudge's food down for him, so Robin didn't need to worry about that. Good thing, as he could barely work out his own needs. "Morning," he croaked with a grimace.

Jay cocked an eyebrow at him. "Morning," he said. "What time did you party animals get in?"

Robin frowned as he plugged his phone into the wall and fetched a cup of coffee from the pot. "You didn't come home with us? Ohh – no. You left early." He'd also stopped drinking alcohol and switched to water at a reasonable time. Unlike everyone else. "You came here, not your own place?"

"I'm staying here all week," said Jay, flashing a cocky grin. "Besides, I wanted to see what state you'd be in this morning. You're coming to my students' Shakespeare play tonight, remember? No wriggling out of it. So, how'd you get back from the bar?"

Ava whimpered, probably feeling like Robin did about being forced to watch kids attempting Shakespeare with a hangover. He pointed at his sister. "We got an Uber with

Emery and dropped him off along the way. With Dair, of course."

"Of course." Jay smirked.

"What?" Robin's insecurities flared.

But Jay shook his head. "You two were just cute, that's all. He looks at you like you hung the moon."

Robin frowned and blinked. "Must have been the alcohol," he muttered, hunting through the cupboards for the sugariest cereal he could find. When he looked back at Jay, though, he was frowning.

"You mean, he's not normally affectionate when you're out?"

Damn. No, what he meant was 'Dair couldn't have looked at me like that because he's straight and we're just pretending.'

Robin shrugged in what he hoped was a nonchalant way, then fished a carton of milk from the fridge. "I mean, he's still getting used to all of this. He thought he was straight before."

"Oh that's right. He's bi, isn't he?" Jay nodded. "Well, he's certainly embracing his queerness now. Have you guys swapped 'I love you's yet?"

Robin choked on his cereal. "No," he mumbled, wiping his chin. "Of course not. Don't be stupid."

Jay gave him a funny look. "Oh-kay. Forget I asked."

It was time to change the subject to something safer. "What about you? Weren't you dating that waiter guy?"

Jay's expression settled into that purposefully neutral one Robin had seen a thousand times. "That was over ages ago. It wasn't even anything more than a couple of hookups."

It wasn't ages ago. Robin remembered Jay talking happily about the waiter just a week or two back. Robin had assumed Jay wasn't mentioning him as much due to all the reunion pressure. He definitely hadn't said it was over.

Jay hadn't dated anyone seriously in the past couple of years. Usually, he was the opposite of Robin. Since college, he had always had a steady boyfriend, never being single for long. Why the change?

"Really? I'm sorry." Robin chewed down another couple of mouthfuls of his breakfast. He was starting to feel a bit more human again. "Everything okay? With dating, I mean."

Jay shrugged and opened up his phone. "Just working more on myself right now. I'll date the right guy if he comes along."

He clearly didn't want to talk about it – whatever 'it' was. But Robin's curiosity would have to wait as his own phone obviously had enough juice to come back to life. The sound of a text message notification rang through the air from where he'd left it on the counter. It was only a soft 'ding,' but Ava still groaned at the noise.

Robin chuckled at his sister's expense, then drained the rest of the milk and cereal from his bowl in a couple of gulps. After placing it and his spoon in the dishwasher, he stood and opened up his messages with the phone still attached to the charging cord.

It was a text from an unknown number, so he opened it fully to read it and discover the sender.

"Oh," he said out loud, his skin rushing cold for just a second.

"What?" Jay asked.

But Robin didn't know why he was being silly. He shook his head. "It just took me by surprise. It's Mac, on a new number."

He'd blocked the old one, after all. He read the message out for his brother to hear.

"Hey Robin! I hope you don't mind, but I got your number from Sandy on the Reunion committee."

"Sandy?" Jay scowled. "I'll be having words with her about privacy policies."

Robin tutted. "No, look, it's fine. Listen. *I know it's kind of out of the blue, but my company's having some real tech issues. The IT folks keep running around talking about going fishing or some shit. Do you think I could pick your brains while you're in town? I bet you're leagues smarter than our guys lol. Coffee tomorrow?*"

"Bullshit," Jay snapped.

Robin felt a little taken aback. "What? No – he just wants to talk work. I think that's actually pretty cool and mature of him."

Mac had always teased Robin back in the day and called him a geek and a nerd for spending all his time tinkering around with computer software and programming. Robin felt validated after all these years that his ex was finally recognizing his skills.

"Bullshit," Ava garbled into her arm.

Robin huffed. "Guys, it's not like that. He's just asking for help. And I *can* actually help him with that. Easily. I think this could be good for me. I was so hung up on our time together, but it's all fine now, I think. This will be like a fresh start. I can close the door on high school like a normal person. I mean – who is still obsessed with their ex-boyfriend ten years after they broke up? That's insane. No, if I don't go meet him for coffee, *that* would be weird. This is great. Just two adults, getting together to work through a professional problem. And he'll respect me for once. I'd much rather be civil, after all. There's no reason we should be avoiding each other or anything. I want to say yes. I wouldn't just be helping him, anyway. It would be for his company. And is it really so crazy to think he needs my help? I *am* pretty great at what I do."

He hadn't realized how long his monologue had gone on for until he stopped, leaving the kitchen in silence. Jay glowered at him. "Are you done trying to convince yourself this is a good idea?"

"No one's questioning your talent," Ava added. "Only his shady motives."

Robin scoffed and locked his phone screen. He sat back down opposite his twin. "He's not asking me on a date. He just happens to have a problem that I can help with."

"How convenient," mumbled Ava from underneath her mass of curls.

Jay sipped his coffee and cocked an eyebrow. "Agreed. He just *happens* to have an issue like that the morning after he sees you for the first time in a decade? I'm not buying it."

"Stranger things have happened."

Robin knew he sounded defensive, but he didn't care. Jay was being overprotective and it was irking him a little bit. Robin was a grown man. He knew he'd been away for a while, but he could take care of himself. Just because Jay had called all the shots when they were kids didn't mean he got to boss him around now they were twenty-eight.

"Okay," Jay said, tilting his head. "What do you think Dair will say? I'm assuming he does know what an asshole Mac was to you by the caveman vibes he was radiating last night?"

"Huh?"

Jay rolled his eyes. "Oh, come on. Dair was one step away from clubbing Mac over the head and dragging you back to your cave to fuck your brains out."

Robin's entire body quivered at such a visceral image. If only it were true.

"No," he spluttered. "Dair's not like that. He's not the possessive, jealous type. He wouldn't be a dick about me doing something for *work*. Like I said, this is one hundred percent a professional thing. I wouldn't be considering it for a second if I thought it really was a date."

He meant that wholeheartedly. He had zero interest in

being Mac's boyfriend again. But if he was being honest, there was a part of him that wanted to prove to Mac that he'd made something of himself. Yeah, it was nice that Dair had been there pretending to be his gorgeous man. But Robin wasn't so shallow as to just value himself on who he was dating. He wanted to show Mac he had succeeded incredibly well in his career.

Jay narrowed his eyes. "I'd still run it by Dair. If you've got nothing to hide, there's no harm in telling him."

"Sure. Of course I will." Robin was getting annoyed by this conversation. Why wasn't his brother believing him? "Not like it matters, anyway," he grumbled after.

"Why not?" Jay scowled. "Look, all I'm saying is I know we've only just met, but I really like Dair. I don't fucking like Mac, and I never have. Why would you risk things with Dair to prove a point to some asshole you left behind ten years ago?"

"Oh for goodness – it's not real with Dair, okay! It's fake."

Jay stared at him. "What?"

Ava lifted her head. When her eyes finally focused on Robin, she glared. *"What?"*

Robin huffed and folded his arms. "Dair and I are just friends, okay? We live together with Pey, and when he heard about Mac and the whole reunion thing, he suggested pretending to be my boyfriend to keep Mac away in case he started any trouble. But there's no trouble! Mac's not dangerous. He's obviously grown out of that shit, otherwise he wouldn't have apologized. So there's no reason for Dair to get jealous or worried. We're not dating. He's *straight.*"

Jay was looking at him like he'd just sprouted another head. Ava rubbed her eyes and scowled even harder.

"You *lied* to us?" she said.

"Only a little," Robin squeaked. Damn it, he really wished he hadn't said anything.

Jay shook his head. "He's...no, he's not straight, Rob. I don't care if you guys are dancing around being official or whatever bullshit. But he's crushing on you hard."

Robin barked a laugh so hard it made his hungover head throb again. He winced and rubbed his hand against it. "Dude, no. Look, we *are* friends. We just stretched the truth a little in case Mac tried something. But it looks like that wasn't necessary."

"Mom *likes* him," Ava growled.

Jay was nodding. "Yeah, if you concocted some sort of lie, whatever, not cool. Totally unnecessary, actually. But it's also bullshit. I've seen you making goo-goo eyes his way-"

"I never said I didn't like him," Robin interrupted with a hiss. Embarrassed, he cradled his coffee mug for a second, regaining his composure. "But he's totally straight, okay? I'm amazed you guys thought he could be my boyfriend. It would be impossible. But...look, I didn't mean to hurt anyone. Please – *please* – can you just play along for the rest of the week? We'll have a nice pretend breakup back in Seattle and no harm will be done."

Jay and Ava glanced at each other. Ava grumbled something unintelligible and dropped her head back on her arms, hiding under a mountain of hair. But Jay pursed his lips and stared at Robin for several seconds.

"Fine. I'll keep your little secret. But just because you guys aren't really dating or whatever doesn't mean I'm happy with you going to see Mac on your own."

Robin huffed. He was slightly relieved his brother wasn't going to let the cat out of the bag. That would be humiliating. But Robin was still irked by his suspicion of Mac.

"I will talk to Dair about it, I promise. But it'll be fine, you'll see. Mac's changed."

Jay hummed, but he didn't say anything else on the matter.

11

DAIR

It wasn't Dair's place to tell Robin this was a bad idea.

That being said, this was a bad idea.

He'd told Dair yesterday how Mac wanted to meet up to discuss some sort of computer issue for his work. Dair wasn't sure precisely what Mac's job was, other than being a salesman for some sort of home automation company. It could be a legitimate problem. But something was setting off Dair's alarm bells all the same.

However, he wasn't Robin's actual boyfriend, obviously. If it were any of his other friends who were meeting up with a former abuser, though, he would still be wary. Just because Mac had said he'd changed didn't mean he had.

Robin had made it very, *very* clear this wasn't any kind of date, even going so far as to show Dair the message chain. Dair had assured him that wasn't necessary – he wasn't *jealous*, after all. He was just concerned. What did make him happier, however, was that Robin accepted Dair's offer to drive him into town for the meetup.

"This is really kind of you," Robin said as they got out of the truck, leaving Smudge inside for the time being.

Dair intended to walk Robin down the boardwalk to Sunny Side Up. As far as Mac was concerned, Dair was Robin's boyfriend. The way Dair saw it, it wouldn't be unreasonable for him to walk Robin to the door in order to remind Mac not to try anything funny. That was what he would have done if Malory had an unpleasant ex she needed to meet with for whatever reason.

Just as they got to the diner, Robin stopped and faced Dair. "Look. If it makes you feel any better. Mac was never an ass – I mean, he never lost control – never, uh…"

"Hit you," Dair said as calmly as he could.

Robin cleared his throat. "Yeah. That. He never did it in public. So even if he was still like that – which I don't really think he is – he wouldn't try anything here."

Dair narrowed his eyes and ground his teeth. "You don't have to go inside," he began.

But Robin smiled and touched his arm. "I've told you, it's fine. It'll give me closure. I want to see him and prove to myself that I did all right for myself these last ten years."

Dair could have told him that and way more. Robin didn't need Mac to give him approval. But Dair had never had an ex like that. So who knew? Maybe this was something Robin needed to do?

"Just…be careful anyway, all right?" Dair looked toward the magnificent lake and squinted against the sun. "I've got my phone on me and I think I'll stay in town. So just call when you're done and I'll come collect you."

"Oh, you don't have to," Robin said uncertainly. "I don't want to be a burden."

"You're not," Dair assured him sincerely as he looked back at him. "Besides, I'm your fella, remember? If I was really your boyfriend, I'd come pick you up. It's my thing." He winked, secretly pleased when Robin blushed.

"Okay, fine," Robin relented, rolling his eyes. Then he

looked through the window of the diner. "Mac's watching," he murmured, casting his eyes down.

Dair's skin prickled. "All right," he said practically. "Let's remind him not to do anything stupid, then, shall we?"

If he couldn't be there to physically sit between Mac and Robin, he'd leave Mac an image seared into his eyes. Let him know exactly who was on Robin's side, should he do anything dumb like lose his temper.

Before he could second-guess himself, he touched his thumb to Robin's chin, encouraging him to tilt his head up.

Then Dair leaned down and touched his lips to Robin's.

It was an extremely chaste kiss. Nothing more than one mouth pressing lightly against another. But electricity shot up Dair's spine. He tried not to jerk back in surprise and give the game away. Huh. It *was* the first kiss he'd had that wasn't his ex in almost thirteen years. It was probably just his body reacting to the sensation on sensitive skin. Pure biology.

"Well, um, have fun," he said gruffly before Robin could pick up on his weirdness.

Robin blinked a couple of times, then nodded. "Oh, yeah, sure. I doubt 'fun' is the right word. But, yeah. Um, thank you."

He scurried into the diner.

Dair caught Mac's eye. He'd been watching them, naturally. But Mac smiled and gave him a salute-wave. Dair simply nodded at him, hoping it conveyed enough of a warning.

Behave yourself. Or there will be hell to pay.

There was nothing for Dair to do but walk away and leave them to it. He thought the hard part of this escapade would be trying to stop a civilian with no military training if a fight broke out. Not willingly leaving Robin with the very person Dair wanted to keep him away from.

He sighed. Without knowing how long he had to kill, he figured he'd better get a move on.

He had a plan.

While he'd been desperately trying to stay awake the previous evening, hungover and forced to watch a Pine Cove High production of Much Ado About Nothing, he'd had an idea. Unfortunately, it involved putting a considerable amount of strain on his credit card, but he'd made the decision Robin was worth it, so he wasn't going to dwell on that anymore. Which was how he and Smudge ended up walking through the door of Turkish Delight for the second time in so many days.

There were a few customers currently being seen to by the barbers. But the guy they had spoken to before looked up from behind the desk. His dog, Pom, ran to greet Smudge excitedly. "Hello again," he said in his soft voice. He crouched down without hesitation and fussed over Smudge as well as his own dog. Anyone who was kind to animals was okay in Dair's book. "Can I help?"

"You don't have room for a walk-in, do you?" Dair asked.

He felt a bit self-conscious – like a bull that had wandered accidentally into a china shop and was trying its best not to break anything. This place was way fancier than anywhere he'd gotten a haircut in his life. But that was why he was here.

The chairs were bright red leather and the walls naked white brick with bold, black decals of flowers painted on them. Each station had an enormous mirror hung at it with an ornate black frame, and black glass chandeliers hung from the ceiling. A local radio station was playing and Pom encouraged Smudge to help her chase tufts of hair around the wooden paneled floor. Spicy grooming products filled the air, and the lights were dimmed more than a usual salon, almost like a nightclub.

Dair was definitely out of his comfort zone. But that was okay.

If Mac was Robin's type, Dair needed to sharpen up if he was going to do him proud at the big party on Saturday night. It was bad enough he'd been to the LGBT night and the play looking like a hillbilly. From now on, the people of Pine Cove would see Robin's new boyfriend and hopefully be impressed.

"Absolutely," the guy said. He stood up again and offered Dair both a hand and a warm smile. They shook. "I'm Taylan. This is my place. I'd be delighted to accommodate you."

"Your place?" Dair asked as he allowed himself to be seated in a chair. The guy – Taylan – seemed kind of young to be a business owner. But then again, he was around Dair's age, so early thirties. For people who hadn't gone into the Marines, that gave them around fifteen years since high school to get their act together.

Taylan smiled as he stood behind Dair and looked at him in the mirror's reflection. "My father opened Delight when he and my mother emigrated from Istanbul," he explained while he played gently with Dair's unruly hair. "Unfortunately, health issues forced him to retire early. But it was my joy to take over from him. I hope people think of Delight as a little escape from everyday life."

"Like a sanctuary?" Dair suggested.

Taylan inclined his head. He was close to six foot, but he was slim, and his features were delicate and refined. Dair liked to think he was getting a reasonably good gaydar after living with Robin and Peyton, especially after his jaunt to the gay bar on Tuesday night. His military training had taught him how to read body language well. But he couldn't make up his mind regarding Taylan.

"A sanctuary, exactly," the barber agreed with a soft smile. "Modern life is so hectic. Everyone should get the chance to unwind and feel their best. So. Are you looking for just a shave, or may I please do something with your split ends?"

Dair laughed unabashedly. "Um, well, I've never even heard of a Turkish barber before, let alone been to one. What's the difference?"

"It's a very close shave with a hot towel relaxation, massage, and a couple of other quirks." Taylan winked. "I promise, you'll never have another shave like it."

Dair nodded. "Let's go for the full works, boss. I trust you. I'd like to look somewhat respectable again, if that's possible."

"Like a gentleman?" Taylan suggested.

Dair grinned. "Sure, why not. I've seen more impossible things in my time."

Taylan rested a hand on Dair's shoulder. "You undersell yourself. We'll have you polished in no time. Now, just relax, and I shall work my magic."

He held his hands up to wiggle his fingers. Pom barked, dancing around by their feet with her tail wagging. Smudge was looking at her like he'd found his first true love. Dair laughed.

To start, Taylan trimmed his scruff with an electric clipper so it was short enough for the proper shave. Dair watched in fascination as Taylan took care lathering up his fat round brush with shaving soap. Then he applied it to Dair's face in a circular motion that already felt soothing.

"This is your first time having someone else do your shave?" Taylan asked.

Dair grunted. "You could say that." His dad had taught him as a teenager, and then it just became something you did out of necessity. Not a luxury. Although when Taylan produced his straight razor, Dair couldn't help but shift just fractionally in anticipation. He'd been in a couple of knife fights during his service, enough to leave him with the sensible impression that if someone came at him with a blade, he should stop them.

Taylan paused immediately, obviously sensing Dair's hesitation. "I assure you, it's perfectly safe." He held the razor out for Dair to inspect. "The sheaths will protect you. I've been administering shaves since I was fifteen. But if you would prefer, we can wash everything off and simply stick with a haircut."

Dair shook his head, the feeling of mild panic fading. He wouldn't say he had PTSD from his time in the service, but every now and again something would catch him. He was fine, though.

"No, I'm good." He smiled at Taylan. "Thanks, though. Let's give it a go."

After the first few scrapes to his neck, Dair was surprised how quickly he relaxed. Taylan flicked his wrist expertly as he removed both hair and shaving cream from Dair's face. They were quiet as he worked, the radio playing softly in the background, leaving Dair to zone out into a sort of meditative state.

Until he heard his name called.

"Dair, baby! Fancy seeing you here!"

Dair cracked his eyes open to see Emery skip across the barbershop and drop into the empty chair beside him. He looked genuinely happy to see him, and Dair smiled as much as he could while someone had a blade to his throat.

"Hey, Emery. How's it going?"

Today he was wearing full-length jeans, but his T-shirt was still a crop that read 'Masc 4 Masc' in extremely swirly letters surrounded by flowers. He pulled off an expensive-looking pair of sunglasses and bit the end of one of the arms as he grinned at Dair.

"Wonderful, thank you, darling. I approve of this." He

swirled his hand in front of Dair. "Taylan is a dream. You're in safe hands."

"Thank you, Emmerich," said Taylan without looking away from his work. Now all the foam was gone, he wiped down Dair's face and started buffering it with a hard block of some kind of white soap.

"So, where's our lovely Robin?" Emery crossed one knee over the other and bounced his foot. "I hope you're taking care of him?"

Dair sighed. He didn't want to talk about Robin behind his back, but he couldn't miss out on an opportunity to get an insight from someone who had known both him and his ex at school.

"He's meeting Mac for coffee. Apparently, Mac needed some computer-related advice. Robin said he wanted to go, so…"

Emery huffed and flopped against the leather chair he was curled up in. "He always was a charmer. I was so fucking jealous of Robin when they first got together, you know?" He didn't wait for Dair to answer. "Don't get me wrong. Mac isn't some brutish wife-beater. Not that I know of. It's more that he likes to rough-house and doesn't always think about who he's with. But…" He rubbed his button nose and locked eyes with Dair. "When he and Robin were together, it was like everything was always Robin's fault. I don't know how to explain it better. Just a gut reaction, you know?"

Dair hummed in agreement. He wasn't sure exactly what it was that put him on edge about Mac, but it was there, whatever it was.

"I don't think too much can happen over coffee." At least he hoped.

Emery nodded eagerly. "You're a very understanding boyfriend, Alasdair. Do you like Alasdair, or should I call you just Dair?"

"Either's fine," said Dair with a shrug. Taylan appeared to be shaving him again, but this time *against* the grain. It felt kind of weird.

"Alasdair, I'm curious. Jay said you've never been with a guy before Robin. What's that like, that moment of 'ohhh'?" He placed a hand on his chest. "I'm pretty sure I flirted with the male OB-GYN that helped delivered me, so I never had to think about it much."

"Oh, um." As carefully as he could while Taylan finished up the second shave, Dair repeated the little story he and Robin had concocted about him being so clueless and not even realizing they were dating until they were literally on a date. That seemed to tickle Emery.

"So, would you say you're bi or pan?" he asked Dair.

Dair blinked at him. "Uhh..."

Emery held up his hands, clearly going to explain. "Bi is attraction to all genders – male, female, nonbinary, all of that. Like, something you're actively aware of. Pan is when you fall for someone and gender isn't really a consideration. Like, you're not really bothered what's between their legs. You fall for them as a person."

Dair frowned while Taylan used the hard bar of soap again. He was listening to every word they said, but he was either tuning them out or quietly processing it. Dair wasn't getting any aggressive vibes from him, though, after hearing Dair was supposedly queer, so he felt safe enough to continue talking.

"Maybe that second one? Pan, was it? I just like Robin for Robin." That was true, after all. In fact, he'd go so far now as to say he was extremely fond of his friend after these past few days together.

"Lovely," Emery said dreamily, resting his chin on his fist and propping his elbow on the chair arm. "That's so romantic. Robin was so special he literally made you question your sexuality." He gasped and clutched his T-shirt. "So many guys wouldn't be brave enough to do that."

Dair gave him a bashful half smile. "I wouldn't call it brave."

Emery's expression became the most serious Dair had seen it yet. "It takes a great deal of courage to be unflinchingly authentic. Trust me. I'm very happy Robin met you."

They had to pause talking as Taylan wrapped a warm towel around Dair's head and face, leaving him covered for a couple of minutes. It gave him time to brood on what Emery had just said.

Robin *was* special. He totally deserved to have someone question their whole world just to be with him. Emery was right. That was hella romantic.

It was just a shame that person wasn't Dair.

When the towel came off, Dair was surprised to see Emery just hanging around, still on his phone. "Um, do you have an appointment too?" Dair asked as Taylan dusted his face with some sort of alternative to talcum powder.

Emery shook his head. "I just came in when I saw you. I've got a pretty light week. Why?"

"Well…"

Dair looked upward as Taylan winked and began massaging his cheeks and jaw with an aloe vera balm. "You ready for the best part?"

"Uh, sure?"

At that moment, Smudge and Pom made their appearance. Apparently, they'd been in the back of the shop. Dair suspected someone must have been feeding Smudge to keep him occupied for that long. But now they found Emery and he was more than willing to make a big fuss over them.

"Oh, there's *two* fur babies today! Is Dair your daddy?" he asked Smudge. "Emery wishes Dair was *his* daddy, too. Oh yes he does, yes he does!"

Dair blushed, but Emery was clearly trying to wind him up on purpose. It felt kind of nice to be teased. In the military, ribbing was definitely a form of acceptance. Dair was happy if Robin's friend felt comfortable enough to give him a hard time.

Emery scooped up Smudge into his lap and waved his paws at Dair. "Look, puppy! Fire!"

Dair whipped his head around to see Taylan holding a stick with cotton wrapped around the end. There was a faint smell of alcohol in the air, which was probably how Taylan had lit the cotton on fire.

"You said you wanted the full works. You still want the ultimate grooming?" Taylan asked, giving Dair that alluring wink again.

Dair wasn't sure what was about to happen. But then an image of Mac floated in front of his eyes, looking every inch of perfection.

"Do it," Dair said firmly.

Taylan proceeded to bat at Dair's ears in quick succession with the flame, each time brushing his hand down the skin afterward. It didn't exactly hurt, but it was still a strange sensation to feel the touch of briefest pain, then have it soothed. The faint whiff of burnt hair filled the air. After half a dozen taps on each side, Taylan blew out the flame, and all Dair's rogue ear hairs had vanished.

"Wow." He'd never thought of doing anything with those before. Along with his extremely smooth chin, he'd never felt neater, and Taylan was only just starting on trimming his hair. Little blond tufts floated to the floor. Dair watched them, feeling like the old version of himself was drifting away too.

Emery was busy on his phone, but he'd said he didn't

have much going on. So Dair decided to be brave. If this was a new version of himself, he wasn't to go all the way with the makeover.

"You wouldn't have somewhere to recommend for a nice suit, would you?" he asked. If he was going to pound his credit card, he might as well do it right.

Emery's gaze snapped up from his phone. His face lit up and he clutched Dair's knee through his slippery hairdressing gown.

"Careful," Taylan growled, pausing with his scissors.

"Sorry," Emery whispered, not sounding sorry at all. "Oh em gee. Alasdair, baby. Are you asking me to take you clothes shopping?"

"Well…" He'd only been asking for a shop recommendation, if he was honest. But Emery's excited face made him change his mind. "I mean, sure. If you've got time?"

Emery snatched up his phone again, hastily swiping across the screen. "It would be my honor. I've cleared my afternoon. You're my top priority. Do you want a look for the reunion?" Dair nodded and Emery squeed. Above, Taylan chuckled and shook his head. "This is going to be epic! We'll get you looking so fucking gorgeous Robin won't even *consider* getting coffee with that asshat Mac again, business or not. Sound good?"

Dair felt a grim determination settle over him and he smirked. "Definitely."

It was suddenly very important to Dair that he look better than Mac for the big party. He wasn't entirely sure why, but he decided it probably came back down to taking care of Robin again. If Robin was proud to stand beside him, he would be easier to keep safe.

That had to be it.

ROBIN

IN CONTRAST TO HOW HE FELT THE LAST TIME HE WALKED INTO Sunny Side Up, Robin's gut twisted. For all he'd argued this would be good for him to meet Mac, now he was here by himself he was suddenly feeling like he was eighteen again, trying to stand up to his boyfriend and convince him it was over.

Except Mac waved happily at him from the booth he was sitting at, then gave Dair a salute out on the sidewalk. He appeared cheerful and at ease. Not the pent-up ball of stress and anger Robin remembered from their breakup.

Robin forced himself not to look back anxiously at Dair. He understood that the kiss had been purely for show, but his knees were still trembling. Dair had *kissed* him. It didn't matter that it had only lasted barely a second or that it was basically a warning to Mac.

Dair Epping's lips had touched Robin's.

He needed to focus. Right then, the most important thing was this meeting with Mac. But it was very hard to shake Dair from his mind.

Mac stood to greet Robin with a warm hug. "You look

great, Robin. Thank you for meeting me. I ordered you a cappuccino – you still like those, don't you? With three sugars?"

Robin couldn't help but laugh as he sat down. "Yep. Guilty as charged."

"Still sweet," Mac said with a wink.

Robin's heart skipped a beat, but not in a good way. Shit. Was Mac flirting? Oh no, that wasn't what he wanted at *all*. He decided to totally ignore it and pick up the menu. He looked around for Sunny or Tyee, hoping to order some kind of pastry quickly to distract himself. They weren't anywhere in sight, however. Neither was Peri, who was usually hard to miss with his mountain of fluff.

Robin felt strangely abandoned. But that was stupid. Dair had specifically offered to come with him, but this was a work meeting. So they should get down to work.

Robin opened his mouth to ask about the phishing (because that was totally what his IT department had been talking about, not *fishing*) Mac had mentioned needing help with, but Mac beat him to it.

"You're wearing your glasses?"

The statement – presented as a question – threw Robin totally off guard. "Uh, yeah," he said, feeling stupid. Obviously he was wearing them. They were sitting right there on his face.

Mac shrugged and looked a little confused. "I just thought you always looked better with your contacts, is all." He laughed and touched Robin's hand with his fingertips. "You're gorgeous. You should show the world that, not hide behind a pair of glasses like an old man."

"Oh." Robin touched the side of his glasses. Yeah, Mac always did encourage Robin to wear his contacts. He'd forgotten. Robin didn't mind wearing them from time to time, but honestly they were so much hassle. He just liked his glasses, usually. "I've got my contacts with me," he offered. "I'll probably wear them to the party. Get a bit dressed up."

"Excellent." Mac beamed.

"Welcome to Sunny's. Here are your drinks. Can I get you anything to eat?" The server was a gangly teenager with dark hair down to his shoulders and painted black nails. He placed two china mugs down with a pot of condiments, then cocked an eyebrow at Robin. "Robin Coal?"

It took Robin a second. "Saul Perkins? Good god, you've grown!" Saul was one of Sunny and Tyee's grandkids. They had a whole brood here in town, so many that Robin had lost count years ago. There might even be one or two great-grandbabies by now. "Jeez. What are you? Seventeen now?"

"Eighteen," Saul said, proudly nodding. "Got a scholarship for Seattle Pacific University. Going there in the fall."

"Holy crap, that's amazing," Robin enthused. "Congratulations. That's really fantastic. Your family must be so delighted."

Saul smiled bashfully. "My mom cried. Pops and Grandpa threw a party here for me."

"That's great," Mac agreed. "I mean, college isn't everything. So long as it's what you want, then good for you."

"It's definitely what I want," Saul said, arching an eyebrow.

Mac hadn't gone to college. He'd had a chip on his shoulder about the whole thing before Robin even left town. He said it was a waste of money for their generation as it just landed them in debt. But Robin had always wondered if there had been an element of jealousy too that Mac's family hadn't been able to afford it for him, despite sending his older brother.

Saul tapped his pen on his notepad. "So, any food for you guys?"

"I'd love a blueberry muffin." Robin smiled at him and folded up his menu.

Mac tapped his muscular stomach. "Not a cheat day, sadly. I'll just stick with the coffee."

Saul swept away, leaving them alone. Mac picked up his cup, swirling his drink. "So Dair seems nice. How did you guys meet?"

Robin licked his lips. "I thought you wanted to talk about work?" It wasn't that Robin was desperate to talk about work himself. His own company had contacted him *again* this morning, begging for help, so Robin would have to deal with that later as well. But he wanted to keep things strictly professional with Mac.

However, Mac scoffed. "Oh, really, Binny? We haven't seen each other in ten years. Would a little chitchat kill you? Come on, give me that. You were the one who broke up with me, after all." He stuck out his lower lip in a childish pout.

Yeah, because you cheated on me, Robin thought. Not that he'd ever told that to anyone, because then he might have to admit what had pushed Mac to fall into another guy's bed in the first place. That was just too humiliating. But it did mean that people like Peyton and Jay latched on to the temper thing a bit too much.

Robin would *never* have stayed if Mac had ever actually hit him. Rough-housing was normal in teenage boys. But knowing Mac had been unfaithful had really woken Robin up to the fact that they just weren't compatible. If they didn't make each other happy, they needed to end it.

He had needed to end it.

Why not talk about Dair? Robin's whole motive in coming here was to prove to Mac that he'd moved on with his life and he was worth something. What was the point of putting himself through the hardship of pretending to date his crush if he wasn't going to big it up?

"He took one of the rooms in the apartment I rent and we just hit it off."

Mac's eyebrows shot up. "Oh, you still rent? Okay." He sipped his coffee. "Buying is such a ball ache anyway, not to mention expensive. Good for you. So, was it love at first sight? He is pretty stunning."

Robin didn't miss the edge of incredulity. What Mac was really saying was 'how did you bag a guy like that?'

"It took a while," Robin said, sticking to the story they'd come up with on the drive over. "It was like it happened by accident. Neither of us realized we were on a date until we kissed."

"I love it." Mac chuckled. "I was worried you might not date after we broke up. You're too shy! I'm glad you found someone new."

"Thanks," Robin mumbled. "So, um, are you seeing anyone?"

Mac scoffed and held his hands up, indicating not only the diner but also Pine Cove at large. "Like there's any decent ass in this dump of a town? You ran away and left us, remember?" He laughed and slapped Robin's arm hard enough to leave a slight sting.

Robin scowled and pulled his arms in, cradling his coffee. "I'd actually forgotten how beautiful I find it around here."

Mac frowned. "Oh. I thought you'd agree with me about city life. I'm looking at a big promotion very soon. I'll be heading out to Portland. It's about time I left all this behind."

Leaving town had always been something he'd resented Robin for. Still, Robin couldn't fault him if that was what he wanted for himself. There were plenty of opportunities out there in the big wide world, not to mention hot guys. Just because Robin hadn't had any luck finding one didn't mean Mac wouldn't.

"That's exciting about the promotion," he said to shift the conversation topic back in a work direction.

Mac nodded, looking out the window of the diner. "It's basically a formality at this point. They want me for the position, but legally they have to interview other people as well." He rolled his eyes. "How about you? You jump up the ladder recently?"

Robin stalled. How did he explain that he was almost as high as he could go without making the leap into management? He loved where he was because although he worked in a team, he wasn't responsible for anyone. He could just put his music on and get on with his own thing. The thought of having to navigate people and politics and drama made him break into a cold sweat.

Thankfully, his muffin arrived and he was grateful for the distraction. Carefully, he pulled the wrapper off the base, then tore little chunks off to nibble.

"I'm good where I am," he said eventually, hoping that was vague enough. "Okay, so these phishing attacks. Did they succeed? Was someone able to get sensitive data or a backdoor installed? That would give me more of an idea of the problem."

Mac scoffed. "Oh, I've got no idea. I can ask the guys in that department the right questions for you, though? Just email them over to me."

Robin almost pointed out he didn't have Mac's email anymore.

But he didn't want Mac's email. He didn't want Mac to know *his* email. "How about I write them down now?"

Shame crept through him as he pulled a pen from his pocket and started scribbling on a clean napkin. Perhaps Jay had been right. Mac didn't really need his technical expertise. He'd just used that as an excuse to worm his way into spending time with Robin.

Fuck. He felt like an idiot.

Well, he'd still done what he came here to do. He'd shown Mac he had a great job and a great boyfriend.

Except, he didn't really have a boyfriend, did he?

He swallowed, desperate for his eyes not to get itchy as he continued to write his list and Mac chatted obliviously about his job in sales.

Mac may have led him on to get him here, but at least he actually *wanted* to date Robin. He was a viable option.

As wonderful as Dair was, he was still straight. Robin was just fooling himself by indulging in their little fantasy.

One day, Dair was going to meet a fantastic girl and move out, leaving Robin and Peyton to fill the third bedroom yet again. Dair was clearly the marrying kind, Robin could tell. He'd get hitched in a church, then have two or three kids and move out to the suburbs. Hopefully when that day came, they'd laugh about that time they'd pretended to date.

And Robin wouldn't feel heartbroken at the idea of him with someone else.

Growing up gay, it was harder to picture yourself married with a family. Things were changing rapidly nowadays, but it was ingrained in Robin from childhood that his path would be a different one than his parents. But then, he had Sunny and Tyee.

Speaking of which, Robin realized with a thrill they'd reappeared. It was silly, but he felt less alone with them around. He glanced over his shoulder to see Tyee fussing over his husband's apron tie at the entrance to the kitchen, Peri wagging his tail by their feet.

They got their happy ending. They'd adopted several kids in spite of adversity from local government for a time. They ran a business that was the heart and soul of Pine Cove. They were a success, whichever way you looked at it.

So maybe Robin could have that too. Just not with Mac, urgh. But sadly, not with Dair either.

He almost rose his fingers to touch his lips. Damn, that kiss had been unexpected. He knew logically Dair had just been proving a point in front of Mac to keep him in line. But Robin's body didn't seem to get that message.

His cock certainly didn't as it perked up again at the mere thought of it, just like it had when their mouths had come together. Fuck, Dair had tasted like coffee and minty chewing gum and something else warm and spicy. Robin couldn't help but wonder what else he might have tasted if their tongues had met.

That would never happen, so he needed to get a fucking grip. He could pine over the man he couldn't have, go back to the only other boyfriend he'd ever had, or get over them both and find somebody new.

But he hadn't found anyone new in ten years. He'd just had a series of silly little crushes and hookups that had led nowhere. It was kind of cruel that his crush on Dair was the strongest he'd felt by far over the years, just in time to coincide with his reunion with Mac. But in a few months, it would fade, just like all the others had. That didn't mean he had to fall back into Mac's arms to rid himself of it.

"Am I boring you?" Mac laughed, but Robin could tell he was hurt Robin had tuned out from whatever he'd been saying.

"Sorry, sorry." Robin shook his head and glanced over the questions he'd penned. "There you go – I think that should help. If they can't work out the issue from that, just let me know."

Mac took the napkin from him, his face breaking into a Hollywood-worthy smile. "I can still read your awful handwriting! That's cool." He sighed and pocketed the list. Before Robin could move, Mac reached out and placed his hand over Robin's. "Damn, I've missed this. Let's not drift apart again, yeah? We can stay in touch this time?"

Robin wanted to wrench his hand away, but he didn't want to cause an argument. However, at that moment Saul returned, slapping a slip of paper down onto the table. Robin jumped, automatically letting Mac go.

Saul looked pointedly at Robin. "Your check," he said with a raised eyebrow.

Mac waved his hand, already reaching for his wallet. "No, no. I've got this. My treat."

He produced his credit card with a flourish and Saul took it to use on the machine.

"Well, I better get back to work," Mac said once he got his card back, rolling his eyes. "Busy, busy, busy. It was amazing seeing you, though. Hopefully I'll catch you at a few more events before you leave us all again?"

"Uh, sure." Robin allowed Mac to hug him as they rose from the booth.

He watched Mac go, buttoning up his suit jacket as he strode confidently down the street and out of sight. After a minute, Robin followed.

"Hey, kid?"

Robin looked over to the server's station where Tyee was rolling silverware. Peri plodded over, sniffing Robin's sneakers. Then he looked up as if asking where his new friend Smudge was. Robin petted his head absently.

"Everything okay with the check?" Robin asked. If Mac's card had bounced, he could cover it no problem. He'd just be embarrassed.

Tyee shook his head. "I was just wondering where that handsome boyfriend of yours was."

Robin winced internally. *Not my boyfriend,* he thought sadly. So far, Jay had kept his promise and not altered his behavior in the slightest or said anything to anyone. Ava was in a mood with him for lying, but so far, Robin and Dair's charade was still going strong.

It just kind of sucked to constantly be reminded of what he didn't have but so desperately wanted.

"Oh, he's doing errands," Robin said, nodding. "He dropped me off for my meeting."

"Uh-huh," said Tyee dubiously, focusing on the silverware he was wrapping in napkins.

"It was just a meeting," Robin said firmly.

The very last thing he wanted was for anyone to get the insane notion that he was cheating on Dair. They may have been fake dating, but Robin would never, *ever* do that to anyone.

Not after the way Mac had made him feel.

Robin pushed those feelings deep down. When he'd seen the messages from that other guy on Mac's phone, it had broken him. It was crazy to think Mac had been so careless as to allow Robin to see them over his shoulder, but he had, and he'd finally broken up with him. That had been a dark time.

"Mac needed help with a technical issue. You know I work with computers still, right? So, yeah, that's all done now. So I'm going to meet Dair."

Tyee looked up and fixed Robin with a stern gaze. "Good. He seems like a lovely young man."

Oh, how true that was.

Robin bid him farewell, then sighed as he walked back out into the brilliant sunshine.

A glance told him that Dair's truck was still there. Seeing as there wasn't either a Dair or a Smudge inside, Robin assumed he was still busy doing whatever it was he was doing. Rather than call him and let him know he was done at Sunny's, Robin turned right and headed toward the lake.

He had to put his sunglasses on to look at it. It was always so dazzling in summer, a thousand little ripples dancing and playing with the golden light streaming down from up above. He looked along the shoreline to the country club where they would be having their big Saturday night bash. It was a damn sight nicer than the school gym where they'd had prom. Robin was mesmerized by a quaint rowboat bobbing where it was tied up on the short dock.

But after a while, his thoughts couldn't simply be preoccupied watching the boat do its dance.

The meeting with Mac hadn't quite gone as expected, but it had thrown Robin's dilemma into sharp relief.

He could pretend all he wanted. But after this week, he was still going to be that isolated, awkward kid from small-town Washington. He could go back to Seattle and get swallowed up by the crowd, but that wouldn't hide the truth.

He was all alone.

13

DAIR

DAIR WAS SURPRISED THAT BY THE TIME HE AND EMERY WERE done shopping, he still hadn't had a call from Robin. "Do you think he's okay?" he asked Emery as they walked with Smudge up to where his Ford Ranger was parked. They'd passed Sunny Side Up and knew he wasn't inside.

Emery frowned and looked over the top of his sunglasses. "Call him."

It rang through to voicemail. But as Dair loaded his shopping bags into the back of the truck, his phone pinged with a text message.

I felt like a walk. Everything's fine. I'll see you back at my parents' place.

Dair tapped the phone screen with his fingernail once he'd locked it. "Do you mind if I take off?"

Emery shook his head, crouching down to pet Smudge goodbye. "Not at all. You go, baby. He might be a little rattled after seeing Mac."

Or he might be remembering why they used to date in the first place. The thought made Dair glum. Didn't Robin get he was worth so much more than a smooth-talker with a temper?

The sooner he saw him, the sooner Dair could assess the situation. It was a fair walk back to the Coal place, but Dair had been in the barbers, then shopping for a while. If Robin's meeting with Mac had been quick, he might already be back there.

"Thank you so much for your advice." Dair shook his head and patted one of the many bags sitting in the truck bed. "I wouldn't have even tried half this stuff on."

Emery jumped up from where he'd been fussing Smudge and fanned himself. "Oh, she knows a thing or two, sweetheart. You call on Auntie Em any time, sugar."

With a wink, he spun on his heels, wiggled his tushy, then strutted away down the boardwalk, watching his reflection in the store windows he passed. Dair chuckled softly, but it wasn't long before he remembered his worry for Robin again.

He texted back saying he was driving back to the house now, then helped Smudge onto the passenger seat. Before he started the engine, he decided to make a quick phone call. If it rang out, so be it. But Dair didn't have a mom to ring for advice.

Peyton was the closest thing he had to family.

"What up!" she cried upon answering. It sounded like she was eating potato chips. Dair smiled in relief, rubbing the side of the steering wheel, feeling the warmth from the sun that had been beating down on the leather.

"Hey, hon. How are you?"

There was a slight pause and the sound of a chip bag being crinkled closed. "I'm fine. How are *you?* What's that tone for?"

"Nothing," Dair said hurriedly. "Except, well, I guess I just wanted to bounce something off you and check I did the right thing."

"Okay?"

Dair bit his lip. "Robin met Mac for coffee. Mac said it was for a work thing, but I think he was trying to win Robin over again."

It sounded awful out loud. Dair was specifically here to save Robin from himself when it came to Mac, and he had just walked off and left him to it, too concerned about sorting himself out. He was a bad friend.

But what would the alternative have been? Telling Robin he *couldn't* go see Mac? That was a dick move, Dair was completely certain. No, he'd done the best he could. At least he hoped that was what Peyton would say.

He still half expected her to shout at him, but instead she sighed sympathetically. "Oh dear. Yeah, from what I've heard, he's a charming motherfucker. That doesn't surprise me at all. Right, where's Robin now?"

"Back at his folks' place, or will be shortly. I was just going to go find him."

"Great," said Peyton. Dair could imagine her nodding to herself. "You go do that. He might need you to pick up the pieces. Jay always said that Mac has a way of getting under his skin and tearing him down. If you feel up to giving him a hug, I'd suggest a big one."

A hug Dair could most definitely do. He thought of himself as an excellent hugger. "Roger that. Thank you." Once he'd checked his other fur babies were doing fine and Peyton wasn't too bored on her own, he closed the call, promising to see her on Saturday. Then he started the engine and began the now familiar drive back to Robin's house.

With his bags in one hand and Smudge's leash in the other, he shouldered his way through the front door.

"Gee whiz!" Robin's mom, Deb, rushed down the hall to take Smudge off his hands. "You've been busy, haven't you? My, you do look handsome, though. Robin's already here. He's in his room." She gave Dair a searching look, probably wondering why they had come home separately, but Dair honestly didn't have any good answers for her right now.

"I'll go check he's okay," he assured her. "He had coffee with an old friend, so I went shopping."

Deb hummed and flicked an eyebrow above her glasses, suggesting she knew exactly who he'd met up with. Dair quashed his guilt as he'd already established he'd done the best he could. Now it was his job to make sure everything was okay. Perhaps gently suggest to Robin that he didn't need a shithead like that in his life.

Ever.

His large frame made it a little awkward to navigate stairs at the best of times, but with several boxy bags of varying sizes knocking against his knees it was even worse than usual. But somehow he made it up to the second floor and along the hall without sending anything crashing to the ground.

He paused outside the closed door, but he couldn't hear any noise beyond it. So he shifted all the bags to his left hand, then knocked with his right. "Robin? May I come in?"

There was a second's pause. "Yeah, sure." Robin's tone was cheerful enough, but Dair wondered if it was forced. He steeled himself and turned the handle.

Robin was curled up on the bed, hugging his stuffed koala when Dair entered. His gaze had been focused listlessly on the wall, but he glanced up as Dair closed the door.

Then he froze.

"Holy *fuck*," he rasped.

The koala rolled away from him as he sat up, his mouth hanging open as he gaped at Dair. Heat rose into Dair's cheeks. He wasn't used to people looking at him unless they were checking out how much he was bench-pressing.

But for Robin, he placed the bags on the floor and did a single turn for him to admire his new haircut and shave. He'd almost gotten changed into some of the new clothes in one of the stores, but he'd decided he wanted to shower before that.

"Do you like it?" he asked.

"You look fucking *gorgeous.*" Robin stared for another few seconds. Then he shook his head and closed his mouth with an audible click of his teeth. "Really nice. I love it."

Dair ran his hand over the longer hair at the top and the closer cut around the back and sides. It felt nice to the touch. "I realized maybe I should have made an effort for being your boyfriend. You're supposed to be showing me off, after all."

Robin bit his lip and pawed his hand on the bed for the koala. Hugging it again, he leaned back against his pillows, not quite lying down again, but definitely closing himself off.

Had Dair said something wrong?

He perched on the office chair and clasped his hands together, allowing them to dangle between his knees. "Is everything okay?"

Robin gave him a pinched smile that didn't meet his eyes. "Yeah, fine."

Dair raised his eyebrows. "Yeah? Things go okay with Mac?"

Robin scoffed and stroked the koala's fur. "Mac was Mac. He wasn't particularly interested in the computer stuff, just like everyone warned me. But he was...well, he was kind of the same as he used to be, but no worse." He shrugged again, his gaze not meeting Dair's. He was clearly rattled.

Dair's heart hurt. This time last week, he and Robin had been friends. But now their relationship had moved beyond that. They were close friends, maybe even more. There was something that ached inside Dair to see someone he cared about going through a tough time.

He thought about that hug he'd promised Peyton he'd administer. But Robin was cuddled up on his bed looking vulnerable. Dair didn't feel like he could just go over there, crawl alongside him, and throw his arms around him.

"Well, look," he said instead. "You knew he was kind of a dick. Good for you to go along and try to get some closure. Maybe you'll feel better about him when you go home after this? In the meantime, there's no harm done."

Robin hummed. Dair's skin prickled.

"There's *wasn't* any harm done, was there?"

Robin frowned at him, then his face relaxed in realization. "Oh, no! No...I mean..." He frowned and rubbed his arm before shaking his head. "No, no harm. Physically. I just feel a bit of a fool."

Dair couldn't take it. He moved to the edge of the bed and placed a hand on Robin's outstretched leg. He rubbed his ankle through his sock with his thumb. Dair wouldn't dream of doing that with one of his straight buddies. But from what he'd observed, gay guys tended to be more like women with how tactile they were. Sure enough, Robin didn't jerk away at the contact. Instead, he gave Dair a half smile.

"You're not a fool for wanting to see the best in people," Dair said softly. "Nor for wanting to believe you didn't put yourself through a bad relationship. We all do dumb stuff when we're teenagers, though. The important thing is how you live your life now." He offered Robin what he hoped was a compassionate smile. "And you deserve someone a million times better than that jackass."

Robin laughed, but to Dair's horror he then hiccuped and it turned into a sob. From the looks of it, he attempted to swallow it down as he rapidly blinked away tears, but it was clear he was trying not to cry.

"Oh, hon." Dair stood, intending to move and sit next to him after all. "Look, Peyton pretty much ordered me to give you a hug. Would that be okay?"

Robin laughed and shook his head as he reached for a

tissue to blow his nose and wipe his cheeks. "Yes, please," he mumbled, rubbing his eyes under his glasses. "If you don't mind?"

Dair chuckled and dropped his weight onto the bed. "Get over here." He opened his arms wide.

Robin pulled his glasses off and pressed himself against Dair's side, nuzzling his face against his chest. Dair rubbed his back gently. It was funny how Robin looked more vulnerable without his glasses framing his face. Not better or worse, just different. Dair liked that he was getting to see all these different sides of his friend.

"I, um, just wish someone was interested in me who wasn't a douche," Robin murmured against Dair's T-shirt. His slender fingers played the material, smoothing out little creases. It tickled ever so slightly on Dair's stomach. In a strange way, it felt really nice.

Much like the kiss they'd staged on the sidewalk, Dair realized it had been a very long time since he'd cuddled with anyone. His ex had been his only source of physical comfort for over a decade and he hadn't really appreciated that until it went away. Robin felt so wonderful in his arms. Dair was comfortable enough that he laid his cheek down against Robin's thick auburn hair, inhaling the scent of the shampoo they'd been sharing.

He was filled with a deep sense of contentment.

"There's a guy out there who's just perfect for you, Robin Coal. He'll be kind to you and respect you and see how funny and cute and sexy you are. You'll fall madly in love and get married and have puppies and babies and assemble Ikea furniture together. It'll be so romantic you'll make yourself sick with it."

He laughed and rubbed Robin's arm, expecting him to chuckle too. But Robin looked up at him with those large topaz eyes, blinking once as his gaze searched Dair's face. He frowned slightly, confusion creasing his brow.

"You think I'm sexy?"

The way he said 'sexy' made Dair wonder if anyone had ever used that word to compliment him before. Unfortunately, having met Mac, Dair figured that could very well be true. But for Dair, this was a simple fact.

"Well, yeah, hon. The way you moved on that dance floor on Tuesday night..." He whistled. "Didn't you see all those guys looking at you? You were mesmerizing."

Robin's frown deepened. "No," he said, as if Dair was winding him up.

Dair laughed again in disbelief. "Oh, come on. Now you're just fishing! The way you move those hips..." He shook his head. "Yes, Robin, you're a sexy little minx, and I bet all those guys were thinking about getting you into bed. So no more of this crap, okay? Whoever that perfect guy is for you out there, he's going to tell you you're sexy every day."

He grinned and winked. But Robin was still staring at him incredulously. Worry crept into Dair that he'd said something wrong again. He tried to ask what was wrong, but his voice seemed to die in his throat. Robin was still staring at him, and Dair's heartbeat was speeding up.

He was suddenly very aware of the warm, bare skin of their arms touching. Of Robin's sweet breath ghosting against his mouth. Of the way Robin's lower lip trembled ever so slightly. Dair could feel Robin's heart beat through his chest and realized it was fast like his own.

What was happening?

Dair pursed his lips. All he knew was he and Robin were still looking into each other's eyes, and Robin's smaller body slotted so perfectly against Dair's larger frame. Even despite his confusion at the moment they appeared to be locked in, he still felt that contentment from before. Holding Robin just felt *right.*

And then Robin leaned closer, just a fraction…

"Hey! Are you guys ready to go to the-?"

As Jay burst through Robin's door, Robin launched himself away from Dair like he'd been electrocuted. Dair was too stunned to move. What had just happened? They were supposed to be boyfriends. They weren't doing anything that would get them in trouble. Besides, it had felt so nice, and then the moment had been ripped away.

He couldn't help but feel a little hurt.

Jay frowned, looking between them. Robin was fiercely hugging his stuffed koala again, perched on the edge of the bed. "Um," said Jay uncertainly. "I was just checking you guys were okay to head to the school in about an hour for the basketball game? There's going to be a cocktail reception beforehand."

Dair glanced at Robin, but for some unfathomable reason, he seemed to be frozen stiff. "Sure," Dair replied cheerfully. "Looking forward to it. It's been years since I saw a live game."

Jay gave him a thumbs-up, then shot a questioning glance at Robin. But Robin didn't look at him, so Jay scowled at Dair. Dair tried to silently convey that he had no clue what had spooked Robin so badly when they'd been having what Dair had thought was a milestone moment in their relationship.

"We'll be down in a bit," Dair promised.

Really, he was trying to encourage Jay to leave so he could ask Robin what the hell was going on. Luckily, Jay got that hint and left them to it, telling them not to be long.

"Robin-"

"I, uh, I need a shower." Robin snatched up his glasses, shoving them back on his face. "I'll just, uh, why don't you go to the kitchen and I'll meet you down there? I think Mom's making pregame snacks. Also, she needs instructions for Smudge, as he can't come with us."

"Robin," Dair said more sternly, causing him to stop in his tracks before he got to the door. He paused with his hand reaching for the handle. "Did I do something wrong?"

Robin's shoulders slumped and the tension on his face softened. "No, Dair," he said quietly. "You've been amazing. I just need a minute to myself, if that's okay?"

Dair nodded. "Of course it is, hon."

Robin dashed out into the corridor, presumably heading for the bathroom.

Dair sat on the bed for a while, listening to the sound of the running water and wondering what on earth was going on.

14

ROBIN

Idiot.

Idiot, idiot, *idiot.*

What the hell had Robin been thinking? Clearly, he hadn't been thinking at all.

A scalding hot shower had helped him get out of his damn head a little. But then Dair had also showered and put on a brand-new pair of jeans that clung sinfully to his ass as well as a crisp white shirt that made his tanned skin glow. Robin had never seen him clean-shaven – or even with a haircut – so to see him looking positively dapper made Robin's heart all but stop.

Now here he was in the back of Jay's car, squished between Emery and Dair, holding hands with Dair to keep up their ruse. Ava was in the front seat. She'd offered it to Dair, but he'd replied that he wanted to sit next to Robin.

It was like he was purposefully torturing him.

Did he get he was killing Robin with all this affection? Of course not. He had no idea that Robin's crush was becoming dangerously worse, pushing at the lid of the box he'd kept in his chest for the past couple of months.

This wasn't some silly infatuation. Those were built on ideas of people, not actual relationships.

What he was currently experiencing were real, gut-wrenching feelings. Robin ached physically for Dair when he wasn't around. The sound of his voice sent shivers down his spine, no matter how mundane the topic of conversation was. And his touch? Jesus fucking Christ, Robin couldn't take it anymore.

He'd *never* been held by a man like that in his life. Not by any of his lovers and certainly not by Mac. And all that talk about how sexy he was? Robin felt like he was going to break apart, just replaying it to himself in the back of the car.

He felt Dair's thumb rubbing the back of his hand, so he looked over. It was only because Robin and Emery were so small that the three of them had fit into the back of Jay's Ford Fiesta. Dair was taking up half the room himself and his body was pressed right up against Robin's. When Robin met his gaze, Dair raised his eyebrows, asking that same silent question he'd asked several times since Robin had sprung away from him on the bed.

'What's wrong?'

Robin smiled and patted his thigh with his free hand. *'I'm fine.'*

If he said it enough times, he might very well start to believe it.

"What time does the tennis match start?" Emery asked, not lifting his gaze from his phone.

Jay huffed from the front seat. "It's a *basketball game* between the current team and as many of the team from our class as we could convince to play."

"Oh, honey. I heard 'men in shorts' and I was there. I have no interest in what kind of ball it is." He smirked to himself. "You know, not *those* kinds of balls, anyway."

Ava snorted while Jay huffed. He wasn't drinking tonight,

hence him playing chauffeur for the evening. Even though he'd been taking it easy with partying the other nights, Robin suspected that the stress of organizing this reunion was getting to him on top of his teaching job.

"This whole week has been amazing, Jay." Robin leaned forward and squeezed his twin's shoulder. "I'm proud of you."

Jay hummed, but he at least gave Robin half a smile in the rearview mirror.

Robin wasn't sure what his thoughts were on what happened earlier. Dair didn't know that Robin has confessed to their relationship being fake, so when Jay had walked in on them canoodling Dair didn't understand why Robin would freak out.

That, and Robin had just been about to kiss him.

What the actual fuck? Robin knew Dair was straight. Kissing him would be so way over the line of what was okay. It would be an abuse of his friendship and his trust. Robin would never want to take advantage of anyone like that, let alone Dair.

He should count himself beyond lucky to have such a mature, open-minded, and caring friend. Robin had felt so safe in his arms after the fallout of meeting Mac. He was a moron for thinking that could have worked out. But Dair hadn't so much as *hinted* at an 'I told you so.' In fact, he'd gone the other way and showered Robin with compliments.

If Dair was gay, Robin might even be starting to think he was interested in him at this point. But he wasn't. So he should just take all the lovely things Dair was saying and doing, put them in a box to treasure later, and lighten the fuck up. This was his vacation, after all, and he was determined not to spend it moping or heartbroken.

By the time Jay parked in the school's lot, Robin was

genuinely feeling like he had more of a spring in his step. He smiled at Dair, a proper one this time, and was happy to see relief in Dair's expression. Robin didn't want him worrying unnecessarily.

"So," he said to the group at large as they exited the car. "Basketball's the one with the sticks with the nets on the end, right?"

Emery hooted with laughter while Jay and Ava huffed. Dair chuckled at his silly joke, though, warming Robin's heart. There we go. Back to normal.

"That's lacrosse. Do you really need me to explain the rules of basketball?" Jay threw him an impatient look. Robin shook his head.

"Nah. I'm going to be joining Emery in seeing if Zack Foster is still as hot as he used to be."

"Oh em gee," Emery wailed. He slapped his hands to his cheeks. "How could I forget him?"

"Isn't he married now?" Ava asked as they walked toward the school gymnasium.

"Hush, you," Emery chided. "Let me have some fun."

Robin looked up at the Pine Cove High sign as they approached. Wow. It had been a very long time since he'd walked through these doors. He'd come to every single one of Mac's basketball games, always the doting boyfriend. Funny, Mac hadn't mentioned playing tonight.

Robin soon forgot his Mac-related thoughts as he found himself in the gym foyer. Jay's reunion team had done a great job decorating it with shiny streamers and paper garlands. There was even a balloon arch in the school colors leading into the hall. Around the foyer were several large cardboard displays propped up on art easels. Each featured a former student from their class who had been a sports star, detailing what they'd done after graduating. Robin and Dair grabbed themselves a beer each, then Robin took him on a tour of the posters, talking to Dair about his memories of each student.

It all felt so normal. After his meltdown earlier, Robin realized he was having a perfectly lovely time holding hands and walking down memory lane with Dair. He even introduced him to several former classmates as his boyfriend without stuttering or blushing.

Good. This was how it was supposed to be. Just two friends hanging out who happened to be holding hands just in case Mac reared his ugly head again.

For all Robin enjoyed winding his siblings up, he actually did appreciate basketball a fair bit. It was one of their family's favorite sports, illustrated by the fact their group met up with Swift, Kestrel, and their parents to all go find seats together. It felt like half the town had turned out for this friendly game. He and Dair waved to Taylan the barber, who looked to be with his elderly father. Sunny and Tyee were being fussed over by several members across generations of their large family. Robin only remembered about half their names, there were so many of them.

Dair insisted on getting them popcorn to watch the game. Robin worried that not living at home he hadn't been eating enough the past couple of days to keep up with his regular workouts. The man was a disposal unit for carbs. So Robin insisted he get a hot dog for himself as well from the concessions stand that had been set up especially for the anniversary game. Emery and the rest of Robin's family went on ahead to get seats together before they were all gone.

Dair insisted on ordering. "Could we get a hotdog, a large popcorn, a pack of regular M&Ms, and could we possibly get another empty popcorn bag?"

The young woman serving them grinned. "Sure," she said, already getting their order.

Robin nudged Dair's arm. "What are you up to?"

Dair gave him that wink that made Robin weak at the knees. "You'll see."

After they'd paid, they stepped aside and Dair placed his hotdog on a table along with their fresh beers. Then he tipped half the popcorn into the empty bag. Robin felt a little pang. He'd quite been looking forward to sharing, but splitting it was probably more practical. Except, then Dair opened the M&Ms and poured half the bag into his share of the popcorn, screwed up the top, then shook it all up together.

"You wanna try my secret popcorn recipe?" He held the bag out with a grin.

"Chocolate *and* popcorn?" Robin chuckled. "Okay, sure, why not." He grabbed a small handful, making sure he had a mix of both, and tipped some into his mouth. For a second he just chewed, then he moaned. "Oh my god," he mumbled, popping the rest of his handful into his mouth. "The chocolate's melting! But it's still inside the shell! And the sweetness with the salt and butter – gah!"

He grabbed the rest of the M&Ms from Dair while he laughed at Robin. Robin didn't care. He just grinned as he tipped them into his own popcorn while it was still hot and shook it up vigorously.

"Perfect." Dair sounded proud. Then he surprised Robin by taking his popcorn back and tipping the two bags back together. They hopped back and laughed as a couple of kernels fell to the ground, but then they had one bag again.

To share.

They got rid of their trash and picked up their drinks and Dair's hotdog. Robin beamed as they walked arm in arm into the hall. It was pretty packed by the time they made their way inside. But Robin's mom obviously spotted them first because she stood up from where the family had their seats and waved her arms over her head. "Honey! We're here!" she bellowed.

Robin tried not to die of embarrassment. Wasn't this sort of thing supposed to end after high school? Dair threw back his head and laughed, then tugged Robin up the steps to their row.

It had worked out that there were three seats left on the end of their line. Dair went in first, followed by Robin so he was closest to the aisle on the assumption that if someone sat down who was by themselves, Robin was more likely to know them.

He should have really seen it coming.

They'd been seated just long enough for Dair to wolf down his hotdog when someone dropped into the empty seat by Robin.

"Oh hey! That was lucky!"

Robin's blood ran cold as he turned to look at Mac. "Oh, hi," he said as pleasantly as he could with a smile. Just what he needed to drag his mood back down.

But only if he let it. Suddenly his smile became bigger and more genuine. He didn't have anything to fear from Mac. He was here with his true friends and family. Yeah, Mac might be irritating, but they'd soon have the game to distract them.

"Hey, Dair. Jay." Mac waved down the aisle. Jay nodded, but Dair apparently wanted to show how many fucks he didn't give either. He stuck out his hand for Mac to shake.

"Good to see you again, man," he said warmly. They pumped hands once with such force Robin was concerned for Dair's tendons. But then they let go and Robin was amazed neither of them wiped their palm on their jeans.

"You, too." Mac nodded and looked around. "I'm glad I found you. I kind of assumed I'd be asked to play. But they must have remembered about my bum knee. It'll be weird to watch a game in here and not take part."

Jay ignored him, leaning in to say something to Swift. Robin guessed Mac hadn't been forgotten about at all.

"Hopefully it'll be fun for you," Robin said, not knowing what else to say.

Dair put his arm around Robin's waist and held their special M&M popcorn between them to share. Robin did his best not to freeze, but it took him by surprise all the same. Dair leaned in closer, grazing his lips over Robin's ear.

"Don't give that asshole the time of day," he murmured over the cheer from the crowd. "He just wants your attention."

The current cheerleading squad ran onto the court, pom poms waving as they greeted former members from Robin's class. Dair's words were almost lost in the noise, but he leaned in even closer so Robin could still hear.

"I've got you."

Then he kissed Robin's cheek.

Robin stared ahead as a shiver rippled through his body. He wasn't sure if Dair felt it, but Robin hurriedly took the popcorn from him for something to do. Now they both had a hand free to eat it with.

Robin must have devoured half the bag by the time the cheer routine was done and the principal had welcomed their class back for the game and the big reunion on Saturday. Robin didn't hear a word of it.

His whole world was reduced down to feeling Dair's muscular arm holding him safe once again. To the glances Robin snuck of his neatly sculpted profile from the haircut he'd gotten to please Robin. To the spicy smell of his cologne and a masculine musk that was purely Dair.

To the way their fingers brushed as they both reached for the popcorn at the same time.

Each touch made electricity shoot over Robin's skin. He knew logically that Dair was simply doing all of this for Mac's benefit. But yet again, Robin wondered if he was also secretly trying to kill him. He was losing his mind being this close to Dair and yet not actually being able to have him.

No wonder he'd almost cracked and tried to kiss him earlier.

Mac tried to get his attention continuously throughout the first half of the game, but Robin wasn't able to answer him with much more than grunts. It was like everything except Dair was in a blurry, underwater haze.

At halftime, Mac disappeared, probably frustrated with his lack of attention. But Robin hardly noticed. Because despite the lack of Robin's ex to impress, Dair still spent the second half of the game with his arm around Robin.

Again, if Dair was gay, Robin would suspect he was possibly interested in him by now. But he wasn't gay. There was no way after he'd spent over a decade with Malory. Things might not have worked out, but Dair had been happy for most of that time and they'd definitely had plenty of sex from what he'd said. If Dair was into men, not women, he would have worked it out by now.

Unless…unless he was into men *and* women?

Robin felt like time stopped.

Despite it being their cover story that Dair had suddenly realized he was bi, Robin had never stopped to consider that he *might actually be bi.* He tried to glance at Dair without it being obvious, but his heart was going like a jackhammer.

That was insane, though, surely? Even if Dair was more queer than they'd both previously assumed, he wouldn't be interested in someone like Robin. He was a computer nerd. A geek. Dair was a badass ex-Marine who spent his days covered in grease in the bellies of cars and trucks. They were nothing alike, shared nothing in common. Just because

Robin was infatuated with Dair in no way meant Dair would be interested in him for anything more than friendship.

So why was his arm still around Robin's waist?

The end of this damn basketball game couldn't come quickly enough. Robin needed answers.

If he was brave enough to ask the questions.

15

DAIR

THANKFULLY, WHATEVER HAD BEEN TROUBLING ROBIN SEEMED to have vanished by the time they got to the high school. Although Dair caught him looking preoccupied a couple of times, he was generally all smiles and laughs for the night.

For some reason, the fact that he approved of Dair's childhood popcorn recipe made Dair ridiculously happy. But Dair's main takeaway from the whole evening was how fucking proud he was of Robin for brushing Mac's attempts to get his attention off like a pro. He was polite, but he wasn't looking for Mac's approval anymore.

Putting his arm around Robin had been for show, especially when Mac was beside them at the start. But it felt natural to keep it there. Just for this week, Dair hoped it was okay to take advantage of a little bit of the real human contact he'd been lacking since Malory. So long as Robin was enjoying it too. It was nice to be hugged, wasn't it?

After the game was over, Dair had a bounce in his step as he joined the buzzing crowd out of the hall. He kept hold of Robin's hand so they wouldn't be separated as the throng emptied out through the exits into the night. Ava and Emery were talking about going for a Chinese, then hitting up The Aquarium again, but Dair and Robin both seemed to agree they felt like heading straight home. It had been a pretty long day.

"I need to pop to the bathroom," Robin said apologetically with a laugh. "Those beers went right through me! I'll meet you back by the car?"

"Sure." Dair gave his hand a double squeeze, then let him go so he and Jay could continue out to the parking lot.

Dair breathed in the cooler night air gratefully, strolling toward Jay's Fiesta. Emery and Ava had already scampered off into town, and Jay was speaking to someone else from the reunion committee. So for a minute, Dair leaned his back against the car and looked up at the stars. You could see so many more out here in the countryside. It was beautiful, and something about the vastness of the sky was oddly comforting.

"Hey, Dair." He looked down to see Jay approaching. He had a slightly pensive look on his face.

"Hey, dude. What's up?"

Jay slipped his hands into his jeans pockets as he stopped beside Dair and nibbled on his lower lip. "All right, I'm just going to say it because I like you, but I don't want my brother getting hurt."

Coldness rushed through Dair's body and he stood up straighter. "Why would Robin get hurt?" That was the last thing Dair would let happen if he could help it. Was this about him going to meet Mac for coffee?

Jay sighed. "Look, he told me you guys are just doing this as a show, a charade, whatever, to keep Mac away. That it's not real."

The coldness that had swept through Dair a second ago returned ten times worse. "Jay, I swear there's nothing untoward going on-"

161

Jay held his hands up to interrupt. "It's cool. I mean, I don't really get it. The faking part. Why don't you just date for real? But it's none of my business. I guess I just feel like I have to tell you not to mess with Rob's heart. He deserves better."

"You and me both agree on that," Dair said firmly. "One hundred percent. I promise, I care about Robin a lot. But that's just not the way it is. I'm simply here as his friend to make sure Mac doesn't try anything." He shrugged and felt his lips tug in a half smile. "I also think Robin kind of wanted to come home and show everyone that he'd made something of his life. A boyfriend helps with that. Reunions are weird."

Jay nodded. "That they are." He waved, and Dair looked to see Robin jogging across the parking lot, weaving in between the people still milling around after the game. "Like I said, I like you. But maybe you should really think about what's going on between you guys?"

Robin returned before Dair could reply, so he simply gave Jay a nod of understanding. Dair wanted him and Robin to be okay just as much as his twin did.

As they drove back to the Coal house in the much less crowded car, Dair found himself chewing over one thing in particular Jay had said. *Why don't you just date for real?* If he knew about the ruse, then he presumably knew Dair was straight? Why would he say something like that? To make things worse, Robin seemed preoccupied again, bouncing his knee for most of the ride back.

When they arrived, Jay didn't get out of the car when he and Robin did. "I think I'm going to stay at mine tonight," he said out the window as they stood next to the car. "Got lots of papers to grade. I think Mom, Dad, and Kestrel have gone out to dinner. But you guys have keys, right?"

Dair looked at the mostly dark house. That meant they were going to be on their own for a few hours, just the two of them. For some reason, that made him feel...not anxious, exactly. But there was definitely a heightened sense of anticipation that tugged at his chest.

Robin pulled his set of keys from his pocket. "Yeah, we're good," he confirmed. "Are you sure you don't want to stay, though? I was thinking of making hot chocolate."

Jay glanced at Dair. It felt like he purposefully caught his eye before looking back at his twin.

Ah. Did he want the two of them to make sure they were crystal clear about their fake relationship? Dair was happy to do that if it put Robin's mind at ease.

"Nah," Jay said. "I'll feel better getting this work done before the weekend. I'll catch you at the fair tomorrow, yeah?"

Robin beamed at him. "Definitely. I'm going to beat your ass at the shooting gallery."

"You wish!" Jay waved them goodbye, threw his car into reverse, then maneuvered out of the driveway.

Leaving Robin and Dair all alone.

Right, fine, no biggie. He smiled at Robin as they walked up the porch.

"Are you hungry or anything?" Robin asked as he unlocked the door and flicked on the hallway light.

Before Dair could answer, a very sleepy Smudge gave a garbled woof at their entrance and rolled backward out of his basket. Dair closed the door behind them while Smudge fumbled down the hall to come say hello.

"I'm not really hungry," Dair replied to Robin's question as he scratched behind Smudge's ears. "But that hot chocolate sounded good."

Robin grinned. "Yes, we need some sugar to go with all that sugar we already had."

"Are you calling me fat?" Dair asked, pretending to be

163

hurt. He flexed his bicep under his shirt and poked it. "Yeah, you're right. I am looking a little chubby."

Robin laughed and lightly slapped his arm before heading into the kitchen. Dair followed with Smudge trotting along by his feet. The little pup had clearly been in the middle of a REM cycle because even though his tail was wagging and he kept running between Dair and Robin, he kept tripping over his own paws. Within a couple of minutes, he'd snuggled back down in his basket.

Dair watched on as Robin poured milk and cream into a pan with chunks of chocolate and stirred it all together. Dair's mouth watered despite the M&Ms they'd had before. Robin's recipe looked divine.

Robin had put the sound system on low as soon as he'd walked into the kitchen and was quietly singing along to a nineties song Dair didn't know. But he didn't care. Watching Robin enjoy himself was enough for him.

After a few minutes, Robin fetched a couple of mugs to pour the cocoa into, then topped it off with a swirl of whipped cream and a sprinkling of mini marshmallows. He turned to face Dair with the drinks…

…then paused. He looked between Dair and the mugs in his hands. "Uhh. Do you want to go watch some TV?"

Dair blinked, unsure what had made Robin hesitate. "Sure," he said amiably. After a fairly nonstop few days, just watching something mindless sounded kind of nice.

They dropped onto one of the couches side by side. Robin used his phone to somehow make the TV work. Dair didn't always follow all the ways Robin could do everyday stuff at the touch of his screen, but it was certainly impressive.

They found a documentary on Amelia Earhart that looked kind of interesting, so Robin left the channel on that and sat back to sip his hot chocolate. Dair shifted his weight so they were leaning against one another. Robin stiffened up for a second but then relaxed.

Dair was only half paying attention to the TV screen. His mind was busy hashing over the events of today. It had been so up and down, but it felt like things were back to being good again. Great even. He loved just lounging around with Robin, getting a slice of that domestic life he missed.

When he finished his hot chocolate (which had been delicious) he placed the mug down on a coaster. Then he wrapped his arm around Robin's chest and leaned his cheek against his hair like they'd done on the bed earlier.

Robin stiffened again.

Dair frowned. Had he done something wrong?

He looked down as Robin pulled away and discarded his own finished drink. He sat up, putting some distance between them, biting his lip the exact same way Jay had done earlier. "I, um, think I might go to bed," he said softly.

Dair felt his stomach drop. Fuck. "Is everything okay?"

"Oh, yeah, fine." Robin pulled at his fingers, glancing at the TV. "I'm just tired. Long day."

He rose, but Dair's gut told him something was definitely Wrong with a capital W. So he reached out and caught Robin's hand with his own. Robin stopped, looking down at Dair from where he was standing. Their knees were practically touching.

"Did I do something wrong?" Dair asked for the second time that day. Robin shook his head and went to open his mouth, but Dair squeezed his hand twice to get him to listen. "Please," he whispered. "I'm worried things might have got a bit blurred...or complicated? If I've done anything to upset you or make you uncomfortable, I want to know. If I overstepped the line with Mac, I'm really sorry, but-"

"No, no." Robin sounded pained as he screwed his eyes

shut. "Dair, I promise. You haven't done anything wrong. It's me. I – I can't explain. I just need some space."

"From what? Me?" Dair wasn't sure how to interpret that other than him having fucked up in some way.

Robin screwed his eyes even tighter and clenched his jaw. Dair was horrified when a single tear escaped from under his lashes and rolled down his cheek.

Immediately, Dair was on his feet. He kept hold of Robin's hand with one of his, then brushed the tear away with his other thumb. Then he cradled Robin's shoulder.

"Talk to me, hon," he said in little more than a whisper. The documentary rumbled quietly on in the background, but as far as Dair was concerned, it was just the two of them alone in the world. "I hate seeing you sad."

"I'm just…" Robin winced, like he was debating what to say. "I'm just a bit confused. There's a lot going on. I'll feel better after some sleep."

Dair rubbed his arm, wanting to hug him close but also wanting to still see his face. "Confused about what?"

Robin took a moment to respond. When he did, his voice was barely audible. "About us. This."

As soon as the words left his mouth, he looked horrified. He shook his head and broke away, heading toward the door. But Dair reached for his hand, snagging a couple of fingers. It wasn't any kind of hold, but Robin stopped all the same. Dair could feel himself frowning in confusion.

"Please. Don't go. Talk to me. What's confusing about us?" He also shook his head. "I thought we were becoming closer friends? Is that bad?"

Robin's fingers were still hooked on to Dair's by mere millimeters. He inhaled shakily. "We are. That's the confusing part." He bit his lip. "If I were crazy, I…I might think you were into me."

"Into-?" Dair stopped.

Robin thought Dair was attracted to him?

That was...

It was as if his brain just ground to a halt.

He loved Robin's company. Being physically intimate with him felt totally natural. Wonderful, even. He had gotten jealous when Mac showed up.

If Robin were a woman, would Dair have admitted he had a crush on him by now?

Did it matter that Robin was a man? What had Emery said about Dair being pansexual? What had Dair's *exact* words to him been about that?

I just like Robin for Robin.

Holy shit. Had he accidentally done *exactly* what he'd made up for their imaginary getting together? Had he actually not realized they were dating until they were *already dating*?

Robin shook his head, still not looking at Dair. "Forget I said anything. It's stupid. I don't know how to be normal with people." He moved toward the door, pulling his fingers free from Dair.

Dair seized them again, spinning Robin around in a dance-like move and cupped his face with his palm. They stood chest to chest. Robin looked up at him through his glasses with enormous shining topaz eyes.

"You're not stupid," Dair said, his voice hoarse. He immediately relaxed his grip on Robin's fingers, then ran his hand up his arm so it was just resting on his elbow. "Please don't go."

Robin blinked, his chest rising and falling rapidly. "Why should I stay?" Slowly, he raised his hand and placed it gently on Dair's chest. "What are you saying?"

"I don't know," Dair rasped. His mind was still reeling. "I – this is all new. But I don't want you to go. I want you to stay with me. I – I want to hold you. Is that okay?"

Robin stared at him for a couple of seconds, then nodded.

Dair moved his hand from Robin's arm to the small of his back. Robin naturally moved forward, so their stomachs were touching. Robin was looking up at him intensely.

"I don't know what to do next," Dair whispered.

Robin glanced down at his mouth, then back up to his eyes. "What do you want?"

Dair took in a long breath. What did he want?

To keep this simple. Not overthink it.

So what *exactly* did he want?

"More," he said.

Robin's eyes widened fractionally. Then he dropped his gaze back to Dair's lips, his long lashes sweeping against his cheeks. Rising on his tiptoes, he moved closer, giving Dair the signal to lean down.

Their mouths crashed together, and Dair's whole world changed in an instant.

16

ROBIN

FOR A MOMENT, IT WAS NOTHING BUT BLISS. THEN THE reality of what he was doing hit Robin, and he sprung back, looking at Dair in horror.

"I'm sorry," Dair blurted, instantly looking concerned.

Robin shook his head. "Don't mess me around. Please. I – I really like you, Dair. But there's no one here to pretend for. It's just us."

Dair licked his lips. "So…I think I might be pan after all."

"Pan?" All Robin could think of was a cooking utensil.

"Pansexual." Dair looked anxious, his gaze flickering over Robin's face. "Like bi. Emery explained it to me. I think – I think I really like you too, Robin."

Robin tried not to get his hopes up. But that was hard when everything he'd been trying to cram in his damn crush box exploded against the lid, desperate to escape.

"In what way?" Robin wanted to be crystal clear about this.

Dair frowned as he considered. "In a way like…I can't stop thinking about how I want to run my hands over every inch of your body. Is that bad?"

Robin launched himself into Dair's arms.

He'd never done *anything* like that before. But he knew Dair would catch him as he wrapped his legs around his tree trunk-like waist. As soon as his hands grabbed under Robin's ass, Robin's lips crashed back against Dair's, his tongue slipping out as the kiss became heated immediately. Dair's abs were pressed against Robin's rapidly hardening cock.

"It depends." Robin gasped for air as Dair squeezed his back and ass, kissing down his throat. "Are my clothes on or off while you've got your hands on me?"

Dair's usually warm brown eyes were scorching as he turned his gaze back to Robin's. "Off," he growled.

"Take me to bed," Robin pleaded.

His hands were in Dair's beautiful new hair as he ravaged his mouth again. He was so turned on by how easily Dair carried him from the living room, like he weighed nothing. They got into a little trouble when they reached the stairs. As Dair took the first step up, Robin's shoulder bounced against the wall. But he giggled into Dair's mouth, making him smile back.

"Careful," he mumbled against his lips.

Dair brushed their noses together in an Eskimo kiss. "Always."

Dair's mouth tasted of chocolate, his neck of salt and musk, and his cheeks had a lavender tang from his shave earlier. Robin's hands didn't stop roaming across his sculpted shoulders and back until they reached his bedroom. Dair kicked the door closed behind them, then fixed Robin with a positively sinful look.

"I don't know what I'm doing."

Robin was so surprised he snorted. "Yes, you do." He grinned and caught Dair's lip between his teeth, tugging on it just for a second. "We're getting into bed."

Was this truly happening? Robin questioned in the moment

it took Dair to reach down with one hand and rip the covers back. He sent Robin's koala tumbling off the bed and out of sight. It was probably for the best. The little guy was too innocent to witness what was about to happen.

Robin could hardly believe it himself as Dair set him on the carpet and ran his large hands along the hem of Robin's Henley. His fingertips just skimmed where the top met his jeans and belt, touching sensitive skin.

Robin placed his hands lightly over Dair's, encouraging him to pause. This was his first time with a man, and that was a big deal. "We don't have to go too fast," he assured him, even though his heart broke at the idea of stopping now. Who knew if he'd get this chance again? He had no idea if Dair really was bi and attracted to him or if this was a moment of madness. If it *was* a moment of madness, Robin was not going to take advantage of him.

He was going to double-check it was both what they really wanted. Robin had hooked up with a couple of so-called straight guys over the years, and they could get really nasty post orgasm. Not that he thought that was what Dair would do, but he wanted to make sure.

Dair blinked in confusion. "Um, what if I want to go fast? Do *you* want to slow down?"

"Oh, no, I'm full steam ahead." Robin nodded vigorously, then proved his point by grabbing the hem of his Henley and yanking it over his head.

Unfortunately, as he did so, he shattered any kind of seductive move by whipping his glasses off his face as well, sending them flying.

"Shit!" he cried, looking hastily around for them.

Dair chuckled and stepped over by the desk. He reached down and scooped them off the carpet, offering them to Robin as he stood back in front of him. "Do you need these?"

Robin gulped. His was half-naked, half-hard, and fully turned on. But he was also a little bit scared.

What if this ruined everything between them? Well, if it was going to do that, the damage was probably already done. So he shook his head and touched his hands to Dair's hips.

"I can see you just fine. That's all I need."

Carefully, Dair folded the arms and placed Robin's glasses on the dresser. Then he cupped both sides of his face to kiss him again.

It wasn't long before desperation crept in. Robin hadn't had sex in months, and he knew for Dair it had been even longer. Robin got his hands on Dair's nice white shirt, yanking it free from the jeans, his hands skimming the rock-hard muscles underneath. Dair moaned into his mouth, the sound going straight to Robin's cock. As fast as he could, Robin's nimble fingers worked their way down Dair's buttons, freeing his chest.

As the shirt floated to the ground, Robin gasped. His hands and lips couldn't seem to decide where to settle as they fluttered against the expanse of perfectly molded flesh. A swathe of light, curly hair dusted his pecs and trailed down his stomach, reaching below his waistband.

Fuck, Robin wanted to lick all of it.

By mutual, wordless agreement, they broke apart to scramble out of their pants, leaving them just in their underwear. Then Dair dropped onto the bed, taking Robin's hand and dragging him down after him. Robin giggled as he practically landed on top of this hunk of a man. For a fleeting second, he wondered if he should be embarrassed by his slim physique. But then Dair's hands were caressing *everywhere*, and for once in his life, Robin couldn't care less that he was skinny.

For once in his life, he felt fucking *gorgeous*.

He knew that was thanks to the hungry way Dair was

looking at him. The way his hands were stroking and squeezing him. The way his kisses were impatient and hard and so goddamned hot.

Robin ground his cock against Dair's through their briefs, delighted with the way Dair gnashed his teeth and moaned. Dair's hands gripped his ass tightly, kneading the flesh like warm dough. Robin whimpered against Dair's mouth. His lips were throbbing from kissing, and he fucking loved it.

Dair wrapped his arms around Robin's back, dragging him down so his whole body was lying on top of him. Then he rolled so Robin was underneath, and Robin dropped his head down on the pillows in ecstasy. This was *exactly* where he wanted to be. Pinned under Dair's tremendous weight, feeling every inch of him against his skin.

Robin grabbed Dair's significantly shorter hair and tugged as they kissed fervently. He felt like he was on fire in the best possible way.

Recklessness overcame him. Dair made him feel strong and brave. Normally during sex, Robin was always worried about opening up too much and giving too much away. But he wanted to give Dair everything, even if it was just for one night.

"Do you like my cock?" he whispered, rolling his hips provocatively.

Dair gasped, looked down at where they were both straining hard against their underwear and rubbing against each other.

"Oh my god," he rasped. "That's so fucking hot. Can I take them off? Can I see more?"

He hooked a finger under the waistband of Robin's briefs, running it along against Robin's stomach, making the muscles spasm and contract. Robin kissed Dair's mouth again and again. "You want to see me naked?"

Dair gripped the back of his head and pushed their groins

together with delicious force. "I want to make you come, beautiful. I want to watch you unravel. Let me take care of you."

Robin had to swallow and snatch a second to compose himself. His dick was throbbing, and he could have very well orgasmed in that moment with no other stimulus. But he desperately didn't want to rush this. He wanted it to last for as long as it possibly could.

He gasped a couple of breaths. "Yes, Dair. Yes."

Dair reversed down the bed, not taking his eyes off Robin's. He slipped both his thumbs over the waistband, then slowly and carefully lifted Robin's briefs over his hard, leaking cock, making it bounce. Robin groaned as he watched Dair slowly drag the underwear over his ass, then down his legs. The way he flicked them aside like they were no longer of any relevance made Robin's stomach flip and his cock throb.

He watched ravenously as Dair stood, pushing his own underwear off in one easy motion. Robin had glimpsed the outline of his magnificent cock their first night here, but nothing compared to seeing the real thing in all its glory. It was thick, just like Robin has suspected, and just the right length. The tip was bright red and shiny with precum. Fuck, Robin wanted to get his mouth on it so badly.

But for now, he was more than happy when Dair crawled back on top of him, rubbing their now completely naked bodies together again. Their wet, hard cocks bounced and slid together. It was good, but Robin wanted it to be the best it could. So he took Dair's large hand and guided it between their bodies.

"Hold us," he said.

Their lips were almost touching, but not quite, as their panting breaths mingled together. Dair looked down as he took both their cocks and wrapped his fingers around them.

As one, they thrust into the fleshy tunnel, crying out in pleasure.

Robin was making Dair do that. His body was reducing this incredible man to a gasping, trembling, dripping mess. Fucking hell, he'd never felt so powerful.

"Fuck, yes, Dair," he hissed. "Fuck me like that. Holy shit, I'm going to come."

He still had a little way to go before he climaxed, but Dair made him want to whisper the filthiest things. Things he'd never in his life had the guts to say out loud, only in his mind while he jerked himself off to private fantasies.

"I'm yours. Play with my body. Fuck me, Dair. I want you to come all over me. Do it harder. Fucking claim me."

Dair moaned and kissed him so hard their teeth clashed and Robin's lips probably bruised. He was jerking them off at a frantic pace, grunting so loudly Robin was incredibly glad they had the house to themselves.

"Robin," he whispered. "Oh my god, you feel amazing. So perfect. I think – I'm gonna come."

"Me too." Robin dug his fingers into Dair's back, not wanting to lose their pace. "Don't stop, holy fuck."

They sped up until Robin crashed over the edge. His orgasm dazzled him momentarily as he squeezed his eyes shut so hard he saw stars. Dair yelled, burying his face into his neck. Warm cum splashed between their bellies, painting them both with the evidence of their pleasure.

Dair clung on to Robin, smothering him with his gorgeous arms and falling down so their bodies were completely pressed together. But Dair held his weight up enough so Robin didn't feel trapped. As their cocks softened, he breathed deeply, staring at the ceiling while gently running his fingers through Dair's damp hair.

Exhaustion was washing over him rapidly. Already, he was struggling to keep his eyes open. They needed to clean up. They needed to talk about what had just happened. But today had been an emotional roller coaster, and Robin's body was shutting down whether he liked it or not.

The last thing he remembered was Dair gently kissing his cheek. "Sleep, hon," he murmured.

At least, that was what Robin hoped he said before he slipped into slumber.

17

DAIR

After four nights, Dair was getting used to waking up in Robin's bed now.

What he wasn't used to was waking up naked.

For a moment he froze, thinking he'd drunkenly forgotten to put on his pajamas or something. But within a second, his memories came flooding back of the night before.

"*Fuck,*" he whispered as quietly as he could to himself. He blinked in the morning sunshine streaming around the edges of the curtains. It was a lot to process, but the panic Dair expected never materialized.

Much like their first selfie on Instagram, holding hands, sharing a bed, or their first staged kiss, it just felt good. The 'wrongness' that Dair would have anticipated simply didn't arrive.

As Dair turned to look at his sleeping lover, all he felt was a fullness in his chest. Robin smelled sweet and warm. There was a faint lingering of their lovemaking from the night before in the air, but nothing overpowering. Just human scents of two people who'd spent the night together.

Dair bit his lip and reached over to very gently brush a tuft of Robin's auburn hair from his forehead. He was snuggled up on his side with his hands under his head, hugging the pillow possessively and breathing softly.

Fuck, he'd never been sexier than he was last night. It was like he'd come alive under Dair's hands in a way he would never have thought possible. He was playful and alluring and hot as sin. The way their two cocks had felt rubbing together inside Dair's fist had been a totally new and awesome sensation.

Dair couldn't wait to try it again.

Would Robin, though? Although they'd both confessed to liking each other, that didn't mean Robin would want to do anything more with someone inexperienced like Dair. And he didn't just mean sex with a man – because he was pretty sure that had a lot in common with sex with a woman.

Dair didn't know anything about being LGBT. Only what he'd gleaned so far from Robin, Peyton, and the experiences he'd had this week. It was an alien culture to him and it didn't feel right striding in this late in the game. It was like he was cheating. He wasn't even really certain how he felt about the whole labeling thing or what he'd say to people if it came up. Yes, Emery had called him pansexual, but was that right?

What he *did* know was that lying here beside Robin after their night of passion was making him feel calm. He scooched over and slipped his arm over Robin's waist with the comforter between them. Their heads rested on the same pillow and Robin's hair tickled Dair's nose.

Dair thought he might have heard people moving in the house beyond. It was so strange for him not to have alarms set and a strict schedule. In the Marines, they'd lived and died by the clock, and back in Seattle, he was always trying to cram workouts in between shifts at odd hours.

It was like being in Pine Cove was helping him to breathe again.

At some point, he dozed off again, curled around Robin's warm, lithe body, all wrapped in the comforter like a hotdog. He could still taste Robin's mouth on his tongue, sweet and tangy from the chocolate and beer. Images of their night replayed in Dair's mind as he drifted in and out of sleep. Dair had forgotten how damn alive he felt having sex.

Eventually he was pulled into consciousness again as Robin stirred under him. Dair smiled before he even opened his eyes, nuzzling his face against Robin's thick hair. "Morning, beautiful," he murmured.

Robin snuffled and rubbed his eyes adorably. When he looked at Dair so close to him, several emotions appeared to fly across his face. "Oh," he said softly. "Hi."

"Is everything okay?" Dair asked. He'd be crushed if Robin regretted last night, but he'd absolutely respect that if he had to.

Robin squeaked and glanced downward. "We appear to be naked."

Dair laughed. "Yes. It was a lot of fun."

Robin exhaled and relaxed in Dair's arms. "You don't, um, you're cool with that? Like, uh, that we, uh-"

"Had great sex?" Dair supplied. "Yeah, I'm pretty thrilled about it, actually. I was surprised for half a minute, but I quickly got over that."

Robin bit his lip, then grinned. "Oh my god," he hissed. "Wait – wasn't there a lot of..." He gestured between their stomachs. Dair grinned.

"Mess? I hope you don't mind, but I cleaned us up a bit. You passed right out."

Robin grimaced. "I'm so sorry."

"Don't be." Dair shook his head. "It was cute. You had this

179

little smile on your face, and I took it that you were pretty satisfied."

Robin stared at him for a moment. Then he laughed and covered his face with his hands. "I can't believe this happened. Is happening." He peeked out from behind his fingers. "It *was* great, wasn't it? I mean, I thought it was, but, oh…" Color drained from his face. "Holy fuck. What did I *say* to you?"

Dair pulled Robin's hands down and stared him straight in the eyes. "You were confident and slightly outrageous, and I fucking loved it. Potty Mouth Robin is my new favorite Robin."

"Oh, shut up." Robin giggled and squirmed, trying to hide again.

So Dair pulled him into a kiss.

Instantly, Robin melted in his arms, his lips soft and malleable against Dair's. Their previous kisses had been filled with fire and fight. This morning it was tender and gentle. Dair felt his heart swelling…as well as other things.

He hummed and grinned against Robin's mouth as their morning wood bumped together. This was something different and exciting for him. He thought back to how he'd jerked off to that scene between two imaginary guys in the shower. Now he was getting to live it for real.

The kiss slowed naturally, then Dair opened his eyes to gaze into Robin's topaz blue ones. "I don't think this is fake anymore," he said. It felt pretty obvious to him, but it was most definitely better to discuss these things than assume.

Robin bit his lip, worry creeping back into his eyes. Dair rubbed his back. Somewhere during their kiss, the comforter had shifted so their bodies were slotted perfectly together in an embrace.

"You want to, um, be boyfriends?" Robin asked, sounding unsure.

Dair's uncertainty around jumping to any labels yet resurfaced. He caressed the small of Robin's back with little circular motions as he considered his words. "Is it too fast?"

"Maybe?" Robin chewed his lip. "Don't get me wrong. This is, well, it's amazing. But I'm still not a hundred percent sure what 'this' is."

Dair let out a breath in relief. "Me neither. But I like it. How about we just continue as we were? We were telling people we'd only just gotten together, after all."

Robin nodded, a smile spreading over his face. "That's true." His eyes lit up and he got a cheeky look on his face that Dair loved. "Dair Epping, would you like to go on a date with me?"

Dair laughed. "Why yes, Robin Coal, I'd love that. I heard there's a fair in town especially for you."

Robin rolled his eyes. "And a few hundred other people."

Dair leaned in and touched his lips to Robin's neck. "I think the best party is the private one we're having in here." Robin moaned, sending blood pumping down to Dair's cock. "I had a bit of a fantasy the other day," he murmured, feeling Robin's pulse under his lips and tongue. "I jerked off thinking about one guy sucking another off while he touched himself. Do you want to do that?"

Robin gasped. "Oh my god, can I blow you?" he rasped. "Your cock is a work of art. I'm not even joking."

It may not have been a joke, but Dair laughed in delight anyway. He rolled onto his back, pulling Robin on top of him. He ran his hands down Robin's slim sides, loving how he twitched a little when Dair found the ticklish spots. The sheets pooled around them, just covering Dair's legs and leaving Robin completely exposed. He appeared to notice, and self-doubt flickered across his face. But Dair held him firmly on either side of his ribs and looked him in the eye.

"You are seriously gorgeous, Robin. You turn me on a

ridiculous amount. I can't believe it took me so long to figure that out."

Robin blushed beautifully and bit his lip. "Thanks," he mumbled through a grin. "Uh, I mean, you're fucking stunning. I'm sure you know that, but, yeah. It's a ten out of ten from me." He gave him two thumbs-up. It was so dorky it made Dair chuckle and fall a tiny bit harder for him.

"I'm happy with that score."

He caressed the side of Robin's face. A thrill shot through him as Robin caught the tip of his thumb between his lips and sucked in a promise of things to come. He was such a delicious contradiction of shyness and sass. Dair suspected the confidence was closer to who he really was. Somewhere along the way, he'd learned to question how hot he was.

Dair really, *really* wanted to help him remember his true nature. "What are you going to do to me, baby?" he asked, his pulse racing in anticipation.

Robin's pupils were blown wide, leaving just a thin ring of brilliant blue. He bit the end of Dair's thumb. "I'm going to suck your big cock," he rasped. "I'm going to make you come down my throat. I want to swallow it all."

Dair couldn't help but gasp. His erection was rock hard now as Robin ground his ass against it. "Yes, I want it," he hissed. "I want to see you touch yourself. Make yourself feel good for me, hon."

Robin bit his lip as he looked down and wrapped his long fingers around his slightly curved cock. Dair hadn't thought much about anyone else's junk before. But he decided he liked Robin's. It was slim like him, but long enough he could get his whole hand around it.

Dair ran his fingers up Robin's thighs, drinking in the erotic sight of him holding his straining cock. "Look at me, Robin," Dair urged. Robin's gaze flicked up, obediently gazing at Dair through his pretty long lashes. "Good baby. Show me how you fuck your hand when you're alone."

Robin groaned and panted. "Dair," he whimpered.

Dair gripped his thighs tightly. "I'm watching. You're so beautiful, gorgeous. Let me see you touching yourself."

"Like that?" Robin rubbed his thumb over the head, coaxing pearls of precum out to spread down his shaft. He gasped and jerked his fist, pleasuring himself for Dair.

Dair's cock was standing up between the cheeks of Robin's pert ass. God, it felt good rubbing against them. He could have come like that, but they were just getting started.

"Can I suck you off, Dair?" Robin begged as if reading Dair's mind.

Dair nodded, watching in awe as Robin scrambled down the bed in seconds. He threw back the covers so they were now both totally exposed. Kneeling between Dair's legs, he took Dair's cock in hand and wasted no time slipping his lips over the top. He sucked and licked at the head like a lollipop, and Dair had to shove his fist in his mouth to stop himself from crying out.

But he didn't close his eyes.

Robin played out Dair's own personal fantasy, swallowing him down while he jerked off. It was a thousand times better than it had been in his head. Quiet sounds filled the room: Dair's stifled gasps, Robin's little gulps, and the slide and slap of his hand stroking his prick.

Dair carded his fingers through Robin's thick hair, feeling his head bobbing under his palm as he took Dair's length in further and further. He wasn't the most confident at deep throating. He tried once or twice, then backed off. But Dair wasn't that surprised, given his established uncertainties. What he lacked in skill he made up for in enthusiasm, though, and Dair fucking loved it.

"Oh, shit, Robin," he hissed suddenly, digging his heels into the mattress. "I'm gonna come. I-"

Robin sucked harder and rubbed him with his tongue, coaxing Dair's second orgasm from him in less than twelve hours. Dair covered his mouth and swallowed his shout as his climax burst from him. His vision swam and he shivered as Robin drank down everything he'd spent, just like he'd promised. Then he crawled up Dair's body, straddling his hips and hovering over him on his right hand as he finished himself off with his left. Until the moment his orgasm hit, he and Dair locked eyes. Dair felt the ripple through Robin's body as he came hard and fast over Dair's stomach.

That was something he'd not experienced before. Well, sort of last night, but they'd come together and smeared it between them. Watching Robin blow his load over his abs made Dair feel like he'd been painted or marked. Claimed.

He was Robin's now.

Robin, who was trembling above him, his eyes still closed from his high. Dair cupped his hand against his face, gently pulling him down for a kiss.

"Jesus Christ, you're a hot little minx. That was – wow, Robin. Just wow."

Robin grinned drunkenly and flopped beside him. When he saw the mess he'd made, he gave a little 'oh' sound and reached over for a few tissues. Dair stroked his hair while Robin took his turn to care for Dair.

"That's better," he said happily, dropping the wet tissues by the side of the bed, probably where Dair had left his ones. Without being asked, Robin cuddled up against Dair's side. Dair pulled the comforter over them again and kissed Robin's temple.

"You have no idea." He chuckled. "It's been a while."

Robin looked up at him with wide eyes. Then he smiled again and rested his head on Dair's chest.

They dozed a little while together, lying entangled and sweaty and perfect in the damp bed.

After a time, Dair found his mind was being pulled in two directions. On the one hand, he wanted to get out there and be with Robin genuinely. After the charade they'd put on, he wanted to try the real thing on for size. When he introduced himself as Robin's boyfriend to people, he wanted to feel like that was something they might actually be working toward now.

On the other hand, he didn't want to leave their little bubble. In Robin's bedroom, they were safe. Nothing could go wrong.

But what did he really have to fear? They were facing an unknown, but that was what life was made of.

In this room, what had changed between them could be written off as fantasy. But once they went out into the real world, other people would see it too. It would become fact. Solid.

That was what Dair wanted. He kissed Robin's head firmly and squeezed him tight. "Do you want to take the first shower, gorgeous?"

Robin angled himself to grin at him. "You eager to get going?"

Dair nodded. "I am."

In more ways than one.

18

ROBIN

NOTHING HAD CHANGED.

And yet everything was different.

During the day, Robin and Dair took Smudge for a walk in the park before going to Sunny's for lunch. They wandered around town where Robin pointed out places he used to hang around as a kid, and Dair showed him a couple of the shops where he'd bought his new clothes. He had the jeans on again with a tightly fitted T-shirt that showed off his body. They held hands and talked with people that remembered Robin from his school days and made each other laugh with silly little jokes.

The only thing that wasn't the same was that every time Robin looked at Dair, he remembered what it was like to kiss those lips, to touch that hair.

To see his expression when he came.

Out in the bright sunshine, it didn't seem possible that Robin had uttered those devilish, filthy things to Dair. But then Dair would catch his eye with a positively smoldering look, and it would all come flooding back.

They'd had sex. Twice. Dair might still have been unsure

of his exact label, but he wasn't straight. And he was still here, with Robin.

He couldn't wait to drop this bombshell on Peyton, but he wanted to tell her in person when she arrived in town tomorrow morning. Until then, it was like Robin was walking around with a marvelous secret, which was kind of crazy because in theory, everyone already knew.

Except they didn't know anything at all.

They didn't know what it felt like to enter the town fair and get their photo taken as a couple with Smudge between them, feeling so complete. They didn't know the thrill Robin got when Dair touched the small of his back or murmured something in his ear. They didn't know how a simple, chaste kiss to the corner of the mouth could mean so much.

They didn't know because Robin hadn't had a clue until now himself.

He'd always thought he'd been in love with Mac, because when you were with someone for a year and a half you were supposed to love them, weren't you? But he'd never felt as content as he was after one day being with Dair than from after a year and a half as Mac's boyfriend.

Not that he was in love with Dair. That was crazy. It took a person ages to fall in love. You had to make sure and really test those feelings.

Or so he assumed. As he'd recently come to appreciate, he wasn't sure he'd ever been in love before. How would he know what it felt like?

Thankfully, Dair seemed to be on the same page about not rushing into anything like labels. They could just explore whatever this was slowly and see if it was really a good fit.

Robin had to say, though, if they'd had sex twice already and Dair hadn't made a run for it, that was a pretty good sign.

Plenty of people stopped to fuss over Smudge, who

lapped up the attention, especially once school finished for the day. Kids poured into the first day of the three-day reunion fair during the afternoon. It felt like all of them wanted to say hello to their excitable ball of fluff. When people asked his name or how old he was, Dair would always glance at Robin as he replied. Robin also noticed he didn't say 'my dog.' He said 'ours.' Robin supposed he lived with both of them, but he was still touched Dair would include him like that.

During the summer months, Pine Cove always seemed to have some sort of fair going every weekend. The attractions changed around a bit as did the food stands, but there were always the staple stalls that Robin remembered from his youth.

He dragged Dair over to buy him a funnel cake from Mrs. Charles. Now her daughter was selling the sweet treats with her, learning the secrets of how she got them so light on the inside but crunchy on the outside. Dair had his sprinkled with powdered sugar and drizzled warm chocolate sauce. Robin got his favorite combo of apple and honey, insisting that Dair try a bite from his wooden fork. When Robin missed a dash of honey on his lip, Dair kissed it off.

As afternoon started to become evening, Dair spotted a stuffed koala that was almost three feet tall. Lucky for them it was a strongman game, so Dair dragged Robin over to the stall to get it. Robin tried to protest that he didn't need a koala almost as big as he was, but secretly he was thrilled when Dair hit the mallet onto the reader, sending the lights blinging all the way to the top where it set off a horn. Dair looked like he'd won an Olympic medal as he presented Robin with his prize.

Of course, that meant Robin had to carry the damn thing for the rest of the evening, but he didn't resume his previous protesting. It was one thing to make a fuss of Dair making a big deal over him. But now the deed was done, he cuddled his koala to his chest, relishing in the way people laughed and smiled at him.

He was hard to miss with his new giant furry friend. There was something about standing next to Dair that meant Robin didn't mind finally stepping into that spotlight.

"Oh my god," Jay cackled by way a greeting as he approached them. They had agreed to meet at the shooting gallery at eight o'clock, just as the sun was starting to set. He bent double and hooted with laughter. "That is amazing. Dair, please say you won that for him?"

Dair preened and puffed his chest out like a pigeon. "Only the best for my man," he said, kissing the top of Robin's head.

Jay smiled. No, he smirked. Robin knew that look.

He did some extremely fast mental gymnastics. Jay was pleased – but specifically pleased with himself. Like seeing Dair kiss Robin made him happy. But he thought they weren't really dating. Didn't he?

Ohh…

Jay had left them all alone last night. The crafty little shit.

Robin huffed, half-proud that his brother sometimes knew what was best for him better than he did, but half-mad that he'd been played.

"Get over here," Robin said, narrowing his eyes at his twin. "I promised to kick your ass."

"Yeah, yeah, tough guy. You're all talk. If I win, I get the koala."

"No deal," Dair growled in a surprisingly hurt voice.

Robin threw his head back and laughed. "Relax, baby. I got this."

Jay knew it. That was why he'd made the empty threat about the koala. Robin let him go first with the toy rifle, where he wildly missed all the pictures of goldfish traveling across on the conveyor at the back of the stall.

"It's a fix," he cried dramatically, winking at the guy running the stall. The guy shook his head and grinned as he reloaded the gun, then offered it to Robin.

Robin tingled with anticipation and tried not to look at Dair, who was standing to the side with Smudge and the koala, watching on.

Then he fired.

One. Two. Three. Four. Five.

He snapped down a moving goldfish picture with each shot.

"Fuck!" Dair cried.

Robin flushed with pride. It had always been a quirky talent of his. His grandpa had taught him to knock tin cans off their back fence with a BB gun as a kid. He'd also destroyed Jay and all their friends when they'd gone paintballing for their fourteenth birthday.

He glanced at Dair, unable to hide his massive grin. "Beginner's luck?" he joked.

"Oh, shut up!" Jay grabbed Robin around the neck and ruffled his hair, then kissed his cheek. "All right, show-off. Pick your prize and I'll catch you later."

Robin raised his eyes at him. "Oh, you're not hanging around?"

Jay shook his head and winked at Dair. "You guys don't need a third wheel. Besides, I have places to be, people to see."

"What people?" Robin demanded as his bullshit meter went off. This wasn't just Jay leaving them alone again. This was something more. Who was he meeting?

But Jay just waved at them, walking backward with a grin.

Dair soon caught Robin's attention again with a hand on his hip. "You're a real crack shot," he marveled. "No wonder you always beat me at Modern Warfare. That was awesome. What prize are you going to pick?"

A couple of teenage girls were playing the game now with surprisingly loud battle cries. Robin stepped to the side of them and looked around at the stuffed animals and plastic toys the stall had to offer.

Then he saw it.

"Oh! Excuse me, sir, may I take this one?"

The old guy smiled at him, his tanned skin crinkling with leathery laughter lines. "Sure, son. You win it for your boyfriend?"

Sometimes, Robin forgot just how awesome this town was.

"Yes, sir." He bashfully accepted his prize, then turned around to swap Dair his koala for the little tank he'd just won him. "Look," Robin said excitedly pointing at the top. "There's even a mini you inside!"

Dair smiled down at the silly toy, accepting a bag from the stall owner to put it in. "Aw, hon. I love it." He touched the dog tags around his neck, hidden under his shirt. Robin hadn't expected him to appreciate such a trivial thing that much. He couldn't help but feel proud that he'd picked something of such value. Unsure how to express that in words, he got on his tiptoes and kissed Dair's cheek. Dair hugged him in return, looking at the tank a little longer before slipping it into the bag.

As they walked away from the shooting gallery, Smudge whined and began tugging on his leash. They both recognized what that meant. "Uh-oh," said Dair, looking around. This part of the fair was on the parking lot by the green. "Okay, if I take him that way past the Ferris wheel, I know there's a poop bin right there. It's a bit far, but better than carrying poop around."

Robin cackled and rolled his eyes. "Way to kill the mood, Smudgy!"

Smudge barked up at him and wagged his tail, then went back to doing his 'I need the potty' dance.

"Here," Robin said. "Give me your tank, and I'll meet you at the benches by the pizza stand we passed earlier. I assume you'll need feeding soon?"

Dair grinned. "Yes, please. Someone's been working up my appetite." His smile was pure sin as he leaned down to kiss Robin on the mouth. But then Smudge yanked him away. "Okay, all right, Mr. Poopy Butt! We'll go!"

Robin laughed as he watched small little Smudge drag a much bigger Dair away.

He kept smiling as he weaved his way back over to the pizza stall where there were a ton of picnic benches. As luck would have it, he spied a family just leaving one, so he dashed over just in time for him and his koala to claim it.

It was almost fully dark now. Fairy lights were strung up everywhere, and all the refreshment stands glowed and flashed in all kinds of colors. Robin spied the pizza place he'd had in mind, but there were also tacos, corn dogs, vegan falafel – *oh! Thai!*

"Wow. You're really fooling everyone, aren't you?"

Ice rushed through Robin. He snapped his head around just in time to see Mac drop down on the bench beside him. His face was like thunder.

"W-what?" Robin didn't care if it was childlike – he hugged his koala to his side. While he had both his legs over the bench, Mac was straddling it, facing Robin side-on.

Mac sneered and shook his head. "Oh, I heard your snobby brother and that soldier of yours after the game last night."

"Marine," Robin corrected automatically. "Heard them-?"

"How your little relationship is a joke. You're just

pretending so I'll stay away from you or some shit. What the actual fuck?"

Panic flared through Robin, even though they were surrounded by people. "Mac, I-"

"How could you do this to me?" Mac's face crumbled, his blue eyes shining as tears pooled, waiting to fall. "Robin, I know we weren't perfect, but I was *so* looking forward to seeing you again and starting over. And you pull this immature crap? Are you still seventeen or what?"

Cold sweat had sprung all over Robin's skin, but then he remembered the current situation. "Look, I don't know what you heard," he said, licking his lips, "but Dair and I are for real."

"Don't give me that!" Mac snapped, slapping the wooden table top. "I heard him with my own ears! He made it sound like I was some sort of fucking threat and he was your damn bodyguard. What the hell have you told him?"

"Mac," Robin said firmly, despite the fact he was trembling. He looked his ex dead in the eye, trying not to flinch away. "Dair might have come here as a friend, but it's real between us *now*. Things changed. And I didn't do this to hurt you. It was just a stupid idea between a couple of buddies."

"Yeah, you're right. It was stupid," Mac growled. "And I'm hurt anyway. God, I bet you thought you were so clever. I know I wasn't perfect, Robin, but I'm *trying*. I've changed so much. Friends tell me all the time I'm like a different person."

What friends? Robin wanted to ask. But that was nasty, and it wasn't like he was Mr. Popular. Instead, he took a deep breath and tried to organize his frantic thoughts.

"I'm sorry, Mac. But this wasn't about you." At least, not entirely. "I'm really sorry you heard whatever it was you heard. But like I said, Dair and I are more than friends now. The situation changed."

"Oh, he decided to have a test run with a gay boy, did he?"

Robin flinched. "Jesus, no. It's not like that at all." He looked around. Where the hell was Dair, anyway? Not that Robin needed rescuing, but some backup wouldn't hurt right about now.

Mac scoffed. "Oh, so he's not straight?"

Robin opened his mouth. But what should he say? Dair had suggested he was maybe bi or pan, but he wasn't totally sure. It wasn't Robin's place to out him, either.

Mac took his hesitation as confirmation and laughed sadly. "Oh, Robin," he said with sympathy. "You *know* what straight guys are like. They all want to scratch that itch and try a cock just once, just to see what it's like. Especially Army guys, Jesus. A hole's a hole to them."

"We didn't-" Robin went to argue but then immediately bit his tongue. The damage was done, though.

Mac sighed impatiently. "Of course you didn't do anal. I see some things haven't changed. Please tell me you didn't blabber at him, at least."

Heat flamed in Robin's cheeks and tears stung the back of his eyes, though he refused to let them spill. Mac's words from ten years ago blared in his mind, as loud as if he was shouting them right there and then.

"Jesus Christ, Robin. YES, I fucked someone else! I've tried to help you be better in bed, but you won't listen! I needed some decent ass. Someone who'll just shut up and let me bang them!"

Robin cringed, thinking about everything he'd said to Dair in bed. God, he was so embarrassing. Why did he have to do that?

Mac shook his head. "Well, congratulations. Your fake-ape-jarhead-boyfriend got his dick sucked. Now who's going to pick up the pieces when he wants nothing to do with you?"

"It wasn't just about sex," Robin snapped, feeling dizzy

with anger and humiliation. But then Dair's words from earlier sprang back up in his brain.

"It's been a while."

For a fleeting second, Robin had panicked that he'd only been interested in sex, but then dismissed it. Because Dair wasn't like that.

Was he?

How well did Robin really know him?

Something on his face must have betrayed him because Mac scooched an inch closer, his expression one of concern. "Robin, I'm so sorry, but I think you've been taken advantage of. Meatheads like that just want to come. They don't really care if it's a pussy or an ass or a mouth. They just want to get their end wet."

"Dair's not like that," Robin snarled.

Mac bit his lip, his gaze flickering over Robin's face. "I don't know him. But I know you, sweetheart. I know you're just trying to impress people, but you don't have to impress me. I love you just the way you are. You're my Rockin' Robin." He put his hand on Robin's arm and rubbed his thumb against the cotton of his T-shirt. "I'm worried about you."

"I'm fine," Robin said automatically.

But his mind was a mess. It did make sense that someone as awesome as Dair wouldn't be interested in Robin for long. Maybe he wouldn't mean to do it, but Dair was bound to get bored once they'd had sex a few more times and he realized Robin was terrible at bottoming. He'd tried so hard to please Mac, but it hadn't been enough, and he'd never tried it with any of his other hookups since.

"I don't want to see you hurt, sweetheart."

Mac leaned in closer. His hand was still on Robin's arm. Robin knew he should shake him off, but he felt so fucking dejected he didn't have the energy.

Things had seemed genuine with Dair, but how could they be? He might be entertained for a day or two. But once they got back to Seattle and the real world, there was no way the two of them could sustain any kind of relationship. Dair's tough mechanic buddies would laugh at him for being gay if he came out, never mind dating a soft little twink like Robin. They had nothing in common. Robin was shy and boring. Dair was a war hero.

"I know we had issues, Robin," Mac continued saying. "But I've changed so much. I don't think anyone could love you like I do. Glasses and all." He gave a soft chuckle. "Don't you wonder if we could have that again?"

Robin was reminded of his thoughts back when he and Mac had met in the diner. What was better? Dair, who was nice but straight? Or Mac, who was gay but made Robin feel like crap? But at least he was outright saying that he wanted to try things again with Robin.

It was tempting to be flattered by that. But Robin didn't reckon he wanted to be with Mac again. He wanted Dair.

The question was, did Dair want him?

Probably not.

He screwed his eyes shut, hot tears escaping from under his lashes.

He heard Mac sigh. "Oh, Binny. Don't cry. I forgive you."

He pressed his lips to Robin's so quickly Robin didn't register it had happened until it was over. Robin whimpered. Shit. That was the last thing he wanted.

"Don't."

"Come on, sweetheart." Mac rubbed his arm again. "You said it yourself. It's not real between you and him. He's had a bit of fun. He'll soon be gone. I need you so badly, Robin. I forgot how much you make me better. You're just like me."

No, he wasn't. But he didn't get a chance to deny it, because Mac pressed his lips to Robin's again.

That broke something in Robin. "Fuck *off!*" He shoved Mac away from him and scrambled to his feet in panic. "I said don't!"

"Robin-"

"No!" He scrubbed his face under his glasses. "Dair might not want me, but that doesn't mean I automatically want to get back together. Just – just leave me alone, okay?"

He started walking before he could think about what he was doing. His head felt like it was full of bees, and everything around him was blurred by tears. He half ran, half stumbled away from the picnic benches until he found a dark, quiet spot behind a milk bottle toss stall to hide. He leaned against the side of the stall, hugging himself in the dark, until he cried himself out.

When the anger and dejection faded into numbness, he realized he'd left his koala and Dair's tank at the table. He might not know what the hell was going on between them, but he didn't want to throw those things away in case there was a chance he and Dair might still be able to make things work.

But when he went back to the picnic area, they were gone.

19

DAIR

SMUDGE WAS SUCH A GOOD BOY. HE WAITED UNTIL THEY MADE it to the grass to do his business, then made friends with a Dalmatian who chased him around some trees for several minutes. Dair was anxious to get back to Robin, but Smudge hadn't had a decent walk or found a playmate in days.

So Dair texted Robin to tell him to grab them a pizza to share with whatever toppings he wanted, and Dair would be back as soon as he could.

As they were walking back, Dair soaked in the atmosphere of this little town by the lake. Even in a big, jostling crowd with music blaring and screams coming from the rides, Dair felt strangely peaceful. The scent of pine filled his lungs along with sweet cotton candy and rich, tangy Chinese food. So many people caught his eye and smiled at him as he walked past, even though they didn't know him. Folks in Seattle didn't do that.

Dair sighed. Only a couple more days and it would be back to 'reality.' He'd be lying if he didn't admit he was kind of anxious what was going to happen to him and Robin once their everyday pressures returned.

And what would Peyton think? Damn, that hadn't occurred to him until just now. Would she be okay with Dair dating the guy she saw as her little brother? He wouldn't put it past her to whack him with a skillet if she thought he was mistreating him.

But Dair had no intention of doing that. In fact, he had to drag himself away from a stall selling hand-painted eyeglass cases. He'd already gotten Robin the koala. He didn't want to overwhelm him with gifts on their first date.

He knew he was also in danger of using presents to alleviate his fear that this was something fleeting. He hoped Robin was into this, but Dair couldn't even trust his own feelings right now. He knew for a fact he was head over heels about Robin. But was that just their friendship? Would they be able to develop a romantic relationship as well as a sexual one?

Was he really pan? Or was he just so blindsided by someone wanting him that it didn't matter if that person was a man?

It was all such foreign territory for him.

There was no pressure so far, though. They'd agreed to take things one day at a time, and if the last twenty-four hours were anything to go by, they were doing fantastic on day one already. He liked Robin a hell of a lot. Of that much, he was certain.

The pizza stand was in a sort of outdoor food court. It was like several square areas joined together by thoroughfares with picnic tables to sit at. Naturally, on a Friday night it was heaving, and Smudge's leash kept getting tangled around people's legs. But eventually, Dair rounded a taco stand and reached the right section. From the looks of the display on Dair's texts, Robin hadn't even seen Dair's message let alone replied to it. Dair hoped he was still here, but if not, he'd call him.

After scanning the crowd for a minute, Dair was ready to phone him, but then he spotted a flash of auburn hair.

It had been so difficult to see because Robin was mostly hidden behind Mac's larger form.

Dair pulled up short, still lingering by the taco stand, his stomach flipping over. Mac was sitting dangerously close to Robin and leaning in. The only lighting was coming from the refreshment stalls and twinkly fairy lights, so Dair couldn't read Robin's face.

Dair had better get closer then. Not that he didn't trust Robin to handle it on his own, but Mac wasn't pleasant company, and Dair was eager to relieve Robin of it. He tugged on Smudge's leash to start traversing through the crowd-

-just as Mac leaned in and kissed Robin on the lips.

Robin didn't seem to react at all. He certainly didn't push him off or walk away. He just sat there.

Dair's heart was hammering in his chest. Seeing Robin kiss somebody else – let alone that asshole Mac – left him feeling like his heart had been ripped out. He knew they hadn't had a talk about exclusivity yet, but he really thought they'd had an incredible connection this week, not to mention last night.

But then...Mac was actually gay. Dair still wasn't sure *what* he was. It would make more sense that Robin was attracted to someone like him because he had his damn life sorted out, even if he was an asshole. Not take a chance on someone like Dair, who was fumbling through, trying to make sense of new feelings.

Dair needed answers.

But then Mac kissed Robin again.

Dair whirred around and walked back the way he'd come without even thinking. He was back by the glasses case stall before he made himself stop and take several deep breaths.

Okay. If he was in any doubt about how he was feeling, he knew it now.

He was extremely jealous.

He was also a bit angry that Robin would throw away what they'd only just started working on. But Dair had been the one to suggest taking things slow. He'd been too chickenshit to consider the idea of committing to be being boyfriends.

But that meant Robin might very well end up becoming someone else's boyfriend if he dithered too long.

When Dair thought about it like that, his own intentions were pretty damn clear.

If he wanted him and Robin to be exclusive, he should damn well grow a spine and tell him that. What was scarier? Coming out and committing to being Robin's boyfriend or seeing him back with that prick Mac?

Dair was marching back to the pizza stand before he'd even finished formulating the question in his mind.

If Robin really wanted to choose Mac over him, Dair wouldn't understand, but he'd make himself accept it. However, if Dair didn't make his feelings crystal clear to Robin, he would be operating under half the information.

But when he returned to that section of the food court, both Robin and Mac were gone. The stuffed koala was still visible at the picnic table, though. A cleaning attendant approached the now vacant table and looked around with a frown, presumably looking for the koala's owner.

Dair hurried forward with Smudge, waving a hand. "Sorry, that's mine," he called out.

The middle-aged woman saw him and raised her eyebrows. "You better be careful. Otherwise you'll lose it."

As Dair reached the table and also saw his discarded tank, he couldn't help but wonder what he'd already lost.

He lowered his bulk onto the bench, hearing the wood

creak under his weight. All around him, people were laughing and chatting while they ate their dinners. The bells and whistles of the nearby games floated over the air, and somewhere someone was playing The Rolling Stones.

Smudge licked Dair's fingers, making him look down. His little face was anxious, and he wagged his tail, asking in his own doggy way if Dair was okay.

"Not really, buddy," he admitted.

Where had Robin gone? What should Dair do now? They'd driven into town together in Dair's truck, but that wouldn't stop him from getting an Uber somewhere.

To Mac's place, perhaps?

Dair lifted the small tank from its bag and ran his fingers over the tread. He'd been so touched that Robin had picked this for him because it had made Dair realize this was the first time he'd felt part of a team again since the Marines. He and Robin made sense to him – they fitted perfectly and worked well together. Or so he'd thought.

"Oh, man, I'm glad you're here."

Dair looked up in surprise as Mac approached the bench. Dair's hackles raised immediately, but Mac looked upset, and he wasn't sure how to read that. So for now, he just asked the most pertinent question.

"Where's Robin?"

Mac paused before sitting down on the picnic bench opposite Dair. He pressed his palms together, then touched his index fingers to his lips. "How long have you been here?"

Dair swallowed. Smudge whimpered and licked his fingers again. Dair sighed and looked up at Mac. "I saw the kiss, if that's what you mean."

Mac sighed. "Okay. Look, I'm sorry you had to find out this way, but it's probably for the best."

"The best?" Dair could feel himself glaring, but Mac didn't seem all that fazed.

"Yeah, I mean, I asked him what the hell he was doing, but he didn't seem to care."

Dair's glare became a frown. "But you kissed *him.*"

Mac snorted. "After he kissed me. I'm only human, man. Look, don't take it too personally. He's more of a magpie than a robin. He likes shiny things. This is what he does."

For a good few seconds, Dair just stared at him. "What does he do?"

Mac shrugged. "He has a thing for straight guys. He plays all shy and coy to get them into bed, then he gets all freaky. I'm guessing he got all freaky, right?" He raised a questioning eyebrow. "He likes to dirty talk and make you beg for a blow job."

Dair clenched his teeth together. "I don't think that's any of your business," he growled.

Mac held up his hands. "Hey, I get it. This is shitty news. But don't shoot the messenger. I'm just trying to save you the heartache I went through. You see, Robin doesn't *do* relationships. He gets distracted by pretty new things – like I said, a magpie. I'm the only one who tried to stick with him, but after he cheated on me…" He whistled and shook his head.

Dair's entire body prickled. "Robin cheated on you?"

"Yeah," Mac said ruefully. "More than once. I'm a fucking idiot for holding a candle for him, I know. But what can I say? I love the guy."

Dair felt sick. Robin, a cheater? And did Mac really love him?

"But he said – his family all said – that you…"

"Hit him?" Mac's face darkened. "For fuck's sake. We had one argument. I was hurt. I saw texts from other guys and I questioned Robin about it. He pushed me, so I pushed him back. It was just a moment of insanity. I'm sorry. I don't know what kind of things he's been telling you."

He rubbed his face and looked over at a donut stand, tapping his finger on the table.

"When he kissed me just now, I was so happy that I kissed him back. But then I remembered you. When I questioned him about it, he laughed. Said it was nothing. But I didn't feel right, and I told him I wasn't interested if he was still a cheat. He got pissed and stormed off. I tried to follow, but I lost him."

Dair shook his head. This was bullshit. *Bullshit.* But Mac seemed so sincere.

Dair wanted to believe he knew Robin well enough to argue he wasn't capable of being that manipulative. But it was true that he'd not had a relationship since Mac. Peyton had said so. And Dair had only known him a couple of months. Really, he'd only begun to properly know him this past few days.

He needed to talk to Robin. Get his side of events.

"I'm going to try and find him," he mumbled, collecting up the koala and the tank.

Mac shook his head. "Hey, I really am sorry, dude. But don't take it personally. Better to find out now rather than ten years down the line. I'm a fucking idiot. If I can help someone else avoid falling for his games, that helps a little."

"Why should I believe you?" Dair asked. Because he sure as hell didn't want to.

Mac shrugged. "You saw that kiss. I'm sorry he played you, I am. But he's not like us. He's really smart. Strategic. But sure, ask him what went down. I doubt he'll admit to making the first move, but why should you believe me over him?"

He knocked his fist on the table a couple of times, then stood. Before walking away, though, he turned back to face Dair.

"But ask yourself – who has the most to gain here? I could

have lied and let you keep seeing him, thinking I was the bad guy trying to make a move. I don't think I want to date him again. I'm just trying to spare you the same pain."

With that, he vanished into the throng, his shoulders slumped.

Dair didn't know what to do or what to think. Surely Mac was talking out of his ass.

Dair needed to talk to Robin, now. But when he dialed his number, the call rang out. So Dair gave one last look around the food court, picked up the koala and tank, then began to walk Smudge in the direction of his truck on Main Street.

Halfway there, his phone buzzed. Robin was calling him back. Hurriedly, Dair answered.

"Hey. I was getting kind of worried. I found our stuff on the table. Are you okay?"

There was a pause. "Oh, good," Robin said heavily. "I thought it had been taken. I'm sorry. I missed your calls and stuff, too."

Dair waited. "What happened?" he asked eventually.

Robin sighed. Dair wasn't sure due to all the noise going on around him, but he wondered if Robin was holding back a sob. "Where are you?" Robin asked.

"Heading back to the truck. Where are you?"

"At the picnic bench again. Dair...I..."

Dair stopped walking near the entrance of the fair. Equal amounts of people were coming and going, jostling around him, so he tried to back in between a Skee Ball game and lemonade stand. Smudge head-butted his shin, probably wondering why they'd stopped walking.

"Robin? What's wrong? Talk to me."

"I'm sorry. I'm a mess right now. My head's all over the place. Maybe this was a mistake."

The bottom dropped out of Dair's stomach. "What was?"

It was agony waiting for an answer. "Us," Robin said

eventually. "I – I think I rushed into it. You don't want to be with someone like me, trust me."

Dair didn't want to believe it, but had Mac been *right*? Was Robin trying to ditch him by saying 'it's not you, it's me'?

"Don't I get a say in who I want to be with?" Dair asked.

"Yeah…but do you really want to be with me? Honestly?"

Dair chewed his lip and stared over the crowd, not really seeing anyone. "That depends. Did you kiss Mac just now?"

The silence told him a lot.

"Robin," he said around the lump in his throat. "I know we said we didn't want to rush this. I think that's for the best. You need to think about what you really want."

He closed his eyes and grimaced. He wasn't sure he could bear the hurt of seeing Robin right now, not with the image of him allowing Mac to kiss him so fresh in his mind.

"I think I might get a motel room for me and Smudge tonight."

"Okay," Robin said in a rush. "Yeah, that's sensible. I'll get an Uber home."

"No, I'll drive you," Dair said quickly, but Robin interrupted.

"It's fine. You're almost back at the truck, anyway. Unless you wanted to get your things?"

Dair just wanted to crawl into a dark hole and not think at all. How had his day gone from bliss to heartbreak so fast? "I'll just grab a toothbrush from a store," he said. "As long as you're okay getting a cab."

"It's fine," said Robin firmly. Dair thought he might have heard another sob, but over the crowd and blaring music, he couldn't be sure. "Dair, I'm sorry."

How had things gotten so messed up? He was sure Mac was at fault in some way, but he couldn't be completely sure Robin wasn't either. He certainly wasn't leaping to defend his actions right now.

"I'm sorry, too," Dair mumbled.

He expected Robin to hang up, but he didn't. "I hope you get a motel room okay," he said quietly.

Dair rubbed his eyes. "We'll be fine. Sleep well, hon."

"Night night."

Dair stared at his phone for a while after they closed the call. He felt wretched in a way he hadn't since Malory and he had broken up. In that instance, he'd known that was the right thing to do. But with Robin, he felt like the opportunity to try was being snatched away before they could even begin.

Maybe they weren't meant to be? Maybe this was Dair's one little fling at being gay, and he'd go back to his regular life now.

The thought didn't bring him any comfort.

Hopefully after some sleep, he'd be able to think clearer. But with his heart hurting and his mind whirling, he doubted he'd get any sleep at all.

He hugged the oversized koala to his chest and slowly, sadly, walked Smudge back to his truck.

20

ROBIN

"Right. Are you going to tell me what the hell is going on, or do I have to tickle it out of you?"

Robin smiled weakly at Peyton as he cradled his cup of sugary coffee, curled into the corner of the sofa in the family living room. It was Saturday afternoon. Robin had slept most of the day away or at least dozed fitfully.

"Mercy," he begged quietly.

Peyton huffed before bouncing over the cushions and wrapping her arms around him. "Why did I run into Dair this morning at the motel looking like someone stole his G.I. Joe? Then stomped on it. And set it on fire."

Robin sighed. The knot that had been in his stomach since last night didn't look to be easing anytime soon. "Mac kissed me. I didn't push him off quick enough. Dair saw. He wouldn't want to be with a guy like me anyway, so it's best if I just let him-"

"No, no, no!" Peyton cried, letting him go. "Back up. Mac *kissed* you?"

"He was just trying his luck," Robin said hollowly. "I told him no, and he did it again anyway, so I got mad and left. But before that…" He sighed again, even heavier. "He said some things that made a lot of sense."

"Such as?" Peyton asked. "And what did you mean about Dair being with you? Do you have a crush on him? Because I have gotten the occasional queer vibe from him, you know."

Robin closed his eyes. He didn't want to admit this out loud, because then he'd have to face that it was also most likely gone.

"We slept together. Twice."

"Shut the front door!" Peyton screeched.

Robin waved his coffee-free hand at her, desperately trying to calm her down. His family was lingering somewhere around the house. He'd lied and told them that Dair and Smudge had gone for a run. But that was hours ago, and they were definitely going to start wondering why he wasn't getting ready for the big reunion party soon.

Peyton leaned forward on the couch, staring at Robin. "You guys hooked up?"

"Yeah, but it was obviously a mistake, okay?"

"Why?" Peyton folded her arms. "Did he say he regretted it?"

Robin's eyes burned, but he managed not to let any tears fall. "He didn't need to. And then he saw that kiss – god knows what he thinks."

"So ask him." She raised her eyebrows. "Have a conversation, like adults."

Robin shrugged. "He texted to say he'd still go to the reunion with me. Maybe we can talk then, but I'm not sure what we'd say. We're not compatible."

Peyton shook her head incredulously but then looked up with a smile. "Oh, hey, Ava! Long time no see."

Robin turned around to see his sister freeze in the doorway at the sight of Peyton. For a few seconds, she didn't seem to know what to do. "Hi," she uttered eventually. "I like your…socks." Then she spun on her heels and pretty much ran out of the room.

Robin frowned. Peyton chuckled. "She's a funny one, isn't she?"

"Not usually that funny."

Peyton slapped his leg through his pajamas. Grown-up clothes had seemed too much of a stretch to put on yet. "Getting back to you and Dair-"

"There is no me and Dair." Robin drained his coffee cup but kept it in his hands, staring at the dregs. "It was just a crazy thing that happened. Hopefully we can both forget about it soon."

Peyton looked confused. "Was the sex that bad?"

Robin cringed, thinking about all the dumb things he'd said in the heat of the moment. The way he'd tried to show off his scrawny body. The way he'd been so thirsty for Dair's cock.

"It was pretty humiliating," he mumbled.

Peyton let out a frustrated cry. "Was it? Or has Mac just gotten into your head? What did he say exactly? And *why* have you been hanging around with him when Dair's whole purpose in coming here was to make sure you didn't have to do that?"

"I haven't been hanging out with him," Robin told her as he put his empty coffee mug down. "Okay, well, we met to talk about work, but the other times were when he came and found me."

Peyton arched an eyebrow. "I'm going to be having a word with Dair about how that happened, I think."

"Oh, shut up," Robin said with a laugh. "I'm not some delicate flower. I can make my own decisions and look after myself. Mac's changed. Not much, but I never felt unsafe with him."

He rubbed his arm where Mac had slapped it. Yeah, that hadn't been great, but Robin hadn't been in any actual *danger.*

Peyton huffed. "This all sounds like nonsense. So, what, you left him at the motel this morning?"

"Actually, he's been staying here. In my room. It was his idea to check into the motel last night."

"Oh, *Robin,*" Peyton cried in exasperation. "You boys are just freaking out over nothing. I swear to god, I'm going to go back over there and bang his head against the wall."

"No, don't," Robin said. However, his lips twitched in half a smile. "Thank you, though. I'll try and talk some more to him tonight. Who knows? Maybe it was all a big misunderstanding?"

Robin wanted to believe Peyton, he really did. But he kept coming back to all the reasons why someone like Dair wouldn't want to be with Robin after one night. Let alone be boyfriends.

Peyton huffed and slapped his knee. "This isn't what I imagined after driving for three hours. I thought we'd all be getting ready together, drinking mimosas, and dancing around the room to Bananarama."

"That sounds great," Robin said, but his heart was in no way in it.

The thought of partying to eighties music made him feel sick. How could he have made such a mess of everything? He should have trusted his instinct the night before last and just gone to bed. Not allowed the stupid box in his chest to break and let out his secret crush. Now he'd lost a friend and ruined it all. He wouldn't blame Dair if he wanted to move out.

Peyton shook her head and rubbed her forehead. "This is all a big fuss over nothing. What did Dair *look* like when you guys talked?"

Robin toyed with the handle of his mug. "We haven't seen each other since…"

Since Mac kissed him. Urgh, that had been gross. Robin had brushed his teeth a dozen times today, he was sure. But he'd been so wrapped up in Mac's words he'd let the kisses happen. He was still to blame.

Poor Dair.

How was Robin going to face him? He'd humiliated himself in bed and confused the poor man with his sexuality…

Or was Mac right? Had Dair taken advantage of Robin's stupid crush?

The coffee rolled around in his stomach like acid. This was why he hadn't dated in a decade. He'd just mess everything up.

Peyton squeezed his knee. "Earth to Robin?"

He blinked. "Huh?"

She looked at him sympathetically. "You really do like him, don't you?" Robin shrugged. "Look, *talk* to him later. Properly. Don't tell him what he's thinking. Ask. I bet you it'll all turn out okay."

Robin sighed. He didn't really believe her, but he appreciated she was only trying to help. "Okay. You still going to crash the reunion?" Robin asked hopefully, trying to shift the subject. "Jay said he'd totally sneak you in as his plus one."

Peyton snorted. "Like anyone would believe me and him were a thing. Yeah, sure. But I might come a little later. If people are full of beer, they might be less likely to point at me and go 'Who's that magnificent lesbian? I definitely would have remembered her from school!'"

Robin laughed, feeling a tiny bit of relief from his melancholy. He could always rely on Peyton to cheer him up. The despair quickly slipped back in, but he tried his best to hide it. "All right, I think I'll get in the shower." And not fret about if or when Dair was going to come back here.

It would be easier said than done.

They stood and Peyton gave him a long, hard hug. "Good man. You'll see. It'll all work out in the end."

The fact she had said something very similar a second ago didn't encourage him, but he appreciated her confidence in him anyway.

He wasn't normally one for fussing over his appearance, but that evening Robin spent over an hour in the bathroom. He showered, shaved, clipped his finger and toenails, and trimmed any wayward little hairs from his ears. Then he spent ages putting his contacts in.

It had been a long time since he'd bothered and he was a little out of practice. But seeing as he was getting all dressed up, he felt like he might as well go the whole way. If he was doing his best not to look nerdy, the glasses had to go. For tonight, at least.

It was like he was afraid to stop getting ready and leave the bathroom. Once he did that, he'd have to face the reality that Dair had probably changed his mind and Robin would be going to the reunion alone.

Maybe he shouldn't go at all.

He tried. He'd supported Jay all week. But what would going tonight accomplish? If he went without Dair, he'd been hyperaware of what he'd lost. If he did, by some chance, go with him, could he face pretending all evening?

That would kill him if he had to introduce people to his 'boyfriend' the whole event, knowing that it was not only fake, but that it *could* have been real.

Urgh. Enough. He couldn't live the rest of his days in his parents' bathroom, no matter how tempting the thought seemed. He splashed aftershave on his neck, then finally vacated the bathroom to head back to his room.

Except his room was already occupied.

He froze on the threshold, only wearing a towel around his waist. Dair was dressed to the nines in a crisp, classic black suit jacket and pants with a fresh bright white shirt. His black shoes were polished so they gleamed, and he smelled of that gorgeous spicy scent he wore.

Robin was amazed his knees didn't buckle.

"Hi," Dair said guiltily. "I did call before I came over, but I guess you were in the shower." Robin looked down at his phone on the dresser. Sure enough, the tiny light was blinking to indicate he had notifications. "My clothes were here. I hope you don't mind?"

Robin tried to stop covering up his scrawny chest, but he was too self-conscious. Only yesterday morning he'd jerked off for Dair on that very bed. He felt deeply ashamed as he hugged himself.

"N-no, not at all. Uh, so, you still want to come tonight?"

"It's the whole reason I came to Pine Cove." Dair raised his eyebrows.

Of course. He was dutiful down to the end. He was a former Marine and had a job to do.

Robin nodded. "Cool. Okay. Well, I'll get dressed, and we can maybe head over? It's starting soon. Jay will want us to be there from the beginning. He's already at the country club doing final prep work. I think he's kind of nervous." Robin bit his tongue to stop himself babbling. "So," he said more slowly, "I can meet you downstairs when I'm dressed?"

Dair nodded and moved toward the door. Robin awkwardly tried to step aside. For a moment, they were chest to chest.

Then Robin scurried further into the room, putting some space between them. Heaven forbid he do something awful like throw himself into Dair's arms again. What the hell had he been thinking?

Dair paused at the door. Fuck, he looked obscenely stunning. There was still a rugged edge to him, but his new look showed he could apply the care he took in looking after others and scrub up himself, too. Robin loved it. He wished with all his heart he could walk over and wrap his arms around Dair's muscular frame, but he just couldn't.

Yes, he'd screwed up not pushing Mac's advances off quick enough. But the bigger issue was that he and Dair were just too different. It would never work, and Robin had embarrassed himself enough already.

Dair looked at him from where he'd stopped. "I was hoping we could talk sometime tonight."

Robin nodded. "Yes, let's talk." With any luck, they might be able to smooth over the last couple of days and try and save something of their friendship. Robin would feel awful if Dair had to move out of the apartment. And – oh *god.* He'd have to find another pet-friendly place! The thought of his taking his little pack of pets with him was even worse than just him leaving. Robin would miss the fur babies just as much as their dad.

No. He'd make things less awkward and hopefully not uproot Dair's life. They might even be able to act normally as friends again after a while.

The thought gave him a little spark of optimism as he put his own suit on, carefully tying his tie and fastening his Space Invader-shaped cufflinks. Looking absently around the room, he realized with a jolt that Dair had brought his giant stuffed koala back and sat him in the desk chair. Considering his size, he would have thought he'd have noticed it right away. But he guessed his mind was distracted.

Robin went over and stroked his soft fur. If Dair and he could get through this awkward mistake, maybe he'd still keep the koala here in his room? But he doubted he'd take him back to Seattle. Every time Robin looked at him, he'd remind himself of what he'd almost had but lost.

Taking a long, deep breath, Robin looked himself over one last time in his mirror with all the rainbow stickers around the edge. No more moping. The theme tonight was 'Prom Throwback.' He'd been a little excited to actually bring a date this time around, considering last time he, Jay, and Emery had all gone stag together. Dair wasn't exactly his date anymore, but he was still accompanying Robin for the night.

Except his mom didn't know that.

"Just one more photo!" she pleaded.

She rearranged them in front of the fireplace for the thousandth time as Kestrel watched on, giggling and playing with Smudge. She was very happy to be on dog-sitting duty for the evening. "Aww, our little baby Robin is all grown up."

"Shut up," Robin mumbled, trying not to feel too awkward. Even if they were actually dating, this would be embarrassing. But after everything that had gone down the past couple of days, it was completely heartbreaking. Before it would have just been bizarre. Now Robin knew what he'd lost, and he didn't know if he'd ever feel like that again.

Eventually, they were released, and Robin ordered an Uber immediately. The sooner they got out of the house, the quicker he would stop having to hug Dair. It was a strange kind of torture.

Why the hell was he still going on with this charade, anyway? He supposed he didn't want to tell the rest of his family he'd been lying to them. He'd just message the group chat next week and tell them he and Dair had decided it would be better if they just stayed friends.

They were quiet on the drive over to the country club by the lake. Luckily, their driver had the radio on loudly playing pop music and kept a mostly one-sided conversation up on his thoughts about the local bat population.

Robin had attended a couple of weddings at The Peaks Country Club growing up. It was a large, one-story complex nestled amongst the pines, backing onto the town's lake. The exterior walls were white and the roof tiles sage green. The Stars and Stripes fluttered gently on a flag pole out front in the evening breeze.

Their Uber pulled up around the circular lawn at the end of the long driveway. Plenty of people were milling around already, and Robin felt a flicker of nerves.

He looked over in surprise as Dair squeezed his hand twice. Double Dair, looking out for Robin yet again. "You've got this."

Robin wanted to ask why he was being so kind to him. As far as Dair was concerned, Robin had cheated on him. Not that Robin would, ever, *ever*, do that. Mac had kissed him without invitation, and in any case, he and Dair hadn't agreed to be exclusive yet. But if this thing between them was doomed anyway, what was the point of trying to clear up the facts?

Mac was right. Robin was fundamentally broken.

But he could be a good friend, he was sure. This way, he was saving Dair from a crappy relationship too. So he smiled back at him and nodded. "Let's go."

The inside of the country club was all magnolia walls, pale wooden floors, and glass chandeliers. Like the basketball game, Jay's team had worked hard to decorate the place in the school colors. They'd hired a photo booth with silly props that people would no doubt make extensive use of later, and there were more boards on display easels depicting events from the four years their class had spent together at Pine Cove High.

For a while, Robin and Dair walked around, holding hands and occasionally talking to other people, but not each other. When Dair excused himself to use the restroom, Robin got lost in the growing crowd, taking advantage of the servers walking around with trays of complimentary Champagne.

He hadn't seen Jay yet, but that wasn't surprising. He was probably run ragged, making sure the catering was on time and the sound system was all set up correctly. According to the schedule, the speeches were due at nine from their valedictorian and prom queen and other important members of the student body. Then the band would start playing to see them through the rest of the night.

It was past eight o'clock, and the sun had just about dipped down past the mountains on the horizon. Alone, Robin pushed his way through one of the function suite doors into the fresh summer air, breathing deeply. There were a few people milling around by the building, but Robin slowly walked down the pier by himself, his Champagne flute dangling from his fingers.

The water lapped all around the jetty as he reached the end, making him slightly nervous. But he was safe here on the narrow dock. In fact, he could take some comfort from looking out over the beautiful rippling waters, the Washington vista rising from the shore in all its glory. It was a soothing view.

Robin really did love it here. He'd be sad to go back to Seattle, but that was where he belonged.

However, he realized with a jolt he *wanted* to belong in Pine Cove. He had never intended to leave and stay away so long. He was angry at how he sabotaged himself for so many years. Despite everything else, he vowed to himself to try and come back and visit more often. He loved his family, especially Jay. Being back with his twin felt so right. Robin didn't want to throw that all away again.

He looked down at the quaint little rowboat still tethered to the side of the dock, bobbing away. Robin had been scared of these waters his whole life, but now he found he didn't want to abandon them again.

A moment of recklessness took over him. He placed his Champagne flute down on the jetty, sat down at the edge, and dangled his legs over the boat. It was only a foot to drop down...so he did.

He froze, his arms flung out for balance. But he remained standing.

He was on the water.

He let out a nervous giggle, quickly grabbing his drink for courage and sitting his ass down in one of the boat's seats to stabilize it again. Below the dock, the party disappeared from view. He laughed again in disbelief at his own bravado. He'd never done anything like this before.

Sipping his Champagne, he listened to the waves lapping around him. The shore was several feet away, so water surrounded the boat. It was scary but kind of freeing, too.

Now he could look up at the mountains around the lake and feel like he was totally alone. For that moment, it brought him comfort. His worries about Dair were briefly replaced with pride at his own bravery.

Of course, it didn't last.

"Hey."

He wasn't surprised to hear Mac's voice come from up behind him.

He was very surprised when Mac dropped into the boat beside him.

There was room enough for two, but irritation spiked through Robin. For fuck's sake, couldn't Mac just let him have a moment to himself? Apparently not.

Robin sighed. What was the point in getting mad at him again, though? He was irrelevant. Robin didn't care about Mac when his heart was full of confusion and regret for Dair. Mac should never have kissed Robin like he had, but his only real crime aside from that had been to tell Robin some home truths about him and Dair. Was that really his fault? He was just the messenger.

So Robin turned to face him. Not with a smile, but not with hostility either.

"Hey."

"Are you okay?"

Robin shrugged and looked back out over the lake. "Yeah. Pretty much."

Mac was wearing cream chinos with a white shirt and objectively did look gorgeous. But Robin didn't feel that spark he had as a teenager, when he'd been overwhelmed by lust and disbelief a guy like that would be with a guy like him.

He just felt neutral, which was kind of nice after the last couple of days. Yeah, Mac was still a dick. But that wasn't Robin's problem anymore.

"I'm sorry about yesterday." Rather than look at Robin, Mac was gazing at the mountains beyond the lake. He sipped his own Champagne that he'd managed not to spill while getting into the boat. "I must have misread the signals you were giving me. I shouldn't have kissed you."

"No," Robin agreed with a sigh. "But I get what you were trying to say. So, thanks for that, I guess."

Mac smiled at him for that. "It's okay. I did mean it about wanting to start over and be friends." He stuck out his hand. "What do you say?"

What *did* Robin say? Well, he wasn't going to be sticking around town, and Mac had talked about moving to Portland anyway. So what was the harm?

"Sure." He shook the proffered hand.

They sat and looked out over the lake for a while together. The music from the party pulsed quietly in the background, occasionally swelling when someone opened a door. The speeches must be soon, so they should probably head back in in a bit. But Robin wanted to enjoy the peace and quiet for a little longer, even if he was sharing the moment with Mac. If he closed his eyes, it was like he was alone, anyway.

"Hey," Mac said out of the blue with a laugh. "Do you remember that time after the Lumberjacks won that big game and we convinced a bunch of other kids to go play water guns out in the woods? Someone bought a ton of beer and a CD player, and we stayed out all night."

Robin blinked. "Oh my god, I'd forgotten all about that! That was so epic. We were like rock stars for a week." He grinned, genuinely reveling in the memory of one of the best nights of his adolescence. That night had shown the best side of Mac, where he was fun and loving and carefree.

If only he could be like that all the time.

He nudged Robin's shoulder and looked down at the rowboat's oars. "Let's do something else crazy to commemorate the occasion."

Robin raised his eyebrows. "Like what?" He didn't want to spoil the moment, but he'd been wary enough just getting into the boat. What was Mac suggesting?

"Just a little ride on the water." Mac smiled and shrugged. "Not quite as outrageous and no worrying our parents sick this time." He laughed. "I'll row. We can finish our Champagne, look at the stars, then head back in time for the speeches."

He handed Robin his glass and picked up the rope, already untying it. Shit. What should Robin do? Try and scramble out?

Robin bit his lip and looked out at the lake. Did that really sound so scary? Yes, even just looking at the dark water made his stomach flip. But he'd already managed to get himself into the boat. There was no need to swim. And he was tired of saying no to things and being afraid all the time. There was more to life than sitting behind his computer working on code or playing video games.

With a lurch, he realized he needed to make up his mind right now, as Mac moved to the other seat, wrapped his hands around the oars, and pushed them away from the dock.

Robin thought of Dair.

If Robin was more adventurous, more alive, maybe there was a tiny chance Dair *would* want to be with him. If he went back with a story of how he'd conquered one of his biggest fears, maybe Dair might be interested in him beyond his disappointing skills in bed.

It was worth a shot.

Robin took a deep breath and nodded. They were several feet onto the lake now, anyway. He might as well go for it.

"Why the hell not? Let's do this."

21

DAIR

"Okay. You can do this."

Dair leaned over the sink and looked at his reflection in the restroom. No one else happened to be using the facilities for that precise moment, so Dair used the opportunity to give himself a stern talking to.

He'd been wallowing all day and it needed to stop, now. It was clear Robin was upset as well, so they needed to sit down and go over everything from yesterday to work out what went so wrong.

Yes, Dair was hurt Robin would kiss Mac so soon after kissing him. That felt awful. But he and Mac had a lot of history, and Dair felt like he could forgive a little mistake if one had been made. Besides, he hadn't even asked Robin for his full version of events yet. What if he told a totally different story?

Dair was angry at himself for letting Mac get under his skin and make his already existing insecurities worse. Peyton had warned him that was what he did, so Dair should have known better.

Robin looked simply gorgeous tonight, leaving Dair

tongue-tied as to what to say. But taking a moment to himself in the restroom had given him the chance to re-center and work out what he wanted to do.

He was going to march out there and tell Robin he was damned crazy about him, beg for a chance to talk things through, then if there was any justice, pull him somewhere dark and quiet to show him just how he felt with his long, luxurious kisses.

Dair couldn't imagine not holding Robin close again or tasting his lips or hearing those beautiful sounds he made when he was lost and free in pleasure. Dair splashed some water onto his face and resolved to do whatever it took to heal the rift that had come between them.

Except when Dair returned to the party, Robin was nowhere to be seen.

He did two full circuits of the function room as it filled with more and more people from Robin's class. The women were dressed in a variety of different colored evening gowns, but most of the men were wearing dark suits. With the lights dimmed for atmosphere, Dair strained to distinguish between the smaller guys. But no, none of them were Robin, he was certain.

Shit. He wouldn't have gone home, would he? Dair wasn't in the bathroom that long. Just as he pulled his phone out to see there were no messages or missed calls from Robin, he sensed someone approach.

"Okay – what's going on?"

Dair pocketed his cell and looked up to see Jay descend on him, flanked by Emery and Ava. She must have been Emery's plus-one for the night. Jay was looking at Dair expectantly.

"With Robin?" Dair guessed.

"Yes, with Robin," Jay said impatiently. "I distinctly remembered you telling you not to hurt him. But Kestrel says he's been acting heartbroken all day and you only came to the house to get changed."

Dair scowled. "I didn't hurt him. Not that I know of. He's the one who's having second thoughts or whatever. I don't know if Mac got in his head or what, but-"

"Why am I not surprised?" Emery interrupted, throwing his hands up in the air. He was one of the only guys not wearing a traditional suit. Instead he was rocking an open fitted blazer, a tank with a gauzy scarf, a slanted knee-length pleather skirt, and biker boots, accessorized with a don't-fuck-with-me attitude and black eyeliner.

"What does Mac have to do with this?" Ava asked, crossing her arms. She was wearing pants and a shirt rather than a dress, which didn't surprise Dair.

He sighed. "I saw him and Mac kiss last night. Mac said they broke up because Robin likes to mess around with straight guys and how he cheated on him back at school. That's why they broke up-"

"The FUCK?" Emery exploded.

Dair took a step back.

"Mac cheated on *Robin*," Jay growled. "Then had the nerve to tell him it was *Robin's* fault because he wasn't good enough in bed."

"Robin doesn't think we know that," Ava added. "But he has a terrible poker face."

"I'm going to kill him," Emery cried, throwing his hands up. "Where is he? My little Asian ass is going to go old-style kung fu on that fucking mother-*fucker*."

"Wow, okay, what did I miss?"

Peyton bounced up by Dair's side, and he immediately enveloped her in a relieved hug. He'd run away from her at the motel, not able to face her wrath for upsetting Robin. But now he'd do whatever it took to set things right.

Were they right? Had Mac been talking complete shit? Dair had suspected as much. He was a goddamned fool.

Ava's eyes were wide looking at Peyton's pretty pink tutu dress and contrasting black leather jacket and knee-high boots. "Oh, hey, Peyton. You look…punctual."

"Aw, thanks, Ava, you too."

Emery clicked his fingers into the middle of the circle. "Back to Mac being a lying little narcissistic shit claiming that Robin was the one who cheated on him and not the other way around."

"The FUCK?" Peyton exclaimed.

"That's what *I* said," Emery agreed.

"Dair, did you actually *see* Robin kiss Mac last night?" Jay asked.

Dair chewed on his lip. "No. Mac just said Robin made the first move. What I saw was Mac leaning in to kiss Robin and Robin not protesting."

"Oh, he protested all right," Peyton scoffed. "How long did you stay? He told me he yelled at Mac, shoved him off, and ran away."

Dair took a second to think. Could that have happened after the second kiss he almost saw?

"That sounds more likely," Jay agreed.

Dair felt like a first-class idiot. "God. Mac told me Robin got his kicks from, um, luring straight guys into bed, then dumping them. I thought I'd been had."

"One hundred percent false," Peyton said, her eyes blazing. Dair felt smaller than her for the first time ever. "If anything, he actively avoids guys who claim to be straight. Who needs that hassle? Why didn't you just ask Robin himself?"

"When I tried to talk to Robin over the phone, he said we'd rushed into things," Dair cried defensively. "It was his idea to cool things off, and he didn't deny the kiss."

Jay made a frustrated noise. "I bet Mac fed him some BS about you using him for sex, then moving on because he convinced Robin he was shit in bed. That was always what he said other guys would do if Robin broke up with him. Fuck. Okay, where's Robin now? And where's Mac, for that matter?"

Dair shook his head. "I looked around the room twice before running into you guys. I'm not sure where he went."

"I don't like this." Emery squinted at the crowd. "My Spidey-sense is tingling."

"Let's split up," suggested Ava. "Meet back here in ten minutes."

Jay checked his watch. "Fifteen minutes until the speeches. Okay, everything's set up and the other guys can handhold the speakers. Let's go, team."

Dair headed to the men's restrooms again to start with, but there was no sign of Robin. Fuck, his guts were twisted with worry. How could he have been so gullible? He'd let Mac play his own anxieties like a damn violin. Now Robin was missing, and for someone with little imagination, Dair's mind was certainly racing.

Had Mac seduced Robin and taken him home? Or worse, could he have him cornered somewhere against his will? Was he filling his mind with poison again that Dair was only interested in him for sex?

Bad sex?

That was especially crazy to Dair. He knew he only had one other person in his life to compare it to, but he was absolutely certain they'd had a mind-blowing time the other night and morning. Damn what anyone else thought, Dair had fucking loved it. He'd been desperate to get Robin back in the sack and see what else they could do.

But that was beside the point. He wanted to snuggle on the couch and drink more hot chocolate. When they got back home, he wanted to hold hands while taking Smudge and Jimmy for long walks. He wanted to come out to his colleagues, even though the thought terrified him. But he didn't want to hide who he was or what Robin meant to him.

He wanted to shout it from the rooftops.

"Hey, have you seen Robin Coal?" he stopped and asked a guy he recognized from the basketball game the other night.

The basketball player frowned for a second, then raised his eyebrows in realization. "That guy Mac used to date? I remember. Mac dumped his ass for cheating on him." He scoffed and shook his head. "Sorry, I can't help you."

Dair seethed. So, he wasn't the only one Mac had been lying to. Just how long had he been spreading rumors about Robin to make himself look like the victim?

"Don't believe everything that asshole says," he grumbled as he moved away from the basketball player. Another sweep of the room confirmed Robin was nowhere to be seen.

Feeling dejected and more than a little concerned, Dair headed back to their rendezvous point just as Peyton got there. "Any joy?" she asked. He shook his head.

"Me neither," said Jay as he approached. He checked his watch. "But hopefully he'll be back in the hall for the speeches. Let's stick together for now and keep an eye out."

"Nope." Ava was holding hands with a fretful-looking Emery as they pushed through the throng back to them.

"Someone outside saw Robin go down the pier," Emery said between pants. Dair hadn't even thought about looking outside. Shit. "Then someone *else* said he got into the rowboat with a blond guy. That's got to be Mac, right?"

"Robin got into a *boat?*" Peyton exclaimed.

"But he can't swim," Dair and Jay cried in unison.

Ava nodded grimly. "We looked. There are no boats there now."

"But he said he'd never go out on the lake," Dair said as if that might change something.

"Let's go look," Jay said just as a woman with an iPad approached him.

"Jay, we need you to-"

"Someone else will have to do it, sorry."

He and Dair weaved past her and the rest of the crowd, leading Emery, Ava, and Peyton through one of the doors of the function suite and outside. Dair's long legs meant he was the first to march to the end of the jetty. But like Ava had said, there were no boats in sight.

He swallowed and resisted the urge to shout Robin's name at the top of his lungs. It sounded like Robin had gotten into the boat willingly. Dair would just wait here until they returned. In the meantime, he squinted in the darkness, desperate to catch a glimpse of anything on the water.

But there was nothing. Just the moonlight reflecting off the ripples. Their small rowboat must be lost in the shadows.

"I hope he's okay." Peyton chewed her thumbnail as she stood beside Dair, the other three congregating around them. "Mac wouldn't...*do* anything, would he? I've never met him."

Dair and the others just hummed and growled.

"Let's just say, I'll be *much* happier when they get back to shore," Dair said.

Anxiously, the five of them stood at the end of the pier listening for any sign for their wayward friend and brother. Behind them, the music died, and the muffled tones of someone speaking into the mic drifted through the air.

"Come on, Robin. Come back to me," Dair muttered under his breath.

His guilt for ever doubting Robin was strong. He couldn't change the past twenty-four hours, though. All he could do was be here for when Robin returned.

And hope it wasn't too late to win back his heart.

22

ROBIN

EVEN THOUGH ROBIN HAD A DEATH GRIP ON THE SIDE OF THE boat, he had to admit it was beautiful out on the lake. All he could hear was the gentle lapping of the water against the wood and the steady *swish-swoosh* of Mac pulling on the oars.

It was calm and peaceful out here. The lights of the country club diminished as they moved further from the shore. The mountains loomed behind Mac, blotting out some of the stars. Robin thought maybe he heard the sound of pine trees rustling across the lake, but that might well just have been his imagination.

He'd held both their Champagne flutes in one hand while Mac had rowed them across the water. They were pretty far out when he stopped, enough that Robin might struggle to point the exact direction they needed to row back in if it wasn't for the faint glow of the party. But they had only been going for maybe five minutes, so they couldn't be that far away.

"Wow, this is amazing. I'm glad I suggested it." Mac let out a breath and looked up at the stars. Robin passed him back his glass, quickly pulling away again so Mac wouldn't try and cheers. They weren't there anymore. Mac just happened to be here, steering the boat. Robin was doing this for himself.

And Dair.

Robin nodded, trying to keep his panic low. Everything was fine. In fact, he was fucking proud of himself for facing one of his greatest fears. Wait until he told Jay that he'd been out on the lake he'd avoided his whole life!

Somewhere overhead, an owl hooted. Robin wondered if the speeches had started. He felt kind of bad for ditching them. But he couldn't even remember who the valedictorian was now, and if he recalled correctly, the prom queen had been a thoroughly unpleasant girl who, rumor had it, had given her competitor food poisoning to snatch the crown.

He wished desperately he could be out here with Dair, but perhaps now he would get a chance to show Dair he'd conquered one of his phobias. Robin would do anything to see that look on Dair's face again like at the shooting gallery. Knowing he'd impressed his crush was a potent feeling. Even if things were rocky between them right now.

"Are you having fun?" Mac asked.

Robin nodded, then remembered how dark it was. His night vision was improving the longer they were away from the lights of the country club, but it was still damned shadowy.

"Yes, thank you," he said. "This was a really fun idea."

"See, we *do* have fun together, don't we?"

Uh-oh. Robin should have really thought this through. If Mac wanted to pitch to him about getting back together again, Robin couldn't exactly walk off. He just hummed in response, hoping Mac would take the hint and let it drop.

Instead, Mac stood up, making the boat lurch and Robin's heart stutter. But they didn't tip. Mac was confident as he crossed the space between the front and back of the boat.

There was just enough room for him to sit down next to Robin.

Shit. Should Robin move to the other end? He really didn't trust himself to stand in the damn boat, though, and he wasn't about to crawl over there in front of Mac.

So he just gave him a small smile that he knew didn't reach his eyes and looked out over the lake.

Mac put his arm around Robin's waist.

Double fucking shit.

"Um, sorry," he said, shifting his weight. "I didn't mean to give you the wrong impression. But I'm still sorting things out with Dair. I just thought we were going to look at the stars?"

Mac chuckled. "Fuck Dair. Oh, wait, you already did that." He grinned.

Shame flared through Robin. He was glad it was dark so his blush wouldn't be seen on his face. "Mac," he said in a warning tone. God damn it. He knew he should have gotten out of the boat when he'd had the chance.

Mac hugged him closer and Robin's heart started to beat faster. "Come on, it's just us out here in our own little world. No one needs to know anything. I've missed you."

He pressed his lips to Robin's neck.

Robin jerked so violently he sent his Champagne flute flying into the water with a splash. Knowing that it was now going to sink all the way to the bottom probably never to be seen again made Robin feel physically sick. But he still managed to use the side of the boat to drag himself off the seat.

"Robin! What the fuck?" Mac cried.

Robin scrambled to the other seat and steadied himself enough to sit back down. His heart was hammering with adrenaline.

"I didn't come out here to make out," he stammered.

Mac knocked back his own Champagne, then flung the empty glass as far as he could out into the water with a faint plop.

"Why do you keep leading me on? Oh my god, I'm such a fool. Robin, if it's that guy Dair, don't tell me you actually think there's something serious between you? I'm the only one patient enough to put up with your crap." He sighed and rubbed his face. "Sweetheart, please," he continued in a softer tone. "You know we make sense. This is so romantic. Don't ruin it. I'm just trying to create some more special memories for us."

Robin balled up his fists, cursing himself for trusting Mac to be selfless for once in his life. Of course he had to go and sully this moment of Robin triumphing over one of his biggest fears.

But perhaps *he* was the selfish one? Maybe he had missed a sign from Mac that this was supposed to be a seduction. He figured if he was out here with Dair, it could have been romantic...

...except he knew for sure that Dair would never pressure him into anything sexual, especially when he was dealing with such a phobia. If Dair was here, he'd hold Robin's hand and tell him he was so brave.

Not try and jump his bones.

"Mac, I don't want to create more special memories. I don't want to get back together."

"Oh, like you could do any better than *me?*" Mac scoffed.

Robin flashed him a scathing look, not caring if it was too dark for him to see it. "Yes, actually, I can. I'm done with you always putting me down. I'm not perfect, nobody is. But I'm all right. In fact-"

He thought of the way Dair had marveled at his aim at the fair or always complimented him on his technical skills.

The way he'd worshiped him in bed.

"-in fact, I'm actually kind of great. And I want to go back to the party now, please."

He folded his arms and refused to look at Mac. Instead, he watched the ripples rebounding off the side of the little boat. No matter what, they just kept on going. They were resilient.

Just like Robin had to be.

A splash of water against his skin made him jump and snap his head back around in shock. Mac was shaking droplets from his hand. He'd obviously hit the surface of the lake in temper, sprinkling Robin in the process.

The cold water was nothing to the coldness that rushed through Robin's body.

Mac looked furious.

"You were nothing without me," he seethed. "Some little geeky virgin who couldn't even fuck right. Still can't, I bet. I made you *cool*. No one would ever have thought twice about you in that room if it wasn't for me. I bet they've *all* forgotten about you!"

Robin gripped the side of the boat tightly and pointed back to the faint light of the party. "I don't give a flying fuck what those people say or don't say about me, Mac. That was always *your* insecurity. I care what my family and friends think. And I know they're going to be livid that I was stupid enough to trust you again. But it's the last time, I swear to god. Now, row us back to shore right this second, or I'll do it myself."

He wasn't sure he'd be able to make the boat move at all, let alone have enough strength to get them across the lake. But he'd damned well try to get himself out of this situation. Genuine fear was creeping into his heart.

With good reason.

Mac lunged forward, grabbing either side of the boat edges and looming over Robin. "I can't believe you," he snarled. "You treat me like shit. This is why no one else will ever want you. You're a *terrible* boyfriend, Robin. But it's okay. I still love you. I'll make it better."

He seized Robin by the chin and smushed their faces together for a painful imitation of a kiss.

Robin shoved with everything he had, sending Mac reeling backward and the boat rocking violently from side to side.

Robin gasped several times, gripping onto the sides for dear life and trying not to let his panic overwhelm him. "I don't want to kiss you, Mac!" he yelled. "I don't want to have sex with you! I don't even ever want to see you again after this! *Take us back!*"

Mac regained his footing and wiped his mouth with the back of his hand. He glowered down at Robin with an awful smirk on his lips.

"You're so fucking selfish. It's always about what *you* want, isn't it? What about me? *My* needs? You *owe* me, Robin Coal. It about fucking time you paid up."

He lunged forward, seizing Robin by the lapels of his jacket, trying to drag him closer. Robin screamed and shoved against his hold, doing his best to wriggle free.

"Get OFF me," he bellowed.

But Mac wrestled him onto his back in the bottom of the boat. Then he dropped on top of him.

Terror like Robin had never known filled his heart. What exactly did Mac intend to do?

Robin had no intention of finding out.

He scratched at Mac's face, making him scream. Robin slapped and pushed at his chest, forcing him up enough that Robin could scramble loose.

"Back the fuck off, Mac!" he yelled.

He realized with a thrill that under one of the seats, among some dried pine needles and old candy bar wrappers, there was a large flashlight tucked away. He grabbed it and swung it, catching Mac on his shoulder with a crack and sending him tumbling back again. He must have accidentally clicked the switch, because the beam of light suddenly cut through the darkness.

"Are you fucking *high?*" Mac screeched. "Why are you *hitting* me?"

"Because I told you 'no,' asshole!" Robin shouted back. He held the flashlight up in front of him like a sword. "Listen to me! It's not happening. Whatever little fantasy you imagined, I'm not your plaything. I'm not your boyfriend – I'm not your anything! So take us back to shore *right now*, and I'll think about not pressing charges!"

"Pressing charges?" Mac laughed hollowly as he rubbed the spot on his arm where Robin had smacked him. "After all that pathetic fuss you made about me accidentally pushing you *one time* you go, and attack me with a blunt weapon! *I* should press charges against *you!* Not to mention the emotional abuse you've put me through. It's too much, Robin. You make me so fucking *mad.*"

He lurched across the boat again. Robin swung with the flashlight, but Mac was almost twice his size.

As Mac grabbed him around the waist, forcing him backward, Robin dropped the flashlight back into the bottom of the boat.

He wasn't so lucky.

The boat rocked, sloshing water over the edge and drenching their clothes. He tried to push free from Mac as they stumbled over the slippery wood, but Mac was too heavy.

The back of Robin's calves hit the edge of the boat. He released Mac to pinwheel his arms, but it was useless. Mac was already falling against him.

They both hit the cold water with an almighty splash.

Robin did the worst thing he could in his panic and gasped, filling his mouth with water. He spat and thrashed, but he couldn't tell which way was up. It was pitch black in the few seconds he opened his eyes, but then he closed them and his mouth against the water.

Holy fuck.

He was going to drown.

He was never going to see his family again.

Or Dair.

Dair.

He'd never get to tell him how sorry he was. He'd never be able to try and make things work between them.

No, no, no! He was going to fight! He wasn't giving up! He beat his arms and legs, desperately searching for the surface.

He wasn't going to leave Dair.

But the darkness was somehow getting darker, and he was going from painfully freezing to flat out numb. His limbs were slowing as the water became heavier.

He didn't know what else to do. His thoughts were slowing down like molasses and his lungs burned.

Dair, he thought, heartbroken.

Then he wasn't sure what happened, but he was pretty sure it was over.

23

DAIR

"He's still not answering his phone." Jay hung up and tapped his cell against his chin.

Dair didn't take his eyes off the lake as he shook his head. "He always has it on silent." He cursed under his breath and chewed his thumbnail. He kept swaying between gut-wrenching dread for Robin's safety and horrible jealousy that he and Mac might actually be having a romantic tryst.

That didn't seem likely considering everyone's reactions and what he knew now about the events of yesterday. But Dair had been pulled from pillar to post over the past few days, and right now he didn't feel like he knew anything for sure. Ultimately, Dair knew it would be better if Robin was having a make-out session with a douchebag than be in any actual danger. But either way, he was going out of his mind.

The speeches were underway behind them in the hall and the sound of the crowd applauding drifted through the night air. It seemed weird that they were all just having a fun time reminiscing the good old days when Dair and the others were out here worrying themselves into a state.

He couldn't help but feel like this was all his fault. If he'd just gotten over himself and *talked* to Robin openly like Peyton had said, none of this would be happening. If any harm came to Robin because of him-

He froze, straining his ears with everything he had.

"Did you hear that?" he rasped.

"What?" Ava asked.

"It sounded like shouting…?"

"Fuck," Emery hissed wringing his hands.

Dair didn't breathe, desperate for more. Then it came, so faint it could have been just the wind. But Dair knew what he heard.

It was a scream.

He didn't even register his suit jacket was off until he'd flung it into Peyton's arms. "Dair!" she called, but Dair was already sprinting the few feet to the end of the pier, kicking his shoes off as he ran.

He dove into the cold lake and started swimming as fast as he could.

No, no, no! he screamed in his head. *Don't you hurt him, you bastard. I'll kill you!*

He was swimming blindly, his muscles pumping as he pushed them against the frigid water. "Robin!" he called out between strokes. He still couldn't see the boat, but he thought he heard more shouting over the water rushing over his ears. "Robin, I'm coming!"

Goddamn it, why couldn't there be a bigger moon? The slim crescent wasn't doing anything to help Dair distinguish any shapes among the waves around him. His teeth chattered as he stopped and tried to get his bearings. His clothes tried to drag him under as he trod water and the cold was seeping into his bones. The fact that it was summer didn't seem to have had any effect on the water temperature. He wondered how deep this lake was.

"Robin!" he bellowed.

He didn't get any reply, but a few seconds later, a light swung wildly, cutting through the inky blackness. Dair's heart lurched. It was maybe thirty or forty feet away from him. It seemed to steady and then point upwards.

It *had* to be Robin.

He started swimming again, praying he wasn't too late. There was more shouting. Dair could discern two separate voices, but not the exact words. He might have heard a 'no,' though, and that made him drive his body through the water even faster.

There was a loud splash and Dair fumbled to a halt. "Robin?" he yelled, terror creeping up his throat. "ROBIN!"

Oh god.

Dair covered the last twenty feet at an inhuman rate. An empty rowboat finally came into sight.

Mac's head burst through the surface a dozen feet away as he coughed and spluttered. "Where's Robin!" Dair demanded.

"What the fuck? What the fuck are you doing here?" Mac spun around. "That *asshole* pushed me in."

"He can't *swim!*" Dair screamed at him, his fury rivaling his panic.

The light. There was something glowing in the boat. Dair sprinted to it. Sure enough, there was a large flashlight rolling around in the bottom of the damp boat. He snatched it up and angled it at the water, desperately looking for any sign of Robin.

"Where is he?" he cried. Fear and cold made the light shake in his hand.

"How the fuck should I know?" Mac snapped. "Fuck, I think my arm might be broken."

There! What was that? Dair shot forward, trying to get a clear view through the churning water. He swore he'd seen the pale flesh of a hand or something…

"Robin!"

Dair had never been very good at keeping his eyes open underwater, but he fucking managed it now as he plunged under the surface of the lake. He used one hand to pull himself down while he kicked frantically, the other hand still holding the flashlight to see by. He hoped it was properly waterproof, but he had no way to know. All he could do was get to Robin's sinking body before the light died on him.

Robin's arms and legs were twitching feebly. He hadn't quite given up, but it looked like he was fading fast. Dair's fingers seized Robin's jacket. However, even his slim form had been weighed down by his waterlogged clothes. So Dair released the flashlight, letting it fall rapidly through the depths as he grabbed Robin with both hands and began kicking with all he had.

His own lungs were just starting to protest.

How long had Robin been under?

There was no time to waste. Dair cycled his legs through the water, hoping he was moving toward the surface. Robin was a dead weight in his arms. Fuck. Dair didn't know what he'd possibly do if he was too late. *Stay with me, hon,* he thought frantically.

What the hell had happened? How had he and Mac ended up in the water? Robin would never have voluntarily gotten in, so Dair couldn't help but assume it was Mac's fault, the shithead.

He could worry about that in a minute. Right then, they suddenly broke through the surface into the night air, and he gasped as deep a breath in as he could manage.

"Robin!" he yelled as soon as his voice worked again. He shook Robin's body and held him close. He couldn't tell if he was breathing or if he had swallowed any water into his lungs. Awkwardly, Dair shifted his arms and jammed his fingers against Robin's throat.

He had a pulse.

"Robin!" Dair jostled him again. Was he going to have to perform the Heimlich maneuver?

All of a sudden, Robin's body jerked violently as he began to cough and splutter. His hands scrambled, finding purchase on Dair's arm still wrapped around his chest.

Dair released a sob of relief.

"Oh my god, are you okay?" he moaned, hugging Robin's freezing body to his own. "Hon, you scared the *shit* out of me."

Robin's teeth were chattering as he twisted in Dair's arms and blinked incredulous eyes at him. *"Dair?* Where – what?"

Dair kissed the side of his neck, hoping that was okay. But his heart was pounding and he still felt like he might cry. For a second, he had been forced to consider the possibility that Robin might truly have been taken away from him.

He never wanted to feel like that again.

"I heard you scream. I knew you'd come out here with Mac-"

Robin burst into tears. He scrambled around so he could fling his arms around Dair's neck. Dair was treading water for the both of them, but the fatigue after his mad sprint was starting to kick in. He began to gently ease them toward the bobbing boat so he could hold onto the edge to help keep them afloat.

"I'm so sorry," Robin cried.

"For what?"

Robin shook his head against Dair's cheek, his fingers gripping on to Dair's sodden shirt for dear life. "For trusting that asshole. I just wanted to be brave and do something crazy. I was so upset, missing you-"

"I'm right here," Dair assured him. "I'm not going anywhere."

They reached the boat and Dair's hand gratefully found the side.

"But last night-" Robin began.

Dair shook his head. "I talked to the others. I think Mac played us both. I'm sorry."

"You're...? But I didn't push him off quick enough."

Dair shook his head. "We can talk after we get out of the water. I just have to make something very clear. If you want to be with me, I want to be with you. No more dancing around. I want to be your boyfriend."

Robin was trembling with his own hand on the side of the boat. Dair hugged him close with his free arm, not willing to let him go just yet. Robin blinked, droplets of water clinging to his lashes, sparkling in the pale moonlight.

"You want...but I'm..."

Dair waited, but Robin didn't seem to know how to finish that sentence. Dair leaned forward and pressed his lips to Robin's temple. "Amazing? Gorgeous? Cute as hell and smarter than that?"

Robin bit his lip. "A dumbass?"

Dair chuckled, the relief still making him feel lightheaded. "We're both dumbasses, all right? So can we move on, be boyfriends, and get back into the boat?"

"What the actual *fuck* is wrong with you assholes?" Mac's sneering voice rang out from the other side of the boat. "You're both psychopaths. Don't think I won't be pressing charges against you both!"

Robin sighed and looked at Dair. "Do I even need to tell you he tried to kiss me, then pulled me into the water when I fought him off?"

"No." Dair hugged his beautiful man close and kissed his cheek. "Fuck him. Let's get you back into the boat, okay?"

Mac continued to mutter and hiss curses, but Dair ignored him. Instead, he gave Robin a boost so he could scramble his way into the rowboat. With his weight over the other side, Dair was able to hoist himself on board without tipping it too much or letting an obscene amount of water inside.

It was absolutely freezing out in the air again. Dair hugged Robin to him, trying to keep them both warm with their body heat. Once he was settled next to Robin, Dair reached his hand down to Mac, who was stubbornly treading water the other side. "Okay, come on. Get in."

Mac seemed to realize he was being addressed. He looked at Dair's hand in disgust. "Fuck off," he snarled. He even backed away a few feet.

Dair rolled his eyes. They didn't have time for this. "Don't be an ass. We're not leaving you out here."

"I'm not getting back in that thing with either of you," Mac shrieked back. "Robin, you've ruined my phone, my suit, *and* my shoes. What the hell were you thinking?"

Robin grabbed both sides of the boat and looked over the edge. "I was *thinking* that I said 'no.' Many, many times. But don't worry. I won't be saying it again, because we're really done this time, Mac. I never want to see you again. Don't call or text or email or slither into my DMs. Now hurry up and get into the damn boat so I can get on with never speaking to you for as long as I live."

He dropped back into his seat with a huff and crossed his arms. Dair felt his heart swelling with pride and…

…love.

He wasn't even surprised. Of course he loved Robin. They may have only been getting closer this week, but they'd known each other a few months now. He meant so much to Dair. No matter what, after tonight he was going to grab on to this relationship with both hands.

If that was what Robin wanted too.

As he snuggled against Dair's side, Dair felt pretty sure they were on the same page.

Mac slapped his hand across the water's surface,

spraying droplets everywhere. If some of them reached Dair and Robin, Dair couldn't tell. They were far too wet and cold.

And impatient.

"Get in," Dair growled.

"Fuck you, Army Boy," Mac spat back. "I'll fucking swim, all right? If you did it, it can't be that hard."

Dair huffed and grabbed the oars. They'd managed to cling on in their rings during the kerfuffle, thank goodness. Dair wanted to get him and Robin back to shore as fast as possible before they caught a chill. If Mac was such a stubborn ass he wanted to swim, screw him. He'd almost let Robin drown. Dair wasn't going to force him to let them take care of him.

It wouldn't be that far back to the country club with the advantage of a boat. Dair expected Robin to move and place himself on the other seat. Instead, he stomped his way in between Dair's legs, sat in the inch of water covering the length of the boat's base, and hugged Dair's calf while resting his head on his knee.

Dair smiled and gently stroked his wet hair back before picking up the oar handles. "Comfy?"

"Extremely," Robin grumbled, then kissed Dair's knee through his soggy pants.

Dair's heart swelled again.

They rowed through the night. As soon as they left Mac behind and his angry splashing, the Pine Cove lake was beautifully peaceful. Dair glanced over his shoulder every thirty seconds to make sure he was heading in the right direction still. But as they got closer, he realized the soft glow from the venue wasn't the golden light he expected.

It was flashing red and blue.

"Oh, crap," he said, not really sure what to expect.

Robin twisted around, sloshing the water around their

feet to look. "Holy fuck!" he hissed. "Oh my god, I'm never going to live this down!"

Dair steered the boat toward the end of the jetty. A pair of paramedics were beckoning them in alongside a cop, all of whom looked concerned with how wet Dair and Robin were.

Dair could hear Jay's voice. "Let me through! Robin, are you okay?"

"I'm fine," Robin called back miserably. He hid between Dair's legs while Dair snorted.

"It's okay, hon. They're just worried about you."

"Because I'm an idiot. What the hell was I thinking?"

He sounded so dejected Dair stopped rowing, even though they were only fifteen feet out. The boat continued to drift gently, but Dair hoped they'd get a few more seconds before they hit the dock.

"Hon," he said firmly, squeezing Robin's shoulder to get his attention. "You went out on a *boat*. I know it ended badly, but I'm so proud of you to face your fear. That was really brave."

Robin's topaz eyes widened. The flashing red and blue lights reflected off the whites. "Yeah – I was tired of being afraid."

Dair encouraged him to come sit in his lap, seeing as he was done rowing. He cradled Robin's cold, shivering body against him. "Well done. And as for the other shit – all I care about is that you're okay. That is all your friends and family will care too. I promise."

Robin scrubbed his face. "Thank you. I still feel really stupid. But – lesson finally learned, I guess. No more Mac." He pulled his hands from his face.

"Oh, no," Dair lamented, realizing he'd been rubbing his eyes. "You lost your glasses?"

Robin looked at him for a moment in confusion, then smiled. "No, I'm wearing contacts."

"Oh, good," said Dair in relief. "You're just not you without your glasses."

Robin's lip wobbled, just for half a second, before he broke into a magnificent smile. "I love you," he said in one rushed breath.

Wait – what?

"Sir, are you okay?" the lead paramedic cut in. The boat had drifted just close enough so that she could seize the edge and drag them against the dock. Then it was a flurry of bodies as Robin and Dair were pulled up onto the jetty. The paramedics were inspecting them for injuries as a firefighter threw a blanket over each of their shoulders and the cop asked them what the hell had happened.

It turned out that Peyton, Jay, Emery, and Ava had been just a tiny bit disturbed when Dair had thrown himself off the end of the pier and into the water. They'd called 9-1-1 and summoned everyone they could, convinced Mac was on a murdering spree. Although they might have exaggerated the circumstances a little bit, Dair was grateful for their proactiveness.

The police were very determined to keep any bystanders back for the time being, and that included Jay and the others. Dair hugged Robin to his side as they sat on the dock, huddled under their blankets as they tried to recount the events of the past hour to the officer. It was a little difficult with Robin's friends and family pushing through attempting to administer hugs. Eventually, the whole throng shuffled up the pier to the safety of the bank. But by that time, people were coming out of the reunion as well, curious as what the ruckus was all about.

"Oh, god," Robin muttered. "I just want to get out of here."

"We can go home soon," Dair promised.

Robin shook his head. "I wish we could have some

privacy," he lamented. "With all this craziness, I'm not sure I want to face all my family right now."

Dair considered for a moment. "Well, I do have my motel room still. There isn't anything really in it, but-"

"We can swing by a store," Robin interrupted, his eyes lighting up like Christmas. "Oh my god, that's perfect. A whole room, just to ourselves."

Dair beamed down at him. "Perfect," he agreed.

"Robin!"

The emergency services personnel finally parted ways and agreed to let Robin's nearest and dearest come through. Dair and Robin had been perched on the edge of an ambulance that had driven over the grass to reach the lake. The country club staff was apparently extremely unimpressed at this, evident from the loud argument one of the managers was having with the ambulance driver. Dair hoped the lawn was okay, but he couldn't say he regretted any of the emergency staff arriving when they did.

He watched on as Jay threw his arms around his twin and hugged him so tightly he lifted him off the ground. "You idiot! I could kill you!"

Robin patted his dark hair. "I love you too, Jay."

There was some shouting back down around the jetty, with various people pointing. From what Dair could make out, Mac had seen the flashing lights and was trying to scramble to shore on one of the pebbled banks so as to avoid capture. But the police had spied him, and now it looked like he was evading arrest. That wasn't a smart move, but Dair didn't have the energy to waste on that dick any longer.

So he turned away and left them to it, focusing on the only person who mattered to him.

Robin.

His friends and family were all tearfully hugging him. But

then Jay relinquished his hold, spun around, and threw his arms around Dair.

"Thank you," he stammered thickly. "You saved my brother."

"Ahh...he pretty much saved himself."

Dair bashfully rubbed the back of his neck as Jay stepped away. As he did, Ava punched him on the arm. Hard.

"Ow?" Dair arched an eyebrow at her.

"That's for being a dumbass." She chewed her lip and rolled her glassy eyes. Then she patted where she'd hit him. "That's for being pretty damn cool."

"So?" Emery demanded as he sniffed and wiped his eyes without smudging his liner. "Are you done being morons?"

"Huh?" Robin said, looking between his brother and sister.

Peyton huffed. "Are you ready to admit you're dating for real? No more pretending?"

Dair held his breath. He'd hoped he and Robin could have gotten more of a chance to discuss that in private.

But Robin just blinked in surprise. "Oh, yeah. We already sorted that." He moved from his siblings to slot under Dair's arm and hug his side. "Everyone, I'd like you to meet my definite, not-fake, amazing boyfriend, Dair."

"Thank fuck for that," Jay cried as the others whooped and clapped.

Dair beamed and kissed the top of Robin's wet hair. They needed to get the all clear from the emergency services, but as soon as they could, Dair was getting them out of here.

He needed Robin all to himself, desperately.

ROBIN

PINE COVE'S MOST POPULAR MOTEL WASN'T SEEDY LIKE THE ones Robin had seen on TV. It was more like a long log cabin with rooms nestled among the trees, tucked away from the road. Kind of similar to the counselor accommodation over at the town's summer camp. It felt welcoming.

Soft lamps lit the walkway as Robin followed Dair down to his room. The bags they'd picked up from the convenience store swung from their hands which weren't connected. Robin's feet squelched in his ruined dress shoes.

Dair rubbed his thumb against the back of Robin's hand, making him look up. "You okay?"

Robin smiled, another wave of relief rolling through him. He was happy for so many reasons, but making things right with Dair was at the top of the list. They'd talked things through, making sure they both told the other their version of what had happened at the fairground.

Unfortunately, that had led to some discussion of how Mac had been able to convince Robin his cheating had been Robin's fault. He hadn't been able to look Dair in the eye when he'd mumbled about how bad he was in bed. Yet here they still were, in a room of their own, half the town away from Robin's family. They had real privacy.

Robin was terrified.

He knew Dair wouldn't hurt him or force him into anything. But it was almost worse thinking about how Dair would react when Robin couldn't do much more than suck him off.

Dair stopped and moved in front of Robin, encouraging him to look him in the eye. "We can still go back to your folks' place?" Dair's concerned voice was a rumble that went straight to Robin's insides, making him quiver. He so badly didn't want to disappoint Dair, not after everything they'd been through. Maybe they wouldn't have sex? Maybe it would be nice to just slip into bed and sleep cuddled in each other's arms.

The trouble was, Robin was *craving* Dair right then. He wanted nothing more than for them to strip down and touch every inch of each other. He wanted to feel Dair inside him. He just didn't know if he could manage it.

"No, no." He squeezed Dair's hand twice, just like he did for Robin. "I just want it to be us right now, with some peace and quiet."

Dair smiled, then leaned down to gently touch his lips against Robin's. "Come on. My room's a few doors down."

He let them in with the keycard that had been safely in his suit jacket when he'd dived into the lake, along with his phone. Robin's was ruined, but he'd made sure everyone had Dair's number who might want to reach them.

It was kind of nice in a way, knowing that his friends and siblings could talk to Dair now if they wanted. Like they'd officially accepted him into the gang.

Dair flicked a couple of the lights on and dropped his bag onto the small table by the window. A couple of spindly-looking chairs sat on either side and the curtains were already pulled. A double bed dominated the room while a small closet occupied the corner opposite the bathroom.

Robin's clothes were still soggy and clinging to him. They'd bought novelty T-shirts from the convenience store, but they hadn't had any sweatpants or anything. Hopefully their suits would start drying overnight, otherwise it might be a little tricky to get an Uber in the morning.

They could think about that then. For now, Robin locked the door behind him, then placed his bag of shopping next to Dair's. He fished out the shower gel they'd bought...

...and Dair promptly took it out of his hand.

Robin turned, raising his eyebrows questioningly. But Dair met him by touching their lips together in a sensuous kiss. Robin squeaked. Dair stopped immediately.

"Sorry," he said breathlessly. "I'm being selfish. Do you need some space?"

The thought of being away from Dair any longer after the last twenty-four hours made Robin physically ache. "No, no," he stammered. "I'm a little disorientated, I guess. It was pretty scary out there. But I don't want to be anywhere else, and I don't want you to stay away."

Dair sighed and brushed the back of his knuckles against Robin's cheek. "Are you sure you don't need to go to the hospital?"

A wave of exhaustion and residual adrenaline rushed through Robin's body as he fought back a little sob. He threw himself against Dair's chest, hugging him tightly while he inhaled deeply and managed to calm himself again. Dair stroked his hair.

"It's okay," he murmured.

Robin believed him.

"No, no hospital. Just you. I'm sorry things got so crazy so fast between us. I shouldn't have let that happen."

"It's my fault, too," Dair insisted. He kissed the top of

Robin's hair. "But all couples fight about dumb stuff. The important thing is how they make up."

Robin grinned, excitement bubbling in his belly. *A couple.* That was what they were. They'd told everyone. It was official, for real.

No more pretending.

He looked up, searching for Dair's lips. Dair grinned just before their mouths met, a spark of fire in his eyes. Fuck, Robin felt so *secure* with him. Not just because of the insanely dramatic rescue that Robin would never forget as long as he lived. But always.

Dair was his safe harbor, his port in a storm. Robin hoped they could drop anchor together and keep each other warm and dry for a very long time indeed.

He felt his shoulders relax as Dair kissed him where they stood, running his large hands up and down Robin's arms, then across his back.

"Can we take a shower?"

Robin eased away from him and looked up into his brown eyes. "Uh...together?"

Dair licked his lips and rubbed Robin's arms again. "Only if you want to?"

"I-I'd love to," he spluttered. "I just...I haven't really done that before with, well, anyone."

Dair's smile was warm and comforting. "Me either. But a buddy of mine back in the Marines always said it was the first thing he wanted to do when he got back home to his wife. Said it was the best way to reconnect." He waggled his eyebrows. "Plus, pretty sexy, don't you think?"

Robin couldn't help but laugh, despite his nerves. Dair's enthusiasm was infectious. "I mean – you're *very* sexy."

He yelped as Dair suddenly slid his hands under his ass and picked Robin clean off the floor.

"As are you. I'm not sure you realize that, so I was hoping to show you instead."

Robin was blushing too hard to think of anything to say in response. Instead, he watched as Dair easily snagged the bag of toiletries they'd bought, then carried him into the dinky motel bathroom.

Unlike the bedroom walls, which were made of log, the bathroom was tiled white. Robin stood back on his own feet near the closed toilet. He winced against the bright light as Dair turned on the bulb that glowed through the flimsy lampshade. Then he watched as Dair closed the door, deposited the toiletries by the sink, and began running the water hot.

Robin had to admit, he'd thought they were just going to shower separately. He was kind of glad he hadn't anticipated this was Dair's plan, otherwise he might have panicked. Luckily, he'd only had a few moments to worry what the hell he was supposed to do.

As it turned out, Dair didn't really expect him to do anything. He turned back around to face Robin, kissing him sweetly on the mouth as he pushed his sodden jacket over his shoulders and onto the floor. It hit the tiles with a splat, which made Robin giggle and relax a fraction more. Then Dair worked his fingers down Robin's shirt, popping the buttons one by one.

Dair hadn't put his dry jacket back on, carrying it to the motel, then leaving it over the chair by the desk. That missing layer somehow made it easier for Robin to raise his trembling hands and rub them against the top button of his shirt.

Robin had gotten into a boat and survived almost drowning that night. He could damn well take Dair's shirt off.

Dair hummed against his lips as Robin also began

popping buttons. The steam from the shower was filling the bathroom, fogging up the mirror, and making Robin's skin tingle. Despite his reservations, his natural urges were taking over, and he was very much looking forward to getting Dair naked again.

He thought he'd lost this. He thought he'd never really had it. He hoped now they were here, together, he could prove himself wrong.

Because, honestly, the way Dair was kissing his neck as he pushed Robin's shirt to the floor next to his jacket couldn't be mistaken for anything but lust. This big hunk of a man was running his hands over Robin's cold skin and sucking against his collarbone with attention bordering on reverence.

"Come on, hon," he murmured as their lips found each other again. "You're still too cold. Let's warm you up."

Robin helped with both their belt buckles. Within a minute, they were both stripped bare and stepping under the water. Dair angled Robin so he was closest to the faucet, meaning they could both get some of the stream. The hot water over his head after the freezing lake was blissful, making Robin moan. Dair smiled and captured his lips for a quick kiss.

"More of those sounds, please."

It didn't feel awkward to be standing in front of each other naked in the bright light. For some reason Robin couldn't untangle, it felt freeing. He grinned back at Dair. Perhaps they could have some fun tonight after all? Dair made him feel *good* like this. Not pressured. Robin would just try his best.

Dair leaned around the curtain and picked up the products they'd bought for their hair and bodies, squirting some shampoo into Robin's waiting hands. He sighed as he massaged his head, rinsing the lake water out of his hair. It felt like several years' worth of hang-ups and stress were swirling down the plug along with the suds.

Mac had been arrested. Robin had meant it one hundred percent when he'd said he never wanted to see his ex again. He was sure Mac would just get a slap on the wrist for his behavior as Robin didn't want to go to the effort of actually pressing charges, but that didn't change anything. Robin was done with him – done worrying about the past. He wanted to live in the present, and right now, the present included his gorgeous, dripping wet boyfriend, who was grinning as he rubbed conditioner into Robin's hair.

Robin couldn't really reach the top of Dair's head without standing awkwardly on his tiptoes. Instead, he lathered shower gel between his hands, then began rubbing it over those magnificent, hard-as-rock abs of his.

Despite his previous exhaustion, Robin's cock perched up, adrenaline pulsing through his veins. "You're *so* hot." He was still disbelieving, and he wondered if the novelty of Dair's body would ever wear off.

He could feel his cock thickening, and Dair was half-hard too. They kissed as the water rinsed the rest of the suds and remnants from the lake, not to mention metaphorically washing away a lot of their earlier woes.

"You're beautiful," Dair rasped, nibbling at Robin's ear and making him whine. "I understand if you're too tired, but I got us supplies at the store."

Robin's breath hitched, and his fingers involuntarily tightened against Dair's hips. Immediately, Dair stilled his playful ministrations and moved around to look Robin in the eyes.

"It's not a problem," he said gently. "I'm just so happy to have you here. We can sleep, nothing more."

Robin bit his lip and blinked against the spray, looking into Dair's concerned gaze.

"I haven't bottomed since Mac," he blurted out, feeling awful where he'd just been feeling so magnificent. "I'm rubbish at it. I want to try, but I don't want you to be disappointed."

Dair sighed with an air of patience. He hugged Robin against him, then pulled back just enough so they could see each other once more. "The only person who's told you you're bad at it is Mac. And correct me if I'm wrong, but he's a compulsive liar, right?"

Robin frowned. "Well, yeah, but…"

His pause was interrupted by a squeak as Dair massaged his ass cheeks, trailing his fingers along Robin's crack.

"Now, if you don't *like* it, that's a totally different issue. Or if you want to try it the other way around, I'm down for that." Dair raised his eyebrows at Robin, leaving the proposition open.

Robin gulped, but he made himself keep eye contact with Dair. "Uh, no. I – I really liked it, actually. I mean, when it went well. Sometimes it just hurt and felt awkward. But the good times were great."

He tried not to get his hopes up. But surely, Dair would be more patient with him than Mac? The fact he had even suggested bottoming while Robin topped was mind-blowing. Mac would have been horrified. Robin had never topped anyone, yet here this gorgeous man was offering to let him try.

Dair licked his lips, looking down at Robin's cock with a positively sinful gaze. "We can see how it goes together. Help each other. But the thought of being inside you…" He hissed between his teeth. "It's pretty all-consuming, hon."

Robin ran his hands over Dair's expansive chest, resting them over his pecs. He could feel his heartbeat under his right palm.

"You make me feel so special," he said reverently.

Dair brushed their lips together. "You're *incredibly* special, that's why. Not just to me. To the world. I feel very lucky to be here with you, Robin Coal."

Robin closed his eyes and smiled, feeling the water run down his warmed body and Dair's solid presence against him. It had been one hell of a night, and he wasn't ready for it to end yet.

"Take me to bed, Dair."

25

DAIR

Dair remembered this from combat situations out in the desert.

Adrenaline made you fucking horny.

He was extremely conscious that Robin was okay with this plan of action. But it was pretty evident by the way he dragged Dair back to the bed after their shower that he was just as eager as Dair was.

Robin's body was perfect. He dropped on the mattress and pulled Dair on top of him, grinding their hardening cocks together. He was warm and solid and so alive under Dair's touch.

A flair of rage almost threatened to rear its head again as Dair contemplated how he'd almost lost Robin forever. But that was done. Dair wasn't going to dwell in the past anymore. There was nothing holding him, and Robin back now. They'd poured their hearts out, and Dair was confident Robin needed him just as badly as he needed Robin. They worked well together. They fitted like jigsaw pieces.

He wanted to see how well they fitted literally as well as figuratively.

Honestly, he wasn't entirely sure of the exact mechanics. He'd never done this before, but he was pretty sure he couldn't just plunge right in. According to his brief internet research this week, when entering from behind, some preparation was required.

"So, what do we do now, boss?" Dair asked from where he was hovering above Robin. As much as he wanted to keep kissing and rubbing their cocks together (it had worked awesomely last time, after all) he felt the need for more.

It made his blood boil that Robin thought he'd let Dair down in any way. Mac was done fucking with his head. Dair was going to make Robin feel spectacular if it took all night.

He kind of hoped it *did* take all night.

Robin snorted. "Boss?"

Dair ran his hand down Robin's ticklish side, making him giggle and squirm. "Yeah. You're in charge. I've never done this before. How do I make it feel good?"

Robin's expression became more serious. He cupped the side of Dair's face and rubbed his thumb over his cheekbone. "You already make me feel good."

Dair's heart swelled. "Good," he murmured before leaning down for another kiss. "Seriously, though. I need some sort of instruction manual."

Robin burst out laughing and hugged Dair to him. "I love you."

Dair bit his lip, then kissed the side of Robin's cheek. "I thought that was what you said earlier."

They pulled apart to look at each other. Robin swallowed, his expression one of resolution. "I do. Love you. I think. I'm not sure I was in love ever before. But I *do* know that today felt like I was missing a part of myself. Like I had a hole in my chest. You...you make me better, Dair. I love the way you care so deeply and how fun you are and the easy way you smile at people." He looked up at the ceiling. "Um, that was a lot of words. Sorry."

Dair chuckled. "I love you too, Robin. I think maybe I have for a while, but I didn't realize it could be like this." He ground his hips, making Robin moan. "Intimate."

"Fuck," Robin gasped. "Oh my god, Dair. We're going to need to have sex soon. I can't last."

"Oh, really?" Dair rolled his hips again and sucked a tender spot on Robin's neck, making him whimper and shudder. "You better tell me what you want, then. What do you desire, Robin? How can I pleasure you, my baby?"

Robin garbled something incoherent that made Dair grin against his neck.

"Jesus fuck, Dair. I want you inside me. I want to ride your big cock."

Dair growled. "There he is," he murmured in delight. He loved sex-crazed Robin. This was what Dair had been craving since their last time in bed. "And how do you want to ride my big cock, darling?"

Robin panted and Dair continued to rub against him. "Uh – need to – uh – stretch first. I can do it – if you want to watch. Or you can do it. Or – oh fuck – how filthy do you really feel?"

"God, filthy, trust me." Dair laughed. His cock was painfully hard right now. He was up for almost anything Robin could suggest, he was certain. But Robin was blushing again and he covered his face with his hands. "What?" Dair asked, his interest piqued. "You can say it, hon. I want to hear all the gorgeous things from your dirty mouth."

Robin moaned and bit his lip, his eyes still hidden. *"Do you want to eat me out?"* he asked in one rushed breath.

Shit. Dair wasn't entirely sure what that meant – *ohh.* Did Robin want Dair to stretch his hole out with his tongue?

Dear lord, that was hot.

"Forget it," Robin blurted. "It's gross-"

"No, it's fucking not," Dair growled, gently encouraging Robin's hands away from his face. His topaz eyes peeked out to look at Dair. "It's sexy as hell. Will it feel good?"

Robin squeezed his eyes shut again, but at least he didn't pull his hands back from Dair's grip. "I've only seen it in porn. But it looks – it looks so amazing."

Dair's heart flipped. "You want to try it with me? For the first time?"

Robin sighed and finally opened his eyes properly. "Yeah. I trust you. But only if you're into it?"

"I am *so* into it." Dair laughed. "Holy fuck. How do we do it? Like this? On your front? Sitting up?"

Robin barked a laugh, relief clear on his face. "Maybe...if I lie on my front?"

He wriggled around onto his stomach and Dair kissed his way down his spine. Every groan and shiver went straight to Dair's cock, keeping him hard and ready. He settled between Robin's legs. Robin tilted his hips and raised them slightly in anticipation.

Dair caressed his cheeks and thighs. "Oh, you want this badly, don't you, beautiful?"

"Yes, Dair. Please." Robin's voice was strained. His body trembled and glistened with perspiration.

Dair nuzzled his nose against the crease between Robin's ass and leg. "Fucking hell, you're gorgeous. Tell me if you like it, okay? What feels nice?"

Spreading Robin's cheeks, he exposed his puckered entrance, making Robin gasp. "Oh, fuck, Dair. Yes." He hadn't even touched it yet. Surely this could only get better?

Dair kissed his away toward the tender flesh, licking and nipping at Robin's pale skin. His hole was darker, inviting Dair inside. But to begin with, he simply kissed his entrance, then ran his tongue along it.

The sounds Robin made were delicious. He bucked against the mattress and grabbed at the sheets.

Oh. Dair loved seeing that. He was causing his beautiful man to react like that?

He was going to keep doing it.

"Holy fuck! Dair!" Robin panted and squirmed as Dair used his hands to keep Robin's ass spread while he kissed and sucked and worked his tongue inside the freshly cleaned hole. There was a faint tang of their fruity shower gel, but mostly it was Robin's natural musk, and Dair adored it. This flavor was intimately Robin's, no one else's.

And no one else had ever tasted it.

Possession washed through Dair. He gripped Robin's hips tighter and he pushed harder with his tongue. He could feel Robin loosening against him, whimpering with pleasure. Dair was going to do everything he could to look after Robin now. That was his job.

Inside and outside of the bedroom.

"Dair, don't stop. Fuck – *fuck!* Do I taste good? Do you like it? I love it. Don't fucking *stop.*"

Dair hummed in delight, touching himself as Robin babbled dirty words, keeping his cock stiff. He was leaking a little already, so he rubbed precum down his shaft.

Jesus. In a few minutes, it would be his cock pressing against Robin's threshold, not just his tongue and lips.

"Do you want my dick, Robin? Do you want me to fuck you?"

Robin gasped and spluttered, rutting against the mattress. "Yes, Dair. I want it. Please. *Please.* I promise I'll be so good for you. I'll let you fuck me all night. I want you to come in my ass and eat it out again."

Dair grinned. Robin was certainly going to widen his sexual horizons, that was for sure.

"Okay, baby. Do you want it slow and deep, or hard and fast?"

He never would have thought he'd be into this much talking during sex. It was hard not to be spurred on by Robin, though. He made Dair feel bold and wicked.

"Slow," Robin stuttered. "Take your time. Make it last." Dair heard his head move against the bedsheets, so he wiped his mouth and looked up at his lover's concerned face. "If it, um, hurts, can you please stop?"

Dair crawled up the bed in a matter of seconds, capturing Robin's lips in a fierce kiss. "Of course. You don't even have to worry about a thing. Just say the word, and I'll stop. I'll never hurt you, Robin. I promise."

Robin – beautiful, disheveled, sex-wrecked Robin – smiled shakily up at him. "I know."

After another few kisses, Dair retrieved the condoms and lube he'd managed to sneak into his basket at the store. Condoms he was fine with. Lube – well, he figured the more, the better, right?

Once he was suited up, he slathered his throbbing cock with shiny liquid. Then he coated around Robin's hole before pushing two wet fingers inside. Robin jerked against the bed, but he was already nodding before Dair looked up.

"I'm fine. I'm good. Just – fuck me like that for a minute. It's helping."

"I'll fuck you any way you like, gorgeous." Dair pulsed his fingers, feeling the inside chamber of Robin's ass. It was so tight and hot. His balls tingled in anticipation.

Robin looked over his shoulder, trembling as he watched Dair work. "Touch yourself," he begged. "Like I did for you."

"Like this?" He made a show of thrusting his cock against his hand and Robin moaned wantonly.

Jesus, Dair could see why he'd enjoyed this as much as he did from the other side. He felt incredibly exposed as he ran his hand up and down his shaft, keeping his cock steel hard for Robin's pleasure. Their eyes were locked together and Dair had never felt more connected with anyone in his life.

"Do you like that, baby?" Dair asked. Robin nodded. "Do you want it inside you now?"

Robin took a deep breath, then nodded again.

Dair used his one hand to angle his tip against Robin's hole, pushing through the ring of muscle relatively easily. With the other, he propped himself up over Robin and kissed between his shoulder blades.

Robin was whimpering and gasping, but he didn't stop nodding his head, either. *"More,"* he whispered, biting his lip. "I can take it."

"You're doing beautifully, baby." Dair kissed the side of his neck and rubbed his chest against Robin's back. "I've got you. You feel fucking *amazing.*"

He really did. So tight and hot around Dair's aching cock.

Then Dair seemed to go as far as he could, and Robin yelped.

"Holy shit!" He grinned as tears leaked from his closed eyes. "That! That's it. Hit that again!"

Oh, was that his prostate? Dair couldn't really tell through the condom, but if Robin was happy, he was happy. So he eased out a little way, then pushed back inside Robin. He shook and pressed back into Dair, his face contorted in ecstasy.

That was how they continued to move, slow and sensual as Robin relaxed and welcomed Dair completely inside him. Dair could tell when he was more at ease as he turned and looked over his shoulder.

"Kiss me," he begged Dair.

Their tongues and lips moved messily against each other as they chased their increasing climaxes. Dair wanted to speed up, but he'd promised Robin to take it slow. However, the way Robin was pushing his ass against Dair's cock suggested he'd changed his mind.

Dair caught Robin's earlobe between his teeth and tugged. "More?"

"Oh, Christ, yes," Robin replied, half laughing, half sobbing. "Fuck me hard. Go to town. You feel incredible."

Dair gave him a fierce, wet kiss, then leaned back. He grabbed Robin's hips with both hands to give him some purchase, then began to pound.

The motel bed squeaked and rocked against the wall. Dair hoped they didn't have neighbors, but there was no way he was slowing down now. Robin was matching his pace, and somehow they made their way onto their knees. Robin scrunched the bedsheets up in his fists, pressing the side of his face against the mattress.

Dair had enough room to reach down and find Robin's hard, bobbing cock with his hand. As soon as he wrapped his fingers around it, Robin howled, his whole body stiffening.

"Gonna come. Fuck me, Dair. Don't stop, like that, harder – harder!"

The air in the room was damp and hot, filled with the sounds of flesh slapping and men grunting as Dair slammed again and again into Robin. He was just about able to keep his hand on Robin's length, so he felt it right away as he began to come.

Robin screamed a few more choice profanities into the mattress as his whole body quivered, riding out his orgasm. Dair rubbed Robin's cum on his belly and over his softening cock.

This was his boyfriend. And he'd pleasured him like no one else had.

Dair's chest bloomed with happiness as his climax rushed to greet him. He filled the condom inside Robin, gnashing his teeth as his balls emptied. For a few moments, they both simply stayed there, satisfaction slowly creeping through their bones.

Dair rubbed along Robin's sides and kissed his back. "Was that okay?"

Robin laughed, somewhat hysterically, and for a second Dair panicked. But then he shook his head and grinned over his shoulder at Dair.

"Okay? Are you insane? That was *phenomenal*. I'd ask if we could go again right now, but I'm utterly destroyed. In the best possible way, of course. Oh my god. *That's* what I've been missing out on? No, fuck that, it wouldn't have been like that with anyone else. Dair, I..."

He seemed to realized he'd been babbling. His expression softened as he eased himself off Dair's cock. He snagged Dair's hand and tugged him down on the mattress to lie beside him. His skin was damp and his lips red and swollen. He rested his hand gently against the side of Dair's face.

"I love you. That was perfect."

Dair knew he was equally unkempt, but he didn't care. Robin was right. Everything was perfect. "I love you too, hon," he whispered, then kissed his lips tenderly. "I told you, you're magnificent."

Robin threw his head back and laughed up at the ceiling. "I'm not sure how we're going to top that. That was easily the best fuck of my life. I won't be able to walk straight for days."

"I'd prefer it if you never walked straight, in any sense of the word." Dair hugged Robin to him as they both chuckled in exhaustion. "And I'll find a way to top it, don't worry. I want to always be finding ways to make you happy."

Robin sighed and snuggled against him, burrowing his face against Dair's neck, wrapping his arms and legs around Dair's body. "That makes two of us. You make me feel like I could conquer the world."

Dair smiled and kissed his cheek. "Let's conquer it together, then. My little koala."

Robin squawked in horror. "No, you did not?"

"Look at you!" Dair laughed and hugged Robin closer to him. But he was right. Robin was clinging to him like a koala to a tree.

Robin closed his eyes and laughed as well while Dair quickly removed the condom and threw it in the direction of the trash. Maybe next time if they decided to stop using protection Dair would take Robin up on his offer to eat him out again post orgasm. He also knew they'd need to clean themselves up soon and probably get some sleep before sunrise.

But just for that moment, they lay in each other's arms, completely at ease.

And in love.

ROBIN

ROBIN AND DAIR'S BUBBLE OF PEACE AND TRANQUILITY HAD lasted until the next morning. After waking, more naked snuggling and a second much-needed shower, they had decided it was finally time to face the music and head back to Robin's home. They had a lot of questions to answer, after all.

Peyton very kindly gave them a lift, meaning they didn't have to risk an Uber in their still-damp clothes. She was positively bouncing with smug happiness, fully aware of what Dair and Robin had gotten up to in their room without Robin having to say a word. He would have been embarrassed, but he was too loved up to care.

He recalled walking up to the front porch at the start of the week, how nervous he'd been to hold Dair's hand. Now he just felt pride and contentment.

Of course it was Jay who opened the door. He grinned, looking between Dair and Robin before pulling Robin into a hug. "The cat's out of the bag, I'm afraid, love birds. At least Mom and the others are up to date with the rest of us now."

Robin groaned. "How mad is she?"

Jay winked at them and Peyton. "Come see for yourself."

The house was overflowing with people. Robin's mom was bustling fretfully around the kitchen. The rest of his family, as well as Peyton and Emery, had been banished to sit at the table, not allowed to help with the jugs of coffee and mountains of bagels she was distracting herself with. Robin saw one dollop of cream cheese disappear into a mug, and Smudge was dutifully chasing her slippers around to snuffle up all the crumbs.

"I just don't see why you had to *lie?*"

"Sorry, Mom," Robin said sheepishly. "It wasn't really a lie."

"Oh, it so was," Kestrel cried scandalously. "You made up a boyfriend! Which is so dumb because any idiot could see Dair was crazy for you." She rolled her eyes and unashamedly fed Smudge some bacon.

Robin tried not to fidget in Dair's lap. There weren't enough chairs, so he'd only protested feebly when his boyfriend had pulled him down onto his legs. But he was feeling a little sore after last night's escapades. Thinking about that made him blush, though, which would only make his siblings tease him more.

"Okay," Dair conceded. "It might have begun as something different. But I think we've loved each other in some way for a little while now. We just didn't know it could change into this."

"I did," Peyton announced cheerfully. "I've been patiently waiting for this to happen for months. But Robin was *terrible* at letting me leave you guys alone. He had a massive crush on you since day one."

"I – what?" Robin spluttered. "Shut up."

Jay laughed, sipping his coffee. Then he grimaced, possibly having gotten the cheesy mug. "I told you, bro. There was nothing fake from the moment you guys got here."

Their mom banged a plate of waffles on the table. "Oh, sorry, sorry." She flapped her hands.

Emery flinched where he was huddled in Ava's lap. He was wearing sunglasses and looked vaguely green. Robin could practically smell the tequila seeping from his pores. "Mother, mercy," he whimpered, making Kestrel snicker.

Ava appeared to be using Emery as a kind of shield. Usually, Robin's oldest sister was the fiercest of them all. But at that moment she was alternating between sneaking glances at Peyton and hugging Emery to her like a human pillow.

Weird. Robin thought Ava liked Peyton?

"I just feel so silly." Robin's mom was wringing her hands and fussing with the pile of waffles, straightening them up. Robin's dad looked up from his newspaper with a fond smile, then took her hand to hold in his own.

"Youngsters," he said sagely.

Swift leaned over the table and clapped Dair on the shoulder. "Hey, I guess sometimes you just take a while to figure out these things, right?"

Emery snorted. "Not me. I was-"

"Gay in the womb," several people around the table chimed in simultaneously.

Emery smirked and flipped them the bird.

Robin's mom huffed and tapped his hand back into his lap. "And as for this business with Mackenzie-"

"Nope, I'm done talking about him," Robin interrupted firmly. He knew his family would be distressed after they heard what had almost happened at the country club. But in the end, everything had been fine. "I've wasted far too much time over that asshole-"

"Language," his dad grumbled.

"You're right," Peyton said, nodding and patting his hand. "I'd call him something much worse."

"-*and*," Robin continued, "I'm not going to let him affect my life anymore. He doesn't deserve that power. I'm looking to the future, and that includes Dair." He smiled down at his boyfriend. "A lot of Dair."

His boyfriend grinned and gave him a sweet kiss. Kestrel pretended to barf. "Eww! Get a room!"

"Well, I guess you guys are already living together." Jay nodded his head. "That gives you a head start."

"Oh, no, we'll keep our own rooms for now," Robin said quickly. "Dair doesn't want all my geeky crap in his space."

Dair raised an eyebrow at him. "I don't know. I've become quite a big fan of koalas myself recently."

Robin was sure he blushed crimson.

"So, you'll be heading back to Seattle soon, I guess?"

Robin looked at his mom. Her voice was cheerful, but her eyes were glassy as she wiped down the perfectly clean counter.

Robin glanced at Dair as he slipped off his lap, then went to go wrap his arms around her. "Yeah, we'll need to head off soon to beat the afternoon traffic. But we'll come visit soon, okay? I promise."

She hugged him back. "I wish you didn't live so far away."

For the first time in a decade, Robin was shocked to realize that he wished he didn't live so far away either.

It seemed so clear to him now how he'd spent all these years running from his past. But it wasn't Pine Cove he had been avoiding. It had been Mac and the way he'd made Robin feel throughout his whole adult life.

After a week here, Robin had the scent of the forest back in his lungs. The glint of the now conquered lake in his eyes. His family and friends' laughter ringing in his ears. He wasn't sure he was ready to go back to the rigorous hustle and bustle of the city grind, but their lives were waiting for them there. He, Dair, and Peyton all had jobs and...well, they were probably each other's closest friends, but they had their apartment waiting for them. Not to mention all of Dair's many pets Peyton had entrusted their neighbor to pop in and feed for a couple of days.

They couldn't extend their trip, even if they wanted to.

But Robin's heart filled with joy as he realized there really wasn't anything stopping any of them from coming back whenever they wanted. Keeping up with Emery and his siblings on social media was nothing compared to making dinner together or walking down the boardwalk or staying up all night talking over beers.

Robin wanted to go to Sunny's for breakfast and challenge Dair to air hockey in the arcade. He wanted to walk Smudge in the park holding hands, not shying away when they ran into someone Robin had once known in town.

He was done hiding himself from Pine Cove. He wanted the people here to see what kind of man he'd become. Because he had a sneaking suspicion they'd all be as proud of him as he was starting to be of himself.

Three hours wasn't that bad a drive, especially if they left super early. They just needed to plan ahead. But still, when they were all packed up and heading out the door, Robin found it harder to say goodbye than he thought.

His mom was openly crying, even though she was laughing at herself. She wiped her cheeks and forced several packed sandwiches into Robin's hands. His dad clapped him on the shoulder and told him how proud he was of him. Then he went to go inspect Dair and Peyton's tires despite them having already done so.

Swift and Ava made him promise to come back while summer was in full swing so they could try and get him in a canoe. They were very keen that his one and only experience on the lake was not the previous night's near-death calamity.

Robin swore he'd give it a go and was surprised when he found he really meant it.

He was largely okay until he got to Jay.

Being back with his twin had felt so right. They were two halves of the same whole. A bit like how Dair made him feel complete, but obviously in a totally different way. Jay had been the first person to champion Robin and always saw the best in him.

Robin felt recharged by all his family. How could he have forgotten the way they made him feel valued and truly seen? Even snarky, hungover Emery got a little emotional when they hugged goodbye.

"This place isn't the same without you," he mumbled before kissing his cheek noisily and leaving a lip gloss stain on Robin's jaw.

Robin chuckled and tried to rub it off. He wanted to tell Emery he might be right, but he wasn't sure he could without getting tearful. "Thanks," he said instead. "Love you."

"Okay, that's far too many feels for this time of the morning. Time to pose!" Emery waved them all in front of his phone, having produced a selfie stick out of nowhere. "You too, Mr. and Mrs. Coal. That's it. Now everyone say 'sparkle'!"

Emery kept them hostage for several more photos, but then it was finally time for Robin, Dair, and Peyton to finally say goodbye.

"Come back soon," Swift instructed.

"And bring Smudge!" Kestrel sniffed and tried to pretend she wasn't rubbing her eyes as she kissed the puppy's head for the fiftieth time.

The three of them promised faithfully they would, waving as they stepped into their cars. Robin was riding with Dair in his truck, while Peyton would follow behind in her banged-up purple VW Beetle.

"Bye!" Robin called out the window. "See you soon! Bye!"

He waved until the house disappeared from view behind the pine trees.

It wasn't until Dair squeezed his knee twice did he realize he was brushing tears from his cheeks.

"Hey," Dair said softly. "We can come back every weekend if you want."

Robin laughed and found a tissue in his backpack to mop his eyes and blow his nose. "Thank you," he said. "I'm really glad you liked my town."

Dair licked his lips, glancing at Robin for a second. "I loved it. I felt like I found myself there."

Robin linked their hands together, then kissed the back of Dair's knuckles. "Me too. It only took twenty-eight years. But better late than never."

Dair squeezed his fingers. "Hell yeah."

Robin bit his lip, looking over Dair's profile as he reclaimed his hand and drove them past the town limits.

Were they leaving the fantasy behind?

Would Dair still feel the same way when they got home? Would he come out as pan when he had to go back to the auto shop and face his very manly dude-bro coworkers? When the thrill of pretending to date dulled down into the realities of dating, would they still have this spark? How would they cope with living together if they needed some space?

If they broke up?

"Stop it," Dair growled with a smile.

Robin blinked himself from his reverie as Dair took his hand again. "What?"

"I can sense all the stress radiating off you. No, I'm not changing my mind. Wild horses couldn't drag me away. This wasn't some holiday romance or whatever. I am very much anchoring my boat in your port, Robin Coal. And if I have to quit my job, I'm really not that attached to it. There are some folks there who might not accept me the way I am now, so perhaps it's better to leave them behind."

Robin frowned. Relief was pulsing through him, but also confusion. "Why would you quit your job?"

Dair shrugged before taking his eyes briefly off the road to glance at Robin. There was a spark of mischief in his eyes. "No reason. But mechanics can always find work anywhere, you know?"

There was a pause while he watched the road as they merged onto the freeway.

"And software developers too. I mean, they work from home half the time, I hear. So even if they had to travel a bit for jobs, it wouldn't be that bad."

Robin could feel his brow knitting together and he tried to smooth it out. "Why would *I* change my job?" He was completely lost. Did Dair know something he didn't?

But Dair just grinned and winked at him. "No reason. I just thought I'd put it out there, so you'd know. For future reference."

Future...

Robin's chest expanded as something warm rushed through his body from head to toe.

Would Dair consider moving for him?

It was such early days they couldn't possibly think like that. But...they had been sharing an apartment for three months like a house on fire. Jay was right. They had the advantage of skipping that step already.

Robin bit his lip as a smile slowly crept on his face. Dair didn't look over at him, but he was still grinning as they drove down the freeway, back toward the city.

Perhaps city life wasn't for them anymore, though?

Perhaps they would be happier in a town with fresh air,

breathtaking views, and more welcoming, loving smiles than they'd ever find in Seattle.

Robin snuggled into his seat, letting Dair have his hand back as Smudge stopped looking out the windows and crawled into Robin's lap. He stroked the puppy's fur, encouraging him to doze off. The radio played softly, and Robin felt a contentment he didn't think he'd ever experienced.

He wasn't sure exactly where their road was going to lead, but with Dair by his side, he was sure everything would turn out just fine.

EPILOGUE

Six Months Later
Robin

"Will the torture never end!" Robin cried, slapping his hands to his face and looking around at the carnage before him.

Dair chuckled and wrapped his arms around Robin's waist, kissing his neck. "This is what you get for having so much stuff," he teased.

Robin huffed, surveying all the many boxes still yet to be unpacked in their new apartment. "You don't understand – I *need* my Doctor Who TARDIS replica phone case from when I was sixteen. And my stackable Game of Thrones mug set. And my thirty-two Goosebumps books. And especially my built-by-hand Lego Death Star!"

Dair laughed again, rocking Robin back and forth gently. "Well, I'm lucky, aren't I? I just need you."

Robin felt his cheeks flush. He rolled his eyes as he lightly slapped Dair's arm. "Shut up, you sap," he mumbled. But he didn't mean it. He loved it.

The truth was, Robin hadn't realized how much of a hoarder he truly was in his Seattle room until he and Dair had moved. Robin had been clinging on to so much junk from his teen and childhood years, not appreciating why.

He was pretty sure now it had been a form of resistance to really embracing his adult life. He'd never felt confident enough to step up to it, retreating back to the safety of comforts from the past.

He'd accidentally spent the last ten years in limbo, afraid to move on.

But Dair had changed all that.

Robin had mercilessly culled a good two-thirds of his junk, only keeping items that genuinely brought him joy. But the rest he'd had let go, as now he was no longer shackled to the idea of a younger, unbroken Robin.

He was the new and improved Robin of the present, who didn't have to run from his past any longer. He and Dair were making memories together, already far eclipsing the time Robin had spent doubting his self-worth thanks to his no-good ex-boyfriend.

And where better to settle down for the next stage in their lives than the home Robin had never wanted to leave?

Their new apartment in the more recently developed area of Pine Cove was small and only rented, but it was all theirs. It had been Dair's idea to come back to where they had fallen in love and really start their lives as a couple. Robin had needed a little convincing, but when he was absolutely sure Dair wasn't just doing this to make him happy – that Pine Cove would make his heart sing too – they'd immediately begun looking for a place.

What had made the decision even easier was the news that Mac was a thing of the past. After the incident on the lake, he'd been released from police custody. Robin didn't want to waste any more time on him by pressing charges, even though he probably deserved it. But this was part of Robin living in the present and looking toward the future. Mac was his past, and Robin wasn't squandering another second on him. Thankfully, though, Mac had been happy to play the victim and blame everyone but himself for events, then apparently moving to Portland. Robin wasn't going to let Mac stop him from coming back to Pine Cove again, but he had to admit life was far more pleasant here without him there.

Dair had found no trouble in locating an auto shop searching for an extra pair of hands. The old place hadn't cared particularly when he'd walked, seeing as Robin had been right and they hadn't paid Dair for the time he'd taken off. One of the first things Robin had done when they'd returned from Pine Cove the first time was pay off Dair's credit card bill. He wasn't going to start their relationship on an uneven footing. Dair soon started making his own money again, and Robin's conscience was clear.

The new garage had been thrilled with Dair's experience, offering him a position on the spot. Robin had been more anxious about his own job prospects, but he quickly discovered that a software and website developer in a town like this could be kept busy for years as an independent contractor. Pretty much every business – from the high school and the outdoor center to the dozens of offices and shops – could all do with a software upgrade or custom website created for them.

Robin's family were ecstatic at the news. When Robin had Skyped Jay to tell him, he'd cried, which had made Robin cry. Then they'd both told each other off for making the other a mess. Having his twin be a ten-minute drive down the road brought Robin a unique kind of happiness. This was how it was supposed to be.

His mom was overjoyed that her wayward fledgling had come back to her. Even only after being here a few weeks, family dinners were already a regular occurrence. She'd almost killed them at Thanksgiving with the monstrous meal she'd whipped up.

Kestrel kept complaining she was going to get fat, but Robin had a hard time believing her complaints when she spent every second she could wriggling around on the floor with Smudge. Robin had it on good authority that their parents were getting her a puppy of her own for Christmas. He couldn't wait to see the look on her face.

Robin and Dair's fur babies were playing chase between the piles of cardboard boxes, the final lot to be delivered from the storage place they had used to tide them over during the move. The two of them continued to hug and laugh as Smudge did his best to corral the cats, but they were too nimble for him, leaping up on top of the boxes and out of the pup's reach. Old Jimmy was asleep on their bed, already accustomed to his new house.

Yep, everything was falling easily into place.

Robin's only real concern in the end had been Peyton. It was a fair drive between Seattle and Pine Cove, but he didn't need to have worried. As soon as he and Dair had worked up the courage to tell her their plans, she'd laughed and said she was already looking for job opportunities at Pine Cove Memorial. "There'd be nothing left to do around here without you losers!" she'd loudly proclaimed, having correctly guessed their intentions. She was good at that, it seemed. Once she'd been reassured Pine Cove also had a decent Thai restaurant, she was completely sold.

For all the jokes, Robin was relieved. He and Dair hadn't taken the decision to move back to Robin's hometown lightly. He had been scared it would drive a wedge between him and his best friend. But she'd jumped at the chance for a change of scenery.

For some reason, Robin's sister Ava had been mildly horrified at the idea. That confused Robin.

"I thought you liked her?" he'd asked last week at dinner when he'd let the rest of the family know.

Ava had immediately tipped over the salt. "I do – I mean, I guess she's all right. She's *your* friend. What do I care?" Then she'd gone to wash her motorcycle. At nine o'clock at night.

Robin just hoped everything would be okay by Christmas, when Peyton got to town. If she couldn't find a place of her own by the time she started her new job, she was going to crash with Robin and Dair – hence the sudden need to unpack and finally make their apartment presentable.

Robin had been making excuses that he'd been too busy with work to properly sort everything out. Then Dair had gently reminded him it was that excuse that had stopped Robin from dating for most of his twenties and had almost stopped him going to his reunion.

From getting together with Dair.

He was more than likely avoiding embracing the start of his new life, afraid in case it might not work out. But that was no way to live. Robin refused to fall into that same trap again and had called the storage place immediately to get all the rest of their boxes delivered that morning. They had been doing okay living out of a couple of suitcases the past few weeks, but now they were going to turn this house into a home.

"I'm still not convinced we needed a second bedroom," Robin said with a rueful laugh. They were sitting on the floor of the spare room, tackling some of the more obscure boxes. "I really *don't* have that much more stuff anymore."

Dair shrugged and pushed another box Robin's way. "Just thinking about the future," he said somewhat cryptically.

That was his favorite expression now, Robin had noticed. It made his head swim and his heart ache with happiness. The fact that Dair took it as a given that they just had a long future to look forward to together. They'd already booked a vacation to Palm Springs in the new year and talked about saving for a house once they were settled in town. Real, grown-up stuff.

Of course, Robin wasn't *entirely* grown up still. Where would the fun be in that?

He let out a laugh so loud it made Smudge bark. But the box that Dair had pushed in front of Robin had contained one single item.

The enormous koala Dair had won Robin at the reunion fair.

"Oh, hello, you," said Robin warmly. He pulled the koala out of the box and hugged him to his chest. When he looked over, Dair was smiling at him. Robin shook his head. "So, what?" he said with a laugh. "The spare room is for him?"

Dair shrugged, biting his lip and casting his eyes down, suddenly shy. "Or someone about his size. Maybe. One day."

Robin's heart skipped a beat. He placed the koala carefully on the floor, then scooched over to hug Dair's side. "Like kids?"

They hadn't talked about this. Robin knew from one of his very first conversations with Dair that he wanted children – that it was make or break for him in a relationship.

Robin was aware that since they'd started dating, Dair had never mentioned it.

Robin had been waiting for it, though. The day when Dair would ask the question that could define them as a couple.

Robin had almost brought it up himself, but it was Dair's place to ask, when he was ready.

Because Robin already knew the answer.

He'd always known the answer.

Dair took in a slow, steady breath, sounding like he was preparing himself. "Yeah. Kids. If that might be something you'd want?"

He finally looked up. Robin was smiling and he saw the hint of relief flutter across Dair's face. "Yes," Robin said with absolute conviction. "It's my dream to have kids. I want a family." He looked around at all the fur babies, then back to Dair. "A *bigger* family. Like I grew up in. Full of love."

Dair's brown eyes were shining. He pulled Robin into a tight hug, rubbing his back. "If we ever had a family, it would be overflowing with love."

Robin grinned, angling himself so he could see Dair's face again. "It already is."

They kissed on the floor, surrounded by everything they needed to begin the rest of their lives together. And for the first time ever, Robin truly believed he stood a chance of being loved forever, by someone he loved more than anything in the world.

It may have started out fake, but in the end, Dair Epping was the best and most real thing to ever happen to Robin Coal. He had come along and smashed that box in his chest, where Robin had tried to hide how he really felt. Not just his crush for Dair, but his feelings on the whole world.

Now love had set him free.

And he was never going back.

THANK you for reading **Robin and Dair's** story! If you would like to be the first to know when the next **Pine Cove** book is coming out, as well as read several awesome and totally FREE stories, please sign up to my newsletter! Emails will only be sent occasionally and you can unsubscribe at any time.

If you enjoyed reading Safe Harbor, I would very much appreciate it if you could share your experience with others online. Reviews, recommendations, fan works and general love is the best way for me to reach new readers.

If you'd like to meet with other HJ Welch fans, why not join our Facebook group? Helen Juliet Books. We're very friendly!

Thank you to: my beta readers John and Mum; editors Meg and Tanja; cover artist AngstyG; cheerleaders Ed, Amelia, Cara, Lucy, Susi and Piper; loving husband; and fur babies Arya and Tyrion.

ABOUT THE AUTHOR

HJ Welch is a contemporary MM romance author living in London with her husband and two balls of fluff that occasionally pretend to be cats. She began writing at an early age, later honing her craft online in the world of fanfiction on sites like Wattpad. Fifteen years and over a million words later, she sought out original MM novels to read. She never thought she would be any good at romance, but once she turned her hand to it she discovered she in fact adored it. By the end of 2016 she had written her first book of her own, and in 2017 she achieved her lifelong dream of becoming a fulltime author.

Safe Harbor is the first book in her Pine Cove series. She also writes contemporary British MM romance as Helen Juliet.

You can contact HJ Welch via social media:
Newsletter (with FREE Homecoming Hearts material and original stories) – https://www.subscribepage.com/helenjuliet
Website – www.helenjuliet.com
Email – helenjulietauthor@gmail.com
Twitter – @helenjwrites
Instagram – @helenjwrites
Tumblr – @helenjwrites
Facebook Page – @HJWelchAuthor
Facebook Group – Helen Juliet Books

Scorch – Homecoming Hearts #1

Blake has never had a boyfriend before. Because he isn't gay. Until recently, he was part of one of America's most successful boy bands. After their record label ruthlessly dropped Below Zero, Blake has no choice but to head back to his hometown with his overbearing family.

Elion never thought he'd get another chance with his high school crush, the pop star hunk Blake Jackson. Not when his life is the opposite of exciting, stuck as a barista in the town he grew up in. When Blake walks back into his world though, Elion feels like there might be something between them after all.

All Blake wants is to pursue his first love of dance again. But in order to do that, he finds himself the star of a reality TV show, and the producers are determined to spice things up. They don't care that Blake isn't gay, not when Elion makes such a cute boyfriend. The pair send the ratings through the roof and find themselves forced to continue the charade. At least for the time being.

As reality and fiction begin to blur, falling in love becomes a tantalizingly possibility. Dangerously so, as a real-life superfan decides that Blake belongs to him and will do anything to claim him.

Elion will have to fight if he's to keep the man who has fallen into his arms. But Blake will also have to fight to keep Elion safe from harm.

***

Spark – Homecoming Hearts #2

Joey Sullivan is hurting. All he ever wanted was to escape his homophobic family. For a time, his dreams of being a popstar succeeded with Below Zero. But when the record label throws the band aside, Joey ultimately has to face the shame of returning home.

Gabe Robinson loves his town. As a firefighter, he'd do anything to protect it. He even tries to help the prickly, fallen-from-grace Joey Sullivan. Gabe is nursing his own broken heart though, so his immediate attraction to Joey can't be anything other than a rebound.

An unexpected road trip forces Joey and Gabe together and the sparks fly between them, but it can't last. Their worlds are too different. Joey plans to get as far away from home as soon as he can, yet Gabe can't imagine any other life. But when Joey hits rock bottom, Gabe is the only one who can save him. Protect him. Keep him warm.

Gabe's saved lives before. But can he rescue hearts?

Burn – Homecoming Hearts #3

Raiden Jones never thought he'd need a bodyguard. His life as a songwriter has been tame to the point of boring compared to his popstar days. But when a malicious hacker starts destroying his career and threatening his life, he finds himself desperately in need of protection.

After leaving the Marines, Levi Patterson takes a place with his uncle's private security firm. The last thing he expected was a dumb babysitting job for the bratty, privileged Raiden. However, the two men have no choice but to get to know each other as they are forced on tour with one of Raiden's remaining clients.

Levi has never told anyone of his secret, occasional hook-ups with guys from his unit, and Raiden's never thought about going with another man before. But it's obvious the increasing chemistry between them is becoming more than physical, and there's only so long they can resist.

As the hacker becomes bolder, Levi finds himself in a race against time before Raiden is taken from him forever. He's no stranger to combat, but with his heart on the line, he finds himself in the fight of both their lives.

Steam – Homecoming Hearts #4

Bad boy movie star Trent Charles is more famous for his outrageous behavior than he is for his acting these days. After one scandal too many, his manager sends him home to the snowy ski slopes of Wyoming to get his life together. No parties, no fast cars, and certainly no women.

Ashby Wilcott is done with bad boys. His heart is broken from his last relationship disaster. A few weeks of peace and quiet in the mountains is just what he needs. He is absolutely not interested in moody Trent Charles, even if he is hot enough to melt snow with his rippling muscles and mysterious ways. Good thing Trent is straight.

But the two men can't seem to stay apart. Trent finds himself pretending to be Ashby's boyfriend, a lie that gets Ashby invited to a wedding as Trent's guest. Regardless of Trent's protests that he's not interested in the beautiful Ashby in that way, the chemistry between the two steams up. With only a few weeks together, what harm can they do having a little fun?

As outside forces threaten to tear them apart, Trent realizes Ashby means more to him than just a fling. In fact, he'll do anything to protect him.

Blaze – Homecoming Hearts #5

International pop sensation Reyse Hickson has it all. Or so it seems. Thanks to his homophobic label, he never expects to find love. But when he's saved from a mugging by a gorgeous stranger, the chemistry between them is undeniable. Reyse can't help but fall into his savior's arms...and his bed.

Corey Sheppard is nobody's hero. He got himself out of the foster system and stands on his own two feet. He could never be anyone's closeted lover. But there's so much more to Reyse Hickson than the world sees. Corey just can't stay away.

When Reyse's dad suffers a stroke, Reyse insists on going home. In desperate need of a friend, he asks Corey to join him. A short time together is better than none. With Reyse's lifestyle, they know it's the best they can manage.

But for the first time in his life, Corey finds a family with Reyse. And Reyse doesn't think he can hide how feels for Corey, even though his label threatens to drop him if he ever comes out. Can Reyse and Corey walk away from the best thing that's ever happened to either of them? Or is this love worth going down in a blaze of glory?

Storm – Men of Hidden Creek

"I can't do this without you"

Chase Williamson was never meant to be a dad. Like it or not, though, he's now the sole guardian of five-year-old Lyla and terrified of messing it up. He needs help, but who wants to rescue a high school dropout? Certainly not the gorgeous newcomer in town, even if he is an ex-Marine.

Hunter Duke is looking forward to a small-town life to drive away his demons. Maybe meet a nice girl? Adopting a puppy begins to fill the hole in his heart, but it's an unlikely friendship with Chase and his daughter that really starts to make Hidden Creek feel like home.

When social services threaten to take Lyla away, Hunter knows he'll do anything to prove that this town is wrong about Chase. Could it be that this is the family he was searching for all along?

Welcome to Hidden Creek, Texas, where the heart knows what it wants, and where true love lives happily ever after. Every Men of Hidden Creek novel can be read on its own, but keep an eye out for familiar faces around town! This book contains a three-legged puppy with attitude, a long-awaited comeuppance, and enough kisses to mend any broken heart.

Ashes – Men of Hidden Creek

"It's always been you."

Kris Novak pours his heart and soul into his job at Hidden Creek's only gay bar. When an arsonist burns the place to the ground, his whole life goes up in smoke and only his long-time crush can save him.

Firefighter Remi Washington never told anyone he's bi, let alone acted on it. But when he temporarily offers his spare room to his best friend's younger brother, he's drawn to the twinky, beautiful Kris in a way he can't ignore. How long before he gives in to this temptation?

Soon Kris stands accused of having started the fire and he has to fight with all his strength to clear his own name. Will Remi risk outing himself to stand by Kris's side, or will that closet door remain closed forever?

Welcome to Hidden Creek, Texas, where the heart knows what it wants, and where true love lives happily ever after. Every Men of Hidden Creek novel can be read on its own, but keep an eye out for familiar faces around town! This book contains a daring rescue, a meddling mommy matchmaker, and enough sparks to start a wildfire.

Masterpiece – Men of Hidden Creek

"I want to trust you."

Koby Duvall always knew his place at school. Art nerds like him were just target practice for guys on the football team. NFL star Vince Russo may never have bullied him, but the two men are still nothing alike. Except when Koby is asked to create a sculpture of Russo, they find themselves stuck together.

Vince is only home for a few weeks over the holidays while he recovers from a head injury. Face to face with his former classmate, he finally has a chance to prove to Koby that he's more than just a dumb jock.

However, sparks fly and Vince realizes he and Koby may have more in common than they thought. But all Vince knows is football, and coming out in the NFL is career suicide. When a violent grudge comes back to terrorize Koby, though, Vince knows he'll do anything to protect the man he loves.

Welcome to Hidden Creek, Texas, where the heart knows what it wants, and where true love lives happily ever after. Every Men of Hidden Creek novel can be read on its own, but keep an eye out for familiar faces around town! This book contains a steamy modeling session, big families with even bigger food portions, and enough chemistry to melt steel.

Lightning Source UK Ltd.
Milton Keynes UK
UKHW011832040220
358150UK00001B/6

9 781916 027244